Merryl Futerman started her c   ....blishing and
then moved into the film ind 
her key skill was looking af
up as a celebrity assistant
years has supported some (
television, often finding heรง..
situations.

Merryl has appeared as a speaker at PA conferences and written for trade magazines, but generally prefers to be behind the scenes.

Based in North London, she fitted her work around parenting two wonderful daughters and wrangling two difficult dogs, alongside a rock of a husband. Now spending more and more time in sunny St Leonards-on-Sea, another book is on the way...

To keep up with the latest updates visit

www.merrylfuterman.com

Twitter @Its_Merryl

Instagram @its_merryl

Don't Make a Scene

Struggles of a Celebrity PA

Merryl Futerman

DEESA
HOUSE

Published in 2023 by Deesa House
40a Chapel Park Rd
St Leonards on Sea
TN37 6HU

www.merrylfuterman.com
Text Copyright © 2023 Merryl Futerman

A CIP catalogue record for this book is available upon request
from the British Library

ISBN: 978-1-7394648-0-6
Ebook ISBN: 978-1-7394648 1-3

All views, thoughts and opinions expressed in this book
are the author's own.

Disclaimer: This is a work of fiction. Unless otherwise indicated,
all the names, characters, businesses, places, events and incidents in this
book are either the product of the author's imagination or used in a fictitious
manner. Any resemblance to actual persons, living or dead, or actual
events is purely coincidental.

To Adam,
for everything

Chapter One

Text from Dani 7.13am:
Babe, its freezing.
Can you get my parka?

It's a straightforward request, so I turn over, keep dozing. This state of bliss lasts about a minute until I remember Dani is in New York and I'm in Muswell Hill. Getting the parka to her is going to take more than a sprint up the Archway Road. My mind starts whirring, working it backwards: get hold of the bloody coat, then a mental scan of my bijou office for supplies and which courier will get it there tonight – latest. What is abundantly clear is that I can kiss the rest of the morning goodbye.

Head down, thinking about Jiffy bags, I bump into my flatmate, Ella, on the way to the bathroom. She is suited and booted, ready for work.

'Not used to seeing you up this early.' There's a note

of surprise in her voice. She also happens to have been my best friend since secondary school. I was obsessed with her neat handwriting; when she admired my curly hair, the deal was sealed. I made her giggle and she made sure I did my homework.

'Yeah, text from Dani – she needs her coat.' I'm still distracted by the logistics of it all.

'Thought she was in the States.' Her tone is genuinely puzzled.

'She is, but she's cold.'

'Seriously? Please tell me you're joking. Can she not buy herself a coat in the whole of New York?' Ella's a high-flying lawyer and, while she's too polite to say it, I know she finds aspects of my job ridiculous.

'Her show opens in a couple of days; she's just stressing.' Ella's logical suggestion didn't actually cross my mind, but my clients aren't looking for the most reasonable solutions.

Entering the bathroom, my breath turns to steam; the radiator isn't pumping out much heat, so I grab the screwdriver I keep on the windowsill for just this purpose. I pride myself on being practical – Ella's more of a thinker – plus it makes me feel better about my mates' rates rent. I twist the screw to bleed it, fire off **I'm on it** with my free hand and so begins a fairly typical day.

Having been freelance for a while, I can confirm there are pros and cons. I thrive on the unpredictability. The thought of going to the same desk in the same office every day fills me with horror, and I get a real buzz out of sorting a situation, so my clients can get on with it. They are all creatives and I truly admire what they do; I love seeing the way they work up-close and hope to pick up some tips and contacts. That's what makes the hassle worth it. I reckon I've carved myself a nice little niche. For now.

Pulling the front door shut and hitting my car fob, I'm rewarded with a jaunty blink of lights just down the road. Parking is a nightmare round here and many's the night I've come back late, tired, and had to abandon my old banger, Betty, down a side road.

Taking in the stunning views, I remind myself how fortunate I am to be living here in the heart of leafy Muswell Hill. Extend that thought – how lucky I am to have Ella; my accommodation is down to her and her 'proper' career. We didn't hang out much while she went to law school and I faffed around in artsy admin jobs trying to break into writing, but I don't regret all the fun and drama I had while she was grafting away in the library. Now, as her lodger, I feel she has the better deal, but remind myself it is not a competition. I like being around arty people; they drive Ella nuts. I give an involuntary shudder at the thought of how much bookwork a law degree demands.

I did have a proper job, at a film PR company. It sounded great – looking after the talent, liaising with the press, seeing the magic happen on set. The problem was that the magic didn't happen very often – mostly it was sitting around, waiting. The main attraction for me was writing press kits. I'd hoped this would get my foot in the door to writing, but it soon became clear that it just didn't work that way and I couldn't see how it ever would. Add to that the fact that actors were wary of me for bringing press on set – the press were always pushing for more. It was a lose/lose situation. The low point was standing in a muddy field in pouring rain at 2am, with an angry journalist who'd flown in from LA to interview the lead, who was refusing point-blank to come out of her trailer. I was not living the dream.

I met Dani in the green room at a chat show. She'd just won *I'm a Celebrity* and her star was rising. We clicked and she suggested I work for her – directly. With a couple of other clients, I could be mistress of my own destiny while trying to break into the scripting side. Dani was good mates with Casper Morris, a TV writer, and promised me an intro. It had to be worth a try. My parents were not impressed, especially as my perfect married sister was scaling the ladder of management consultancy, but I took the plunge, moved out of my smart flat in Putney – Ella was buying this place and needed help with the mortgage – and here I am.

Flinging my Dani bag into the passenger seat, my thoughts turn to my delicious boyfriend, Ed, and the fun weekend we had together. It's a shame we're now living on opposite sides of London or I'm sure we'd see each other more. And then I'm off, like a FedEx ninja. First stop: packing materials; next stop: Dani's.

Each of my clients has their own bag to keep life simple. It holds the essentials for that person, so I can be out the door without faffing around: their keys, my notebook, stamps, cigarettes – whatever they might need. I take pride in finding a bag that suits, so that's why my passenger seat is currently home to a shiny pink pleather one with gold stars embossed on it. It's tits and teeth and jazz hands in bag form, and it screams Dani.

I summon up my imaginary documentary host, Davina, with a hand mic in my passenger seat and we begin:

'So, Maddy…'

I decide I will use my full name for the purposes of my pretend TV career.

'So, Madeleine, how are you finding today's challenge?' She turns to me expectantly.

'Well, this morning was a wake-up call, literally,' (raise eyebrow to camera, pause for laugh), 'but I feel confident I've got this. Barring unforeseen circumstances, I expect a satisfactory outcome by tonight.' I'm keen to make it clear that I am at the top of my game.

'You think Dani will have her parka that soon? Impressive.'

'As you know, Davina, I take my clients' welfare very seriously. I will do my utmost to keep Dani warm on the chilly streets of Broadway.'

I do realise pretending your life is a reality TV show is what happens when you spend too much time alone, and there are definitely times I miss having colleagues, but I am saved by the bell. My phone is ringing through Bluetooth. Caller display shows it's Casper, this afternoon's client.

'Hi, Casper, how are you?' I'm hoping it's nothing urgent.

'Depressed. My ratings from last week are shite. I'm a failure.' He's such a drama queen.

'That's not true, you were up against the football – you have to factor that in.' Having tuned in for the new series, I did notice it didn't crackle quite as much as I recalled. The first was such a massive success, the second was bound to come under scrutiny. Best change the subject. 'Isn't this a bit early for you?'

'Another reason I'm depressed. I've got a new trainer coming – can we shift our meeting? I'll need a lie-down once he's gone. I fucking hate training.' It's all black-and-white with Casper; he doesn't really do grey.

'Sure, but why did you book him?' I'm relieved I'll have a bit more time to sort the parka situation.

'You'd understand if you saw him. He made me an offer I could *not* refuse.' I can picture the glint in his eye.

'To train you?' I'm keeping the tone professional.

'Got to start somewhere,' with a dirty laugh.

'I'll see you at two then. Do you need anything?' Like I said, I'm professional at all times.

'Alcohol? Laters. Use your key.' And he's gone.

I should remind him to send Dani something on opening night. They've stayed in touch since she had a cameo in a show he wrote years ago. They share a similar sense of humour and similar love of a good night out. The tabloids know they'll get a good picture if those two are at the same event and, if you look really closely, you might see a blurry image lurking in the background, probably carrying bags or coats and juggling a phone. The glamour.

✦

Pushing Dani's door open, it's obvious there's a huge pile of post behind it. Might as well run through it while I'm here, but first things first – locate the notorious parka. I'd expected to see it hanging on the hall coat rack, but it isn't. It's not in the cupboard under the stairs either. I head upstairs to check out her luxury walk-in wardrobe. Running out of ideas is making me anxious; there will be real drama if I don't find it soon.

It's not in the wardrobe either – last possibility is by the back door in the kitchen and I'm crossing everything it's there, but it's not. A band of anxiety is starting to squeeze my chest and I'm readjusting my timings while wondering where on earth the damn thing could be. I decide to make a cup of tea and have a logical think about its possible whereabouts before freaking out.

It does cross my mind that Dani might be testing me. She has massive trust issues – and who wouldn't if several mates and half your family had sold stories on you? In the early days, I felt she was constantly trying to catch me out, but I thought we'd got past all that.

Waiting for the kettle to boil, I scan the invites on the fridge door, double-checking what's coming up in case I need to call in clothes or book hair and make-up for a red carpet. So many invites to openings and weddings and parties. Since getting this Broadway role, her popularity has certainly risen. It's interesting how many old friends come out of the woodwork when you're starring in a new show. I'm musing on the nature of loyalty when I spot it – nestled between the Children of Courage Awards and the Dogs' Home Vet of the Year invites. Eureka! A dry-cleaner's ticket.

I turn to my imaginary TV host with a jubilant fist pump.

'Yes, I'll admit I was starting to worry, but I knew that keeping calm and thinking outside the box would yield a result. What do you mean I'm talking in clichés?' I really need to work on my natural delivery to camera. Next 'I'll be giving 110%'.

I make pretty quick work of the post. Fan stuff is easy to clear and quite satisfying. I feel a tinge of sadness for the letters that go straight in the bin, but Dani is brutal with her no stamp/no photo rule. She says people don't realise what it costs her: my time, glossy photos, stationery, etc. and not sending a stamp is adding insult to injury. Occasionally, I take pity on the children's letters and buy second-class stamps from petty cash. I feel less sympathetic towards the male prisoners who send her leery letters and want 'hot' pictures in return. Who knew convicts were such fans of daytime telly?

Fan stuff under control and a pile of envelopes under my arm, I head back to Betty the banger and off to collect the now famous parka. Quick check-in with Davina.

'Yes, I'm on target for a lunchtime dispatch, allowing me an hour before Casper to catch up on some life admin of my own.'

'Sounds like you are on top of this, Madeleine. Does that mean you could meet up with the lovely Ed for a bite of lunch?'

Shut up, subconscious.

The night Ed and I met, the attraction was instant. I spotted him straightaway – he had the tall, dark and handsome look I go for. It was at a gig and I was delighted to find he was with some guys I knew. We started chatting and laughing and didn't stop, peeling away from the crowd and finding a quiet corner. We went back to mine that night (there was never any question) and although it took every ounce of my being to play it cool, within a few weeks our relationship was established. We've fallen into a pattern of spending the weekends together and doing our own thing during the week. Maybe it's just the change in geography, but I don't feel quite as close to him recently. I'm probably imagining things, but suggesting an impromptu lunch feels a bit pushy. I decide if I get the parka on its way safely, I'll spend some time in the gym and clear my head before seeing Casper. Having off-peak membership is a perk of being freelance, apparently.

From Ella, 11.30am:
Can you meet at the Ocado
tonight? I'm stuck here. You're
a star x

Being available to meet deliveries is another freelance perk. Enjoying luxury meal deals from premium supermarkets is not. Ella and Drippy Tom don't have to think twice; they are on obscene salaries at the magic circle law firm they work for. Drippy Tom is becoming quite a regular fixture at our flat – not at all who I imagined Ella would fall for, but she seems happy, so I keep shtum.

✦

Letting myself in at Casper's with slightly wet post-gym hair, I expect a bitchy comment and get it.

'Going for the natural look?' he calls out as I try to sneak past his study into the kitchen.

'Just been to the gym.' Keep walking.

'Indeed, well I've had quite the workout myself.' Still in his rather revealing gym gear, he's followed me into the kitchen and is leaning against the polished concrete counter while he continues dreamily, 'I can't get the sight of his six-pack out my head. I won't be good for anything this afternoon.' Not wanting to hear the graphic details about what he would rather be doing, I try to bring him back down to earth.

'You do remember we need to sort out the paperwork for Mr Accountant, don't you?' Casper can be easily distracted.

'Oh, yawn – you start and I'll come down after my shower.' As he heads up the impressive central staircase to his en-suite wet room, I have to admit he's in pretty good shape for a man in his forties. As his Lycra-clad back recedes, he calls down 'And don't mention the ratings.'

Heading down the less glamorous stairs to the basement, past a shelf of awards and a wall of framed reviews, I'm confronted with a pile of tatty receipts and invoices to sort through and a heap of unopened envelopes scattered all

16

over the table. How did it come to this? I sigh and think of my hourly rate.

Casper arrives a bit later dressed in fancy Japanese jeans, with two fresh coffees, delighted to have the chance to play with his new bells-and-whistles coffee machine. As he is now in a good mood, I mention Dani's show opening, hoping he'll want to show his support. Dani really notices that kind of thing.

'We must send her something,' he responds enthusiastically. 'Let's get creative! Flowers are boring, champagne is wasted on her...' He narrows his eyes while he searches for inspiration. 'I've got it. A vibrator! It will be *hilarious*. Send her a vibrator from me.'

He sits back, delighted, fixing me with a beady stare, hoping for a reaction.

Seems I am going to end my working day in a sex shop. Not one to share with the parents but I do perk up when I realise it means an authorised visit to the all-women's erotic emporium I've heard of in London's trendy East End. Knowing Casper will enjoy thinking he has made me uncomfortable, I show no sign of weakness and politely ask for a budget.

'Top of the range, of course – go wild!' he shrieks as I pack up my Casper bag (Black PVC and studs) to make it to Hoxton before closing time.

The shop is not what I expected *at all* – nothing like the sleazy storefronts I walk past in Soho – and I'm immediately

17

welcomed by a heavily pierced woman at the counter, exhibiting a caring nature by smiling and tilting her head.

'Let me know if you need any help and feel free to browse.'

I boldly announce I want a vibrator and she gestures towards a large table, covered with such a vast array of shapes and sizes I am rendered speechless. She picks up on this immediately.

'Anything you particularly like?' She has come over to stand next to me. Right next to me.

'Oh, it's not for me, it's for someone else.' I edge away slightly.

Her expression shows she has heard this line before.

'Well, what does 'she' like?' Her direct gaze is withering my bravado.

'Um, I'm not sure. What do most people like?' I'm starting to feel a bit hot and bothered.

She raises her studded eyebrows at me.

'Well, you could start with big or small.'

'Honestly, it's just for a bit of fun.' I hear myself and cringe inwardly, but decide to style it out by channelling *Sex and the City*. 'What about a Bunny?' I know that's a thing.

'Do you mean a Rabbit? We have quite a selection.' She's doing a patient voice.

'Top of the range.' I'm doing a Samantha voice.

'Would you like me to run you through the features?' I'm starting to think she is enjoying this.

'No, it's fine. Does it come with batteries?' Ever practical.

'Someone's in a hurry!' she laughs, chummily.

Ignore this and ask for it to be gift-wrapped.

Confident as I like to imagine myself, I pay and bolt for the door, too embarrassed to browse and broaden my clearly narrow mind. This escapade certainly won't feature in my documentary.

From Dani, 5.45pm:
Actually, babes, don't
worry about the parka.
It's warmed up X

Chapter 2

From Dame Annette:
Dressing room. 5pm

Charming. And typical. Since being made a dame, she thinks she's the queen. Since being given her honour, she is, literally, 'The Grande Dame of British Theatre' – and doesn't she like everyone to know it.

Instead of a pootle up to her house in Hampstead Village, now it's a shlep into town in rush hour, carrying all my stuff. What was the point of only taking clients in North London if Her Ladyship has me running all over town after her? I totally fell for her 'I'm-so-charming' act when I went for my interview, seduced by her serving tea in mismatched bone china with a chocolate bourbon. No sign of tea and biscuits these days. I can confirm she is an excellent actress, delightful when she needs to be and a bitch on wheels when it doesn't matter.

On the other hand, this could be an excuse to suggest meeting Ed for a drink after work. Why should I sit around waiting for him to call?

To Ed:
Hey! I'm in town for work,
meet for a drink later? M x

Immediately panic. We saw each other on Saturday and had a fantastic night, but since then: silence. It's not that I need to see him all the time, just to know when I am going to see him. I'm trying to be easy-breezy, but Ed is proving hard to pin down. Probably nothing, just the end of the honeymoon period, shifting into a more settled routine kind of phase.

If I'm reading too much into everything, that is the Ed Effect – making me feel I'm a nag. Hearing Drippy Tom creeping along the landing this morning didn't help. Staying over on weeknights is next level. They haven't even been together for as long as me and Ed, *and* they see each other every day at work. Thinking like this doesn't help.

Not wanting to go down a rabbit hole of self-doubt, I decide to channel my energies more productively. I'll pop into Dani's lawyers and pick up the documents for the sale of her flat in Majorca. If that flat could write a book, it would be a bestseller – or, at least, serialised in the *Daily Mail*. Dani and her gal pals partied hard for a few years and those weekends in Magaluf were legendary. It was before my time, but I remember the tabloid pictures of them falling out of nightclubs, falling out of bikinis, falling out with each other. I wouldn't be surprised if those photos had paid for the flat – Dani is very shrewd at setting up a deal where she can. Reinventing herself as a 'proper' actress means wanting to be taken seriously from now on. No more lost weekends, so time to sell up and she was keen for me to keep the sale moving along while she's away. Having all the legal documents arrive in Spanish has been an interesting challenge.

A couple of hours puzzling through contracts *en Espanol* later and it's time to grab Dame Annette's bag – trimmed with fake ermine – and shoot over to the theatre. Being bustled along by the West End crowds is life-affirming. I'm part of this living flow of bodies, criss-crossing London, mistress of my own destiny. My goodwill lasts a second before a tourist stops dead to take a photo and I'm just another angry Londoner cursing under my breath. Plus, no reply from Ed.

Being buzzed though at the stage door reminds me how much I loved drama at university. I signed up to Theatre Soc straightaway. Some of our shows weren't bad – testament to our passion, commitment and possibly even some talent. I was more devoted to my drama activities than my dreary degree, but still feel the sting of not getting to play Lady Macbeth in the end of second year production. I was made for that part and I swear the only reason I didn't get it was because the girl who did had better hair – long auburn locks tumbling down her back. That and her willingness to tumble on her back with the bloody director, whose name I can't even remember.

They took that play to the Edinburgh Festival and I sulked at home writing a one-woman show I planned to star in – that would show them. It never quite happened, so going into final year I made the excuse of not having the time. I missed the camaraderie – Dame Annette's stories about doing rep are a scream. Truth is, you need a tough hide to make it in the acting profession and the Dame certainly has that.

An imperious 'Enter' and I'm in the stuffy atmosphere of a West End dressing room, pushing past a rail of costumes to find her leaning out of the window, having a fag. Large derrière in the air, she catches me smirking as she reverses back into the room and I am given the death stare. This stare has won Oliviers and I am suitably chastised, so busy myself settling on the end of a cheap saggy sofa surrounded by supermarket bags full of snacks.

Lowering herself onto her make-up chair, sitting slightly sideways on so she can see herself in the mirror, her gaze settles on me. Not sure why, but this makes me feel guilty. Big smile.

'How's the show going?'

She pauses and inclines her head, 'Well, that's a very broad question. I'm not sure I can give you an answer. Personally, I can say my role is evolving nicely, as I believe the critics noted in the reviews. Have you read the reviews?' Back to the stare.

'Actually, no, I don't like to read reviews before I've seen a show myself, so I can make up my own mind.' Surely honesty is the best policy?

'You haven't seen the show?' Her frosty tone implies not.

What I'd like to say is: 'Since you haven't offered me a comp ticket, I haven't splashed out £50 to see you do your thing.' She is the only client who wouldn't think of at least suggesting I come in on the press preview. I note the look of dissatisfaction settle on her face. She continues, her tone sour.

'I'd like to make sure we are up to date with my invoicing. Please raise one for the production company to reimburse me for my expenses.'

I'm on safe ground here. 'No problem, do you have the receipts for your lunches and fares?'

'Taxis!' she hisses.

We both know full well she brings a sandwich from home and uses her bus pass, but she wants me to charge them for sushi and black cabs.

Do I say anything? Of course I don't. I need this job. The best I manage is a direct stare, met with a gaze of steel. She's not backing down. *Is this illegal?* I wonder. I should ask Ella. And then what – report her to the police? I almost smile at the image of the police breaking the dressing room door down and arresting her for fraud, but she's moving on, oblivious.

'And make sure someone from the charity is coming to pay for tea on Friday. I do *not* want a repeat of last time.' She purses her mouth like she's tasted something nasty.

Dame Annette is not one for supporting charities, but she wouldn't have received her honour without showing willing. Cleverly accepting becoming a patron of a charity supported by the royal family, she hosts a tea at The Wolseley once a year for people prepared to hand over thousands of pounds for the privilege of joining her. Last year, she was presented with the bill. Certainly not what she had intended, but in front of the great and the good she had to cough up. It was before my time, but I know my predecessor had to invoice the charity to reimburse her – not a good look.

'Absolutely, I'll make sure they have a representative there to settle up. Will you be wanting hair and make-up?' This is a given, but I need the go-ahead to start organising it. Rachel is good with her, but Rachel gets busy.

'I've asked the girls here to freshen me up after the matinee,' she says, smugly, patting the side of her hair.

Of course she has, as if she'd pay when she can find a way to get it for free. I'll get the theatre people proper thank-you gifts, with grateful cards from the dame. This is part of maintaining diplomatic relations on a client's behalf, even if I fake-sign the cards myself.

She gives me a list of chores for the rest of the week and then, as I am packing up to leave, she throws out, 'Your invoice was a little high this month, wasn't it?' She's smiling but it's not friendly. I've been half expecting this; I'm trying to stop being taken advantage of and I have my answer ready.

'Well, the cost I gave you for a day a week was assuming I was popping into your house. Coming up to town to meet you takes much longer.'

And I'm out the door before she can question me, resolving to add my own fares to the next invoice. I have a goodwill margin for my clients, but she used hers up pretty damn fast and when you're freelance you have to bat for yourself – there's no one else to do it for you.

Starting out, I was grateful for any work, but now I know I'm good at my job. They don't even realise half the stuff I do for them. I strut out of the theatre head held high, until I check my phone. No reply from Ed. I can practically see his office from here. Would it be weird to just turn up? Maybe they mute their phones while they work and he hasn't seen my message.

Imaginary Davina chips in: 'Don't do anything you'll regret.'

It's as if she can read my thoughts.

'This programme is supposed to be about my professional challenges, stay out of my personal life.' Fortunately, my headphones are in, so it doesn't look like I'm actually talking to myself.

Maybe if I just 'happened' to be passing by as he leaves work? No harm in that; I've already told him I'm in town. He usually finishes around now, so I saunter past really slowly, pretending I haven't clocked it's his office. Of course, just then, the light drizzle turns to serious rain.

Sheltering in a shop doorway, I peep round to see who's leaving, but instead I glimpse Ed's slim-legged Levi's and vintage trainers under a huge golf umbrella heading in. That explains it – he's been out at meetings. High with relief, I'm about to call out when, as he moves forward,

I see there is a small, dark-haired woman sheltering with him, clutching his arm and gazing up into his smiling face. My stomach does a flip – and not in a good way. Something about the sharing of personal space sets off alarm bells and before I have a chance to have a word with myself, I'm off, heading straight for the entrance. Blocked by a group of what look like interns leaving, chatting and laughing as if they don't have a care, I'm too late to catch up with Ed and the mystery woman.

A cheery 'Can I help you?' from the receptionist brings me to my senses, as well as the realisation that I must look a complete fright with wet hair hanging down my forehead, flushed pink from the central heating combined with humiliation. I try and cover up by fanning myself and muttering 'Hot in here' under my breath while deciding on my course of action. I have not thought this through.

'Oh, hey! Maddy, isn't it?' My blank face gives me away. 'We met at the summer drinks?'

She does look familiar, but I can't remember her name, so just launch in: 'Yeah, hi! How are you? I was just with a client down the road, so thought I'd pop by and see if Ed was finishing up, so we could grab a drink before heading back to the wilds of North London...' I'm wittering.

'Did he know you were coming?' An innocent question, but it sounds loaded to me.

'Not exactly.' I omit to mention my texts etc.

'It's just that they're on a massive deadline – new client to impress, so it's all hands on deck, chained to their desks. You know the drill.' She's smiling in a friendly way.

'But I just saw him coming in?' I realise too late how stalkerish I sound. Convinced I see a flash of pity cross her face, she continues, 'Yeah, they had to pop over to the client's office to run them through some roughs?' It's not a question but her voice goes up.

'They? I only saw Ed.' A lie but I'm hoping to extract some more information.

'Oh, Mimi went with him. She's the new freelancer?' The upturn at the end of her sentences is increasingly irritating. 'She's amazing.' No question mark there.

'Right. Thanks.' Of course she is, that's all I need to hear. My face must be giving me away because she suddenly goes all professional.

'I'll buzz through and let him know you're here.' Dealing with relationship issues must be above her pay grade.

Shit, I look a fright and now there's amazing Mimi to contend with. A quick scrabble in my bag surrenders a stub of lip pencil, while my coat pocket contributes a scraggy tissue to dab the worst of the mascara running down my cheeks, and it's at that point that Ed appears, looking, well, not actually surprised, but certainly sheepish.

'Hey – this is a surprise!' He leans in for a kiss on the cheek just as I look down to put the pencil back in my bag and ends up kissing my forehead like an uncle. He's wearing a T-shirt I gave him that makes his eyes even greener.

'I tried to get hold of you.' I'm brazening this out.

'Yeah, sorry, we've been flat out, big pitch to prepare. I've hardly looked away from my screen all day.'

Apart from into Mimi's eyes, I think, but manage not

to say it out loud. I realise Ms Receptionist is following the conversation avidly, so I focus on Ed as I'm not sure how to continue this conversation without sounding awkward.

'I'm afraid I'm here for the duration,' he offers.

'Come by for a bite later? I can cook something hearty and nutritious to keep your strength up!' I'm attempting cheery, but fear it is coming over as desperate.

'Nice offer, but work will cover takeaways. It's going to be that kind of night.' And I can see he is trying to end the conversation.

What I want to say is, 'Come on, Ed, throw me a line,' but instead hear myself saying, 'OK, another time. I'd best be off.' I'm reluctant to leave it like this, but unsure where else I can go.

He pats me on the shoulder, awkwardly. Ms Reception looks embarrassed for me. I put on a big old smile and turn to leave before my real feelings show. Because there is no doubt that this has been a very unsatisfactory encounter and has done nothing to assuage my anxieties.

Weaving through the rush-hour crowds, I'm aware of my phone buzzing in my pocket, but can't face checking it until I get to the tube and, sure enough, there are three missed calls and four texts.

From Jess, 6.03pm:
See you at the CHAMPS event later xx

6.15pm:
Hope you haven't forgotten...

6.20pm:
You better let me know if you
aren't showing up

6.29pm:
WHERE ARE YOU???

There in 20, I ping back. The CHAMPS meeting had completely slipped my mind. I wasn't fussed about going, but Jess is trying to get a new job so convinced me to accompany her to the event at the fancy new hotel that just opened in Mayfair. If I hop off at the next stop, I can just about make it. Knowing it will be full of glossy Kensington girls who work in the private offices of high-net-worth individuals, I swerve into Selfridges and head for a make-up counter, where they are only too happy to give my sorry face a makeover. Declining to buy any of the products and leaving with the obligatory, 'I'll think about it,' I head for the hotel. My name is on the guest list thanks to Jess and there she is, hovering by the door, waiting for me. I can see she's made an effort. I love my clothes, but Jess is next level and her style can be, well, bold. There's usually animal print involved and always huge earrings. Her hair changes colour more often than most people change their minds. Today, she is a frosty silver grey and it looks amazing. It's actually great to see a friendly face after the afternoon I've had. We grab glasses of the free champagne that's flowing.

'Do we have to mingle?' I plead with her. I'd rather

find a corner for a catch-up and possibly ask her advice about Ed. She's lived through the whole romance with me and she's hung out with us a couple of times. I usually enjoy these events with other celebrity PAs, and I've made some great contacts, but the high-net-worth assistants are a different breed entirely.

'We do – just a tiny bit. I've looked at the RSVPs. The girl from ASOS head office is here and I think she knows the girl who works for what's-his-name from Liberty.' Her eyes were already raking the crowd.

Fashion is Jess' passion, but she's ended up working full-time for a model who has no interest in fashion and spends her time being late for shoots, missing flights and generally being incredibly hard work. I'd have had a nervous breakdown by now, but Jess seems to manage to not let it get to her.

I'm weighing up my options while Jess starts working the room, when a tall, skinny woman dressed in black looms up, introduces herself as the hotel's PR and immediately asks who I work for. That's how we earn our free champagne and she's not going to leave me alone until I've toured the hotel, the VIP suites and the private dining rooms, made all the right noises about recommending it to clients and, of course, considering booking their next press junket/birthday party/romantic getaway there. At last, Jess joins me and we nod and smile until we can break away, clutching business cards, and find a quiet corner. Before I can start off-loading, Jess blurts out:

'I cannot go through another fashion week with her –

I might kill her or myself. She called me at midnight to say she'd run out of cigarettes and could I just pop over with a pack. Forgot to mention her latest squeeze had whisked her off to Paris. I went to her sodding flat with 20 Marlboro Lights before she thought to tell me where she actually was. I can put up with so much, but she wasn't even remotely sorry.'

Laughing so hard I might pee, Jess's face shows she does not see the funny side yet, so I reign myself in. My clients seem tame in comparison.

Just when I thought we could have a proper chat, I spot a flock of high-net-worth individuals' assistants bearing down on us, led by the awful Caroline. Quite a few of them seem to be called Caroline. Marked out from birth. Anyway, I digress, they think they are better than us because their bosses have tonnes of money and can pay for things, whereas our bosses generate publicity and often get things for free. We coexist uncomfortably and this is clear on Caroline's face.

'Madeleine, Jessica, great you could make it.'

Her fixed grin reaches no further than the tips of her glossy lips, which could be distaste or could be the filler. Probably both. These girls are high-maintenance and their dream career progression is to catch the eye of a banker or hedge fund manager and become one of the set they currently work for. Like a modern version of Cinderella.

'I wanted to introduce you to some new members, Annabel and Charlotte. They work for that oligarch who runs the newspaper – I can never pronounce his name properly,' she whinnies, not noticing the stony looks Annabel and Charlotte are giving her.

'Girls – meet Madeline and Jessica – they work for celebrities; they know all the gossip.' She waltzes off to schmooze elsewhere. Cow. She's trying to suck up to them by providing newspaper fodder.

'Oh, like who?' Annabel does look a bit interested.

I reel off a couple of clients and, as soon as I mention Dani, she launches in, 'Oh, she's a complete bitch, isn't she? I've heard all sorts.'

Everyone has an opinion about these people they have never met and, as annoying as Dani can be, I respect her work ethic, so smile sweetly and say, 'Have you heard that she is currently in New York slogging her guts out in two shows a day? She also employs me, a personal trainer, driver, stylist and agent, keeping us all off the streets, so – no – bitch isn't the way I'd describe her.' I maintain a big smile so it doesn't sound too harsh.

Annabel looks awkward. Jess grabs my arm and yanks me back to the bar.

'Dani can be a bitch, but she's *my* bitch, know what I mean?' I mutter darkly.

'You know I do, sweetie. Come on, let's get you another drink. I'll go and make nice with the fash pack for a minute, then we can get out of here.' I watch in admiration as she sashays her way into a circle of already chatting women.

I first met Jess at a press junket years ago. She was looking after one of the actors in the movie we were representing and I was drawn to her flamboyant looks and easy laugh. I do envy the way Jess manages not to take things too seriously; I tend to go the other way. Straight after the junket, I dashed round the corner to a designer sample sale and Jess was already there in the queue. When she motioned for me to join her, I knew I'd met a kindred spirit. Soon after, we joined CHAMPS together, making these events much more of a laugh. The Carolines take it all terribly seriously, networking like their lives depended on it.

I was quite happy waiting at the bar, sorting through the business cards I'd collected, ready to annotate and file when I got home. I reflexively check my phone and, at last, there's a message.

**Sorry about earlier, let's make
a plan for the weekend.
Saturday night? Ed x**

Chapter 3

I worked on autopilot for the rest of the week, mind wandering, plotting ways to use Saturday to get things back on track with Ed. Veering from suggesting a romantic restaurant dinner to cooking a special meal at home; deciding what to wear, which depended on what we'd do. I mentally rehearsed amusing anecdotes from work and in my downtime caught up on my TV viewing.

We used to watch Casper's hit show, *Just Between Us*, together. It became a weekly ritual. It's set in a fast-moving design agency, not a million miles from the kind of place Ed works. We'd cosy up with a takeaway and he'd howl with disbelief at the goings-on. Once, he suggested I offer his services to the producer as a reality consultant, only half joking. I explained the principals of dramatic license, but he enjoyed his outrage too much to put it aside and just let himself enjoy the show. He did say he wouldn't mind if Edie, one of the leads, turned up in his team, which earned him a sharp punch, which turned into some play wrestling, which turned into... let's call it, a night to remember.

My other aim was to hit it hard at the gym and it was while powering through a spin class, I received:

Hey. Re Sat nite, someone from work having a house party. Sounds fun. Ed x

Oh. Not exactly what I had in mind. I barely know his colleagues with their in-jokes and nicknames for clients. Plus, there's the memory of the summer party when Ed told them I worked for the writer of *Just Between Us* and I had to listen to all their gripes about the accuracy of the way the *fictional* agency was portrayed. All in all, it is not a suggestion for the kind of just-the-two-of-us evening I had in mind. Gazing mournfully down at my phone, the gym instructor yells at me to get moving and I don't have much option.

Perhaps I can salvage something of my precious vision. Sexy cocktails in an underground speakeasy before the party? Suggest we open a nice bottle at mine and then try to discourage Ed from wanting to move on to the party altogether?

I've perked up a bit and, reaching for the fruit bowl on my way out the door to Casper's, I see Ella's left me a note on the windowsill, tucked in among the succulents. Got to love her old-fashioned ways, but who knows how many days it may have been lurking there? I think she overestimates my fruit consumption or the number of meals I eat actually sitting down at the table.

Having people to supper
Friday, very cas, join us! E x

Now I'm all for a jolly dinner party, but it does rather depend on which 'people' she means. If it's work people, will they be super brains who think my job is frivolous and only want to talk about the serious issues of the day? Uni people – that *would* be fun, but unlikely without more forward planning. New people? All that getting-to-know-you stuff takes a lot of energy. I'd been looking forward to a home spa and telly night. There's a surprising amount of effort in maintaining the natural look I was planning for my hot date. Instead, the flat will be brimming with 'people' eating, drinking and chatting, so any prospect of an early night is out of the window. I resolve to be mature, not drink too much and get to bed at a reasonable hour, even if it involves earplugs.

To Ella:
Crazy week – shattered, but
thanks hun. What can I do?
World-famous chocolate mousse?

This is a reference to when Casper invited a major Holly-wood movie star round to his place for a kitchen supper. She specifically asked for chocolate mousse and was certainly someone used to having her requests met, so this fell under my job description. Fortunately, the brief included that it looked realistically homemade – Casper wanted to pass it off as his own. I spent a frantic weekend making mousse after mousse, trying different brands of chocolate and different ways to serve it. Most of my friends and family roped in for taste tests. It was agreed that cheapo chocolate made a better mousse. I got my technique spot on and, on the night, served them in champagne coupes. The star was delighted, Casper was praised and I conferred her legendary status to my mousse. Not sure how this skill would feature on my CV.

✦

A chai latte usually cheers Casper up, but today, as he opens the front door, we are straight into it.

'I'm a failure. My career is over.' I know what this is about. Series two of *Just Between Us* is not going down well with either viewers or critics, and the shadows under his eyes tell me this is keeping him up at night. I go into jolly head-girl mode.

'Come on, you know the expectations on a second series are that much higher. It's only to be expected, like second-album syndrome.' I was quite proud of the analogy.

'Thanks for that Maddy – blah blah blah. Have you even watched it?' Unlike the dame's West End theatre productions, telly is readily available to all, plus I genuinely love it. My dream job would be writing for film or TV. It's the reason I was so excited when I got this job.

'Of course! It's great.' First bit is true; second, not so much – but I don't want to contribute to his nasty mood.

'Yeah, yeah – that's what everyone says to my face, but I want to know what they really think. You're an ordinary person. What do you think?' He doesn't mean to be rude. Following him down the hall, I've been talking to the back of his head, but now he stops and turns to face me. The meanness is gone; his guard is down and his expression is one of genuine pleading.

'What am I doing wrong? Why won't anyone just be honest with me?' I've never seen him quite like this; he's usually the king of bravado. My gut feeling is that he really does want to hear, as does the fact that he hasn't resumed marching down the corridor and is just standing there, shoulders stooped, looking at me beseechingly.

He isn't dressed to his usual snappy standards; he's in a baggy tracksuit and un-ironed T-shirt, and looks so forlorn I decide to take a different tack, because I do have a few ideas. Deep breath, this could be my chance.

'Well, my honest opinion is that it's the female characters causing the problem. They just aren't three-dimensional.'

As soon as the words leave my mouth, I see the storm clouds gathering above his head as his eyes narrow and he spits back, 'Thanks very fucking much, Maddy. Who made you TV critic for the fucking *Guardian*?' Whoah! This escalated quickly.

'Sorry, Casper, I didn't mean to upset you. You asked for my honest opinion. I… I was trying to help.' I'm back-pedalling so fast I wish my spin instructor could see me.

Turning, he stomps down the corridor to his office, slamming the door behind him.

Chai latte cooling in my hand, I honestly don't know what to do. In the first place, I think they're disgusting so can't even console myself by drinking it, but the truth is, I feel awful. This side of him is new to me and I don't seem to have managed it very well. I'm supposed to be on his side, supportive. We banter and it can get a bit close to the bone, but I've never seen him this angry. Should I knock? Should I leave?

I decide this is not an episode for my personal documentary, though I could really do with some sensible advice. What would Ella do? She doesn't take any, what she calls, CFC – Crap From Clients – and is always on at me about not being treated like a doormat. Would she leave and go home? Probably, let the dust settle. What would I advise to Jess if she called with a situation like this? Keep calm and carry on, or something trite like that. Deciding that I am here to work, I settle on going down to the basement to get on with the paperwork and hope things subside.

It's awfully hard to concentrate when your client is so angry with you that you fear you may lose your job, along with about a third of your not very large income. I'd hoped working for Casper would give me some insights into getting into writing, and although he can be tricky, I thought I'd got handling him down pat. It was the first little window of opportunity to be involved in the scripting side and I'd got it all wrong. At a loss, I decided to tackle the bits and pieces that had accumulated in my work area. Cataloguing foreign versions of his shows and signing and sending scripts for deserving charities to auction has a calming effect. Casper has no idea, but sometimes I take these scripts home to pore over, trying to learn the craft before they hit the post. By the time I've sorted the receipts for the accountant, I hear Casper on the stairs and compose myself, ready to make a grovelling apology, only to hear the front door slam as he leaves.

Slumping down into a beautiful, but not very comfortable, Philippe Starck chair, I'm furious with myself for getting into this situation. What on earth gave me the right to criticise an award-winning writer? I'm no expert, in anything really, and just because I'm around these wildly talented people doesn't confer any of their skills on to me. It's usually quite good fun working for Casper, and although I haven't witnessed the creative process as I'd hoped, we have a laugh, plus I get to go to show recordings and wrap parties. If I needed to find a new client, I could end up with someone like Jess's model, Aria, or another dame. You can't pick and choose; jobs like this don't come along often.

Anxiously chewing my thumb nail, my thoughts spiral down a dark hole of despair when I get a text:

Skinny flat white – extra hot?

Surprised he remembered my order of choice, I reply without hesitation.

Yes please!

After the initial wave of relief, I have a go at practising some mindful breathing exercises to calm myself. By the time Casper gets back, I'm a bit lightheaded from hyperventilating, but manage to launch into an apology as he enters. Before I get very far, he interrupts, gruffly:

'You might have a point. You hit a nerve. I know there's something wrong, but I can't pin it down. Let's watch the episode together and you tell me where you think it's weak.'

I am so grateful not be chucked out of the house that I would have agreed to almost anything, but I genuinely like the sound of this.

'Thanks, Casper, amazing, I'd really like that.' What I'm not sure of is whether I should suck up or get real.

'Calm down, sweetheart. I'm not saying you're right, but a fresh pair of eyes can't hurt. And don't pussy-foot around. I'm a big boy. I can take it.' Well, there's my answer. He passes me the coffee and we head up from my usual area below stairs to the luxurious living room, decorated in imperceptibly different shades of white, all chosen by a top interior designer. I paid the invoices and continue to marvel that you can charge that much money for whitewashing an entire room. Perhaps I should consider a career as an interior designer – who has shares in a company that makes white cushions. And rugs.

Slipping my shoes off at the door in case I've brought a bit of leafy Muswell Hill in with me, I follow him to the complex seating arrangement that wraps itself around a 62-inch TV. Too scared to sip my coffee in case of spillage, I lower myself gingerly as he throws himself back onto a reclining section of the don't-call-it-the-sofa and hits the remote.

I'm not sure how to play this, but the intro music has started and we're off.

Luckily, I'd seen the episode, so was able to watch again with a critical eye. Five minutes in, I interject, 'There!' He hits pause, looks over at me and says, 'Go on…' so I point out that given what we already know of Edie's character, she wouldn't behave like that, deferring to her boyfriend on a matter of design, and although I can see what he wanted to happen for comedy purposes, her dialogue doesn't ring true. Edie has way more attitude than that.

I think he would have furrowed his brow at this point, but, you know, Botox. He has a look of concentration, as he says, 'OK, let's go on…' and hands me the remote. 'Stop it when you want to tell me something.' He reaches back to grab a pad and pen off the desk.

There are about half a dozen moments where I hit pause and explain what I thought the problem was, usually issues relating to Edie or Grace, who is one of the bosses. He didn't say much, but he didn't get angry, and I manage not to drip coffee on the soft furnishings, so that's a bonus. Truth is, it was great, engaging muscles I hadn't used in a long while. I consciously tried not to babble, kept it succinct, and one thing I did learn at university is that an opinion is valid as long as you can back it up with evidence. Fair play to Casper, he just listened, which was a bit disconcerting as he usually has something to say about everything. As the credits rolled, he turned to me. I felt quite elated, really stimulated. I looked at him, expectantly.

'Thanks, Maddy, food for thought. You can go. See you next week.'

I guess that's that then.

Chapter 4

It is astonishing how much mess making mousse using just two ingredients can create. There's a light spattering of dark brown mixture over most of the kitchen surfaces, including me, to greet Ella when she rushes in from work. She has the look of someone who is frantic, but trying to be calm.

'Maddy – what the hell is going on in here? I need to get cooking and set up and sort myself out in...' she checks her watch, '... under an hour and a half.' Her words speed up as the sentence goes on. She's dumping her bag with one hand and turning on the oven with the other. I know the signs of a frazzled person.

'Panic not, dear friend. It looks worse than it is and behold...' I present the tray with a flourish and we both pause to admire the eight perfect mousses lined up in her mother's china teacups. 'All they need is a plump strawberry on the top and they are good to go.'

After a respectful moment's silence, I continue, 'You cook, I'll clean, then I'll set the table while you shower. You'll be ready to greet your guests while I jump in the shower and it will all be fine.'

This is the kind of stuff I am good at – calming ruffled nerves and coming up with a plan of action. Ella is meticulous about her work but gets easily flustered if things don't run smoothly. I am very adept at going with the flow – a prerequisite for my job. She gives me a grateful look and, for the next hour, we work around each other companionably, singing along to the cheesy hits on the retro Spotify playlist. Soon, delicious smells start wafting out of the oven and the lids of the pots on the cooker clatter their applause. I realise I never did find out exactly who was coming.

'Well, me and Tom, obviously; the new trainee from work and her girlfriend I haven't met before; and, in the interests of equality, Tom has asked a couple of his friends from college; then you and Ed makes eight.' She is enthusiastically mashing potatoes and doesn't notice my startled expression.

'What do you mean? I didn't think Ed was invited.' I sound defensive. She stops mashing and turns to look at me, quizzical.

'Well, duh, he's your boyfriend, isn't he? Of course he's invited.'

She is contemplating me with a look somewhere between concerned and puzzled. I deflate. Not so much because it didn't even occur to me that she meant for him to come, but more because I don't think of Ed and me as a single unit in that way, and that's sad. Ella senses I'm upset and tries to fix it.

'Text him! He won't want to miss out on your Oscar-winning chocolate mousse. It doesn't matter if he's a bit late.'

Fuck it. Why shouldn't I? Bring a bit of spontaneity back. I fire off a message – light, breezy – implying the dinner is sort of impromptu. I'm heartened when there is an immediate response.

Sorry – no can do. Finishing up on pitch then hitting the pub with team.

I deflate entirely, then rally so as not to let on how gutted I am. It's not just that he's not coming, more the realisation that not even I assume we are a 'proper' couple. When did things start to get so complicated?

I try to shrug it off. 'He's stuck at work, big pitch, but I'm seeing him tomorrow.' Fortunately, she's too busy to read between the lines for once and goes back to energetic mashing.

'Sure, no problem. More grub for the rest of us.' And once she's completely pulverised the potatoes, I pack her off for a shower and get on with laying the table for seven.

Satisfied the kitchen looks tidy enough to receive visitors, I take my time over my shower and prep, partly because I want to look my best for tomorrow, but mainly because the knockback from Ed has left me feeling distinctly flat.

I'm aware of the door buzzer going and the chatter of voices as I try not to think about him 'hitting the pub' and take a moment to process my afternoon with Casper. He didn't say much, but he did listen to what I had to say and I can't deny it felt good. Reminded me of debates we had at uni about literature, looking at characterisation and discussing pace. I wonder if he'll take any notice of my suggestions. The good news is I don't feel on the cusp of getting sacked anymore. He was treating me as more of an equal, less like his PA. This is exactly the direction I hoped we'd move in. I had to earn the opportunity and I think my extensive knowledge of what makes good telly helped. All those hours definitely not wasted then.

There's a sharp rap on my door.

'Maddy – get a move on. We want to eat!' Ella is back in her element and I don't want to let her down.

I join them as they are squeezing round the kitchen table, Drippy Tom carrying a chair in from the living room and Ella filling up glasses. She looks fresh as always in a crisp white T-shirt. Candles shed the only light and it's an inviting scene as Ella makes the introductions.

'Listen up, you lot! This is Maya from my department and Stella, and Dominic and Craig, who were at college with Tom. Everyone, this is Maddy – my good friend, flatmate and provider of dessert.' Business done, she settles into her seat cosied up beside Drippy Tom, who pours her a glass of wine and drapes his arm across the back of her chair.

Giving a little wave, I squeeze into the only gap left, between Dominic and Craig, who politely leans right to let me swing my leg over the bench seat.

'Snug, isn't it?' Dominic smiles and offers to pour me some water. We have a bit of desultory chat about how Friday night used to be party night, but nowadays we are all so knackered from work. I don't ask him what he does because he's bound to ask me and sometimes it can be hard to explain, especially as this lot all seem to be young thrusting professionals with clear career trajectories. I'm enjoying letting the chatter go on around me when Maya catches my eye across the table.

'So, you're the famous Maddy who makes the impossible happen.'

I wonder what Ella has told them about me. 'Well, I am Maddy, not sure about the rest!'

'Ella's told us how you spend your days making the wishes of the rich and famous come true. She says you could provide a unicorn if requested!' She's a bit tipsy.

This is where I come into my own – my job is certainly good for hilarious anecdotes. 'Not exactly, but a colleague did once source a baby elephant for a children's party.' This is the sort of story people generally love. It reinforces the image of a demanding celebrity who won't take no for an answer.

It's Stella who responds, eyes wide, 'Seriously? That's amazing! I would freak out if someone asked me to do something like that.' She seems genuinely impressed.

'Yeah, but I'd freak out if someone asked me to stand

up in court. Give me the baby elephant every time.'
Everyone laughs.

Stella goes on, 'Well, that's unlikely to happen to me. I'm a dogwalker by day and aspiring burlesque dancer by night.'

More laughter at the contrast and I relax into the conversation.

'I'm familiar with performing *one* of those roles,' I throw back, 'but I'm not saying which!'

I tell them about my foray into the erotic emporium, to much hilarity. Then, Stella and I have a companionable chat about the difficulties of walking other people's dogs, and I promise to take her number in case either of the services she offers are required by any of my clients. She is delighted, especially when I tell her she could get double her rate for dog walking, but I know in her heart she is hoping to be twirling her tassels at a star-studded party.

Remembering my manners, I turn to Craig, but he is deep in conversation with Ella about something legal, so I turn to Dominic.

'Are you another lawyer?' It's a neutral opener.

He shrugs and smiles. 'Me? No, nothing like that. I was at college with Tom and Craig, but when they went to law school, I started my PhD.' I seize up as this guy is clearly some kind of super-brain and I have no idea how to have a conversation with one of those. But he's still looking at me.

The silence is about to become awkward when he goes on. 'Your job sounds interesting,' he offers helpfully.

Feeling a bit shallow in comparison, I just smile and busy myself with collecting and stacking up the plates. He offers to help, but I brush him away. 'Honestly, don't – it'll break up the party. I just need to get dessert organised.' And I contort my way from the table, concentrating on holding the pile of plates with both hands.

Standing up, I realise I've done that stupid thing of not noticing how much wine I've drunk. I'd better switch to water so I'm on good form tomorrow. I've booked an optimistically early gym class. Leaning my hips against the counter to steady myself and carefully piping a swirl of cream topped with a strawberry on to each mousse, I feel the familiar buzz in my pocket – not just a text, an actual call. My stomach gives a lurch. It must be an emergency.

With hands covered in cream, I pull my phone out my back pocket.

'Maddy, it's Steven. Can you hear me?'

There's a lot of background noise at both ends, so I leave the room and shout back, anxiously, 'Just about. What's up – are you alright?' My heart is racing. I shouldn't have had all that wine – I may need to drive. Shit, shit, shit.

Steven is an author who doesn't really need an assistant, but hopes to raise his profile and thinks being able to refer enquiries to me makes him seem powerful and successful. He also has a super-aspirational wife who wants to be part of the glitterati and wears a slightly disappointed air that he hasn't lived up to his early promise.

'The lights have all gone out. I'm at Simon Hollerton's book launch.'

He sounds a bit pissed, too. I'm not sure what's required of me.

'OK, are you at your house? The fuse box is under the stairs.' Practical starting point, I reckon.

'Aha, you see – I said my assistant would be able to help,' he shouts, clearly for the benefit of the rest of the party. 'Where's the fuse box?' He's obviously not at home; probably swigging warm wine from a paper cup in a bookshop in Central London.

I can't hear the reply, but I do hear the cheer from the crowd as the lights go back on.

I'm thinking *What a twat* as I say, 'Sounds like you're sorted then,' resolving to charge him an extra hour for interrupting my Friday night for no other reason than to show off. I respect his talent as a writer, but I do need to find a way to reinforce some professional boundaries.

Dominic passes me on his way to the loo and probably heard the whole conversation. Must have sounded ridiculous to a PhD student with an Oxbridge degree. Sounded pretty ridiculous to me.

'You're like the fourth emergency service,' he says over his shoulder, smiling warmly, but the call has brought me down to earth with a bump and I'm in no mood to rejoin the party. I'll just quietly sneak off to my bed. Satisfied Ella won't notice, I slip into my room and gently close the door behind me, effectively muffling the voices from the kitchen.

As long as Steve doesn't manufacture any more dramas, nothing is going to disturb me tonight.

Chapter 5

From Ed, 11am:
Shall we grab a bite before
party? I'll pick you up at 7 x

This is all good. I float through the rest of the day, help Ella and Drippy Tom clear up, half listening as they debrief on last night's dinner. It seems things got a bit heated after I went to bed; Maya and Dominic had a disagreement over a news story that didn't ring any bells for me – a human rights issue about visiting academics or something. I thought Ella was a bit tight-lipped with me for disappearing early, but I blamed it on Steven's call and made out it was a bigger deal than it was. Luckily, Dominic had said something that backed me up. Drippy Tom volunteered that Dominic is a top bloke, but coming from him... Anyway, my world-famous mousses went down well, so all was forgiven. I even put up with some gentle teasing about my date night prep.

Post-gym, I stop off at my favourite independent coffee shop. I browse their heavily curated brunch menu and settle on a kimchee toastie and a skinny flat white. There's a complicated contraption set up on a long table behind the counter that seems to deliver cold coffee a single drop at a time. I marvel at the inefficiency. Hopping on the Wi-Fi, I demolish my toastie – which provides pleasure and pain in equal measures – and browse reviews from Dani's opening night. The play has gone down well and even though she isn't the lead, Dani gets a couple of positive namechecks. This is good on many fronts. If ticket sales go well, she'll be away for couple of months, which is a decline in work for me, but on the other hand she'll be happy, which should mean less hassle. Win/win, I decide, and send her a congratulatory text.

As I sit waiting for my pedicure, I muse on my handling of Steven last night. I can't ever be completely unhelpful, but I have learnt to recognise when something is not my problem to solve. I decide I am particularly good at delivering these pearls of wisdom; perhaps I should write a book? A self-help guide to being a top-notch celebrity PA. I've always wanted to write a book, so this could be it. I'll start jotting down my hard-won knowledge and resolve to buy an inspirational notebook for this very purpose. I could get clients to endorse it with complimentary quotes on the jacket, approach Steve's agent... The rest of the pedicure is spent in this delightful daydream.

From Dani, 4.00pm:
Thanks babe. All good here. Can
you return those Jimmy Choos?

I know exactly the ones she means. The shoes a chat-show host gave her as a thank you for stepping into the breach when another guest dropped out. Dani didn't have anything in particular to promote, but she likes him so she did it. He was so grateful he bought her a pair of fancy sandals – that was a couple of months ago. She doesn't like them, but it's taken until now to decide this. So, we are looking at no receipt, probably last season, and very possibly part of some contra deal with the TV production company.

Exchange? I reply hopefully as this is more likely, but **Refund x** comes back. I'm not going to think about this until after the weekend, as I already know it won't be easy. Anyway, I have my date to think about.

By the time Ed arrives, I am pretty upbeat. My hours of preparation have paid off. I look good, but not too try-hard. Wearing a fancy designer cast-off donated by Dani on a generous day, my hair is behaving for a change and my skin is clear. Hoping we will end up back here, my room is tidy and the bed is freshly made. As a backup, I have the barest essentials for a stayover at Ed's in my clutch bag.

I skip past Ella and Drippy Tom vegging out on the

sofa, watching some true crime documentary, and think I would much rather be me on a hot date going to dinner and a fun party than a boring old married couple, spending Saturday night on the sofa. Right on cue, Ed bips his horn. Sliding into the passenger seat, I take a deep breath of his aftershave – something woody – and leaning over to kiss him, my anxieties melt away. As soon as I'm with him, it just feels right.

Arriving at the seasonal dining pop-up he has booked in Crouch End, I'm looking forward to the eight-course taster menu, glowing with happiness as we order artisanal gin aperitifs from the hipster barman.

'Great choice, Ed. I thought this place was booked for weeks in advance.' Checking out the other stylish diners, I'm chuffed that this is the place to be.

'Yeah, Mimi suggested it and she knows the chef, so they pulled a few strings.'

Course she did. My goodwill glow dims a little, but I push past it and ask how his week has been. Soon, we are chatting and laughing and I'm telling him about the dame's fake expense claims and he says I should be careful – there was a story about a PA being charged by the police for getting rid of sensitive documents – so I tell him about not taking any CFC. Before we know it, we are eight courses down.

Leaning back happily, I say, 'That was delicious, but I can barely move. Are you sure you want to go to this party? We could just head back up the hill to mine...?' I give my most inviting smile.

But Ed is already getting his jacket on and checking the address on his phone.

'I promised we'd go; it'll be super fun. The whole gang will be there.'

Your whole gang, I think.

'Will Mimi be there?' I ask, all innocence.

He gives me a look. 'Of course, it's her party, didn't I say? Housewarming.'

He bloody did not say. That is not a detail I would have forgotten. On the positive side, we ditch the car at mine and catch a cab to Mimi's place, which is part of the new King's Cross development.

'Wow! How can she afford a place like this – a free-lancer?' My eyes are so wide I might pop a contact lens.

'I think her family helped out. They live in some pile in the country and wanted a London base,' he says without envy.

I want a London base. Or a country pile, for that matter, I manage to think rather than say, as I slip my arm round him.

Heading in with Ed's arm round my waist feels good and even though I only recognise a few faces, people are friendly and, annoyingly, the flat is lovely – decorated and furnished exactly how I would do my flat, if I had one. And a juicy budget. It's a mixture of old and new, artfully blended, with a Berber rug and a massive potted fern alongside a mid-century armchair. While I pause to take in all the details, Ed goes off to get us drinks and Mimi appears at my elbow, looking casually elegant, but with clearly a lot of thought put into the outfit. Close up, she looks a bit like Edie from the show, small and delicate with lively dark brown eyes that dart, not missing a thing.

'Maddy, hey, so cool you came.' Although she is smiling, I don't feel any warmth.

'Lovely flat, Mimi, do you live here alone?' I make my mouth curve up into the semblance of a smile.

'For now,' she giggles, putting her manicured hand up to her mouth. It seems appropriate that her nails are filed into points. 'It's so good to meet you properly. I didn't even know Ed had a girlfriend!'

So much to dislike, but I grit my teeth to say, 'Oh, yes, we've been together a while.'

'Funny, he never mentioned you,' she tosses, turning to meet some newcomers. Then she looks back and says, 'Do let me know if you can make the ski trip. I'm booking on Monday.'

I can't put my finger on how it is I am feeling when Ed returns a moment later, bearing drinks, but it's not a nice feeling and I'm certainly on the back foot. I decide Mimi shall henceforth be known as MooMoo, as she is clearly a cow.

'What's this about a ski trip?' This comes out accusingly, as soon as he's close enough to hear.

'Oh, yeah... no, I mean, yeah – I was going to tell you. Mimi's organising a trip. Sounds like it'll be a laugh, just a long weekend.' He shrugs. No big deal.

'Were you going to ask me or tell me?' Peevish, I know.

'Yeah, well, I know you aren't into skiing so...'

'So, what? Go without me? Go without telling me?' I'm getting a bit shrill.

'Of course I was going to tell you... I mean, ask you. Of course you should come. You could do lessons, hang out – après ski!' He's babbling and the more he says, the worse it gets.

'Ed, this is bullshit.' I feel hot and teary. 'I can't ski; I don't have any ski gear; I don't have any money. Actually, I want to go home. Can we go?' I cast around to see where my coat has gone.

'Maddy, don't be so melodramatic. The suggestion only came up the other day. It's just a weekend. You don't have to come if you don't want to.' He's holding his hands out, palms up, all innocence.

Bingo – the Ed effect. Suddenly, it's me being unreasonable.

I look at Ed, he is looking at me. We are both appraising the situation, but also waiting to see which way the other is going to go. Keep cool, Maddy. I don't want to make a scene here at the party in front of MooMoo and the others, so I smile. Deep breath.

'Let's talk about it later. We're meant to be having fun,' I manage, amazed at my self-control.

He looks relieved and takes my hand to introduce me to some of his department, and they are friendly and chatty and seem interested in me, but I can't relax properly as I am constantly aware of Mimi flitting from one group to another, tinkly laugh audible above the noise – it jars me.

At a reasonable time, I tug Ed's elbow, so that he leans down, and whisper, 'Let's go home,' in his ear.

He smiles – the smile I love, when his eyes crinkle at the edges – and says, 'Sure, I'll call a cab.'

'I'll get our coats,' I offer. I can't get out of here fast enough.

Heading into Mimi's understated yet stylish bedroom, still holding a half empty glass of red wine, I can't resist a bit of a nosey, but her room is blank, like a set. No photos or books – nothing personal at all. She's all for show, I decide, then sling the coats over my arm and – oops – a splash of red wine hits the dove grey carpet. Leaving the glass behind on the bedside table, I'm tempted to wipe my fingerprints. Feeling guilty, but not bad enough to attempt cleaning it up, I find Ed and make sure we are holding hands as we say goodbye to Mimi, who pulls a pouty face and says, 'So early?' I manage a smug smile and feel I have won one little point in this unspoken battle.

'Well, that was fun,' I lie as we let ourselves into my flat.

'Yeah, wasn't it?' he replies, genuinely. 'Why did you want to leave?'

'Just wanted you all to myself,' seems to do the trick.

Chapter 6

The phone rings at 3.45am.

'Hello, this is ALB alarm systems. The alarm has been triggered at 22 Barnsbury Square and you are listed as a key holder. Can you attend?'

My heart is racing as I croak out a 'Yes' and I'm out of bed and pulling a onesie on, not really awake at all yet.

'What the fuck?' mutters Ed, squinting as I turn on the bedside lamp.

'Dani's alarm has gone off. I have to go and reset it,' I whisper.

'Don't go, Maddy.' He reaches across to pull me back.

'I have to – I'm the key holder.'

'For Christ's sake, you don't get paid enough for this. It's...' he squints at the clock by my bed, '... 4am and the bloody weekend.'

'I know, but there isn't anyone else,' I reply, slipping into my boots.

'You've got no sense of perspective with your clients. They take advantage,' he says, grumpily.

'I've got a sense of responsibility.' I need to focus and get over there as quickly as possible.

'Has it occurred to you that it might be dangerous?' he says, sitting up, more awake now.

'Could you come with me?' Ready to go, I stand, looking down at him.

'You're joking, right? I've had it with coming second to a bunch of C-listers.' And with that, he turns over, pulling the duvet over his head.

'I won't be long – at least the roads will be clear.' A feeble attempt at lightening the atmosphere, but there is no response.

Turning out the light, I hope I haven't disturbed Ella as I creep down the hall. Throwing on a big overcoat, Dani bag in hand, I let myself out as quietly as I can, locate the old banger and freeze my hands swiping the traces of frost off the windscreen. Ed's comment about intruders has spooked me. Perhaps it isn't a false alarm and I am heading over there in a panda onesie with Ugg boots on.

Deciding some company will take my mind off my fears, I summon up my imaginary host.

'Well, Madeleine, this is exciting. A mercy mission across North London.' She's serious, but with a twinkle.

'Yes, Davina, my clients are secure in the knowledge that I am there for them twenty-four seven,' I say in my efficient voice.

'That kind of reassurance must come at quite a price.'

Even my imaginary reality show host is on my case. Because, actually, no. I can charge an extra hour or two, but there aren't any provisions in my non-existent contract for overtime or out of hours – or even holiday or sick pay, come to that. I've got a creeping feeling that maybe I'm not the strong independent woman I like to think I am. And I'm not sure how far this job can help me get to where I really want to be, anyway.

Arriving at Dani's, my heart is racing and my hands are shaking as I fit the key in the heavy black door. *What if there are burglars inside and I surprise them?*

I text Ed with my left hand.

You awake?

Reply from Ed, 4.27am:
U OK???

Just going in

Reply from Ed, 4.28am:
This is nuts, let me know when you're in

Steadying myself, I cautiously open the door, alert for any noise or movement in the dark, empty flat. Should I put the light on or creep in? I decide lights on so I can bolt back out the front door if I see anything. Or anyone. The entrance hall seems fine and I can't hear anything, so, trying to stay calm, I tiptoe towards the living room, but I've got the fear. I get a vision of myself from outside – a young woman, alone, in a dark empty house at 4.30am. Should I try and find a weapon? There's a golf umbrella by the door I could brandish, but I'd have to put my phone down, and somehow that seems like my lifeline. The house I know so well and usually breeze in and out of now feels ominous.

Freeze! I think I hear a noise upstairs. I should run, but I'm rooted to the spot, my ears straining. I hear nothing more. I put 999 into my phone, but don't call – yet. The alarm display indicates the living room sensor was triggered. I'll go in with my thumb hovering so I can hit dial if there is anyone in there. Courage. I throw the door open and hit the light – element of surprise.

Immediately, I can see a picture has fallen off the wall, activating the movement sensor. *That's it.* I laugh with relief. *I'm sure that's it.* I stand and wait for my breathing to steady.

My phone rings. It's Ed and I feel a warm flush of gratitude – he cares!

'Maddy? What's going on? Are you OK?' His voice is thick with sleep.

'I'm fine – I think it's a picture that fell. I haven't checked upstairs, but—'

'Right, well, I'm heading home now, too.' He sounds grumpy.

'No, why? I'll be back before you know it.' I'm laughing with relief.

'I'm shattered. I really needed a good night's sleep. Do what you have to do.'

'Please, Ed, don't leave.' I'm not laughing now.

'Maddy, I'm done.'

And he hangs up. What does 'done' mean? Done with tonight? Done with me?

He wasn't joking. The bed was cold by the time I got back and, of course, I didn't sleep a wink.

Maybe she'd heard some of it or maybe my face was giving my feelings away, but Ella was being very kind when we met up in the kitchen, late morning.

'Where's Drip… I mean, where's Tom?' One day, I'll let slip.

'Gone to the gym. Where's Ed?' Her back is to me as she butters a bagel.

'He's gone. Home. I think. Just gone,' and before I know it, a hot tear runs down my cheek.

'What happened? You two were doing so great.' She leaves the bagel to come and give me a hug.

'Honestly,' I say into her hair, 'I don't know. Something's shifted. I can't put my finger on what exactly, but the clincher was a work call last night – well, this morning really. He got all pissed off and left.' She smells reassuringly of soap and shampoo.

'I thought I heard something. What kind of work call do you get in the early hours?' She's let go of the hug to look me in the face.

'Dani's alarm went off,' I mutter.

'So you went? Alone? Are you mad?' She's holding my shoulders and gives me a bit of a shake.

I smile and shrug. 'No – just a key holder.'

She's not smiling back. 'Does Dani even know about this?' She sounds cross. *Why doesn't anyone get it?*

'No need, she's got enough on.' *Here we go again. I'm getting sick of having to defend my clients.*

'Being in a show is not saving lives. It's not fair to expect you to run around in the middle of the night. It's not fair to expect you to do half the things you do. Where will it end, Maddy? Do you ever say no?'

Bloody hell, why is everyone so down on me?

'I might not be all qualified and clever like you, Ella, but I am prepared to take responsibility. They don't lead nine-to-five lives, so neither can I.' It makes sense when I think it in my head. 'I just try and do a good job for people whose talent I respect.' Her face softens.

'Stop making excuses. You *are* clever, but you take way too much CFC. Let's not argue; I'll make tea. Maybe Ed will calm down and call.' I'm starting to wonder if it's me that's got things out of perspective.

But Ed doesn't call.

I text him late afternoon.

Sorry x

No response. Why was he so OTT last night? We get on brilliantly when work doesn't get in the way. I put up with it when his job is demanding. Is mine not as important? I know I must let the dust settle. He was probably just knackered. To stop myself from brooding, I go to my default setting – keep busy. I'm long overdue a big clear-out – my boho look is in danger of tipping over into hoarder.

Sitting in my room surrounded by clothes, books and all kinds of stuff, I get waylaid flicking through old notebooks. There are snippets of overheard conversations and ideas for characters scribbled down, pieces from magazines that caught my eye torn out and stuck in. I'd fancied myself as a writer after uni, then parked it after rejections from a couple of short story anthologies I submitted to. Steven is a bore, but seeing how hard he works made me realise what being an author entails, spending years working on the same manuscript. When I first went freelance, I thought about going to creative writing classes, but Jess said it would be full of retired accountants and housewives from Surrey. What Casper does is fast-paced and exciting – much more my thing. I can't bear to think about my real life right now, so I spend the next half an hour daydreaming about being hired as a TV writer while stuffing a bin bag for the charity shop.

From Dani:
Run extended! Xxx

The word of mouth from preview week is good and Dani is getting some attention. She doesn't have the recognition in the States that she does here, but, in this case, it has worked in her favour.

Bravo! X I reply. Superstitiously, she only packed for a couple of weeks in case the show was a flop. Now she'll be there for six months, at least. I can't pretend I'm not disappointed on a personal level; Dani is fun to be around and, work-wise, I'm barely making ends meet as it is. My heart sinks at the thought of finding another client. Can today get any worse?

The door buzzes and my heart leaps – Ed? But it's Drippy Tom, who is actually very nice. He asks how I am and how work is going and all the normal things. I can't be around a perfectly happy couple tonight, so I'll pay a visit to my folks. I know I'll get a warm welcome and some nice food, but I'll also get a grilling about my career – or lack of it. They don't understand the creative industries; they think I should have the security of a 'proper' job. The unspoken question is always: Why can't I be more like my sister?

To Mum, 7pm:
Hi Mum, Can I come for supper?

From Mum, 7.10pm:
Listening to the Archers –
cracking stuff! Baked potato ok?

It's not far to my parents, but it is a foray into the deepest, darkest heart of suburbia. Nobody out and about; shiny cars tucked behind well-pruned hedges and curtains drawn. I couldn't wait to get out of here as a teenager, with big dreams of being an actress. Or an artist. Or a novelist. I

68

was full of ambition and drive. When did I decide to settle for a supporting role?

I tell myself I haven't – that, once in the real world, I gave it a go but recognised my particular skill set and put myself right at the heart of the arts, working alongside truly talented and successful people, soaking up knowledge, making contacts. Sounds convincing, but, honestly, I'd rather be one of them, not just sorting out their admin. What can I do about it now, though? It all feels overwhelming.

Pulling up at Mum and Dad's, I brace myself for the usual barrage of awkward questions. Letting myself in, it's a comfort to see Mum standing at the oven in her Gap jeans and grubby Converse. I think it's been her uniform since the eighties. She was doing double denim before it was a thing.

Supper is ready and I settle down at the scuffed pine table we've been eating at for as long as I can remember.

'Is Dani still going out with that footballer? The one will all the tattoos?' is her opener as she puts an overloaded baked potato down in front of me. She takes a particular interest in my clients.

'No, Mum, she was never going out with a footballer.' I've got a good idea where this is coming from.

'She was! It was in my paper.' I should have guessed. 'There was a lovely photo of them coming out of a hotel in the early hours. I thought you'd know the full story.' She shouts for Dad and then settles down for a dose of showbiz gossip.

'Mum, you know that the papers make up stories to fill space. They were probably just leaving at the same time.' *How many times?*

'Oh, no, Maddy, you could tell they liked each other – she was beaming. Where's your sense of romance? Speaking of which, when will you bring that handsome Ed round again?' Didn't take long. She's looking at me expectantly, escaped greying curls from her topknot framing her face.

'I'm not sure. Soon.' What is it with Mums? Mind you, he turned the charm on full beam when he came for Friday night dinner – he did and said all the right things. 'Everything alright?' She's got Mum-antenna. Her expression has become one of concern; her brow creased with worry lines.

Channelling Dani to avoid more questions, I slap on a big smile. 'Fine! Great! We might be going on a skiing holiday.' *Where did that come from?*

'Skiing? You can't ski.' She looks horrified at the suggestion.

'It's with friends. I'll take lessons.' *I really need to change the subject, fast.*

'I thought you liked a relaxing beach holiday, like me.' She looks almost disappointed, as if she doesn't know me at all.

'I do, but, you know, try something new!' Fact is, having inherited her olive skin, I am a complete sun worshipper.

'True, your father's latest is an instrument. He fancies the trumpet, but I'm suggesting acoustic guitar – much quieter.' She seems to have lost interest already. 'I wish

70

he'd do something useful, like paint a statement wall in the living room.'

Happy to steer down this track, we have a giggle remembering other fads my dad has had, from karate to long-distance cycling. Mostly it's all talk but he does tend to accumulate a lot of gear, which inevitably leads to the perpetual clearing out of 'my' room.

'Maddy, sweetheart, we were clearing the top cupboard and found boxes of old diaries and notebooks. We can't store them forever.'

'Please tell me you didn't read them, Mum,' my insides squirming at the thought.

'I've got better things to do with my time than relive your teenage angst, Maddy. I was there, remember?'

What I now recall is that I was so terrified of anyone seeing them, I devised an elaborate code, of which I can now remember... nothing.

'And to what do we owe the pleasure of your company?' Dad arrives – being, well, Dad – and ruffles my hair in a way I have always hated, but learnt to live with.

'Just thought I hadn't seen you for a while.' I say through a mouthful of tuna mayonnaise.

'Not got some big announcement to make? "I'm getting engaged?" or "I've got a proper job?" That kind of thing?' If there was a prize for insensitivity...

I can feel the daggers Mum is shooting him, but he's managing to ignore her and continues, 'Only kidding, chance'd be a fine thing.'

Like I said.

Chapter 7

From Casper, 8.30am:
Come early – lots to do!

This could mean so many things, so I decide to get my act together and just get over there. Check bag contents, check Instagram (have resolved to become an influencer, or at least amass a bigger following through posting witty tweets and aspirational photos). This is all part of my Stay-Positive-and-Don't-Think-About-Ed strategy. I am going to focus on important things like being really good at my job and generally improving myself. I might sign up for a class. I've been thinking about yoga. Or the much-debated creative writing. Maybe both! Whatever I decide, it will be positive.

I wonder what Casper has lined up for me. Sounds major. Could be home renovations to manage or a party to plan. I did his fortieth and it was a big success – topless barmen handing out tequila shots was a particular highlight. Of course, what I truly hope is that it's more critiquing the show.

Whatever it is, I will bring my can-do attitude, because I am a competent, flexible, capable, woman. This will be my mantra from now on and I will repeat it every time I think of texting Ed. Which I am doing, but I made a solemn vow to Ella that I wouldn't – and, deep down, I know she is right.

'I am a competent, flexible, capable woman,' I self-affirm, giving my warning buzz before letting myself in, but the door is flung open and Casper is standing there. Fully dressed, which is unusual at this hour.

'Maddy – great – you're here!' This welcome is most unusual and somewhat off-putting.

'Er, yes. Everything OK?' Maybe he's met Mr Right. Again.

'Come in, come in. I wanted to have a chat. Come and sit down.'

This is unnerving. Casper doesn't usually surface until much later in the morning and I'm usually ensconced in the basement office, wading through paperwork, before he appears with any special requests, but here I am being ushered into the posh sitting room.

The crisp morning sun reflecting off the all-white soft furnishings is so bright I am tempted to put my sunglasses on. Perching gingerly on the edge of the huge L-shaped sofa arrangement, while worrying about the dye from my indigo blue jeans rubbing off, I adopt a competent, flexible, capable expression.

'You alright, Maddy? You look a bit strange.'

I resume my normal face. 'I'm fine, what's so urgent?' He's starting to make me nervous.

'I had a good think about your comments and you might be onto something. It's too late for this week – it's in the can – but how about we have a little look at Episode 3 together and chat about any suggestions you have?' There's a slight strain in his voice.

'Sure, great. But shouldn't I get through the usual stuff first?' I have committed to being excellent at my job, remember.

'No – now!' Bit snappy! 'What I mean is, if we could do it now, I would have time to make any adjustments before I go into the production company.' He's leaning forward, hands on knees, bit too close for comfort.

'Oh, OK, but you don't usually go in on a Monday.'

'Ha ha, no, very perceptive. It's an extra production meeting, just to talk things through with them. Nothing to worry about.' His left leg is jiggling.

'Why would I worry?' This conversation is getting weird.

'Exactly, no reason. I've had a script printed off. Have a read and I'll make some coffee.'

Thrusting a clean new script and a Sharpie at me, he's off.

Seems straightforward enough. This is more like it; I am being paid to read and comment on a comedy script. And to think I thought he was annoyed at my criticisms. Just goes to show: I should stop doubting myself. I am valued and, by playing the long game, I am on my way.

It's very different seeing a show I haven't seen yet laid

out on paper. I'm so busy congratulating myself on my fortunate turn of events that when Casper reappears, bearing coffees, I haven't actually started.

'Well? Any ideas, character development, dialogue?' For an informal chat, I'm feeling the pressure.

'Oh, not yet, I'm just feeling my way in. It's all a bit new.' He's making me tense.

'Well, crack on, if you come up with anything decent, I need time to incorporate it.'

'Me? I thought we were doing this together?' There's a very different atmosphere to last time, sitting together on the sofa, chatting it through.

'We are, but I don't want to cramp your style. Give me what you've got and I'll let you know what I think.' This is starting to feel more like an assignment.

As a couple of hours fly by, I get really into it and I think the fact that Casper is scribbling away on his script is a good sign. I get more relaxed as we go on, making bolder suggestions, and he is pretty receptive, which only encourages me.

When we reach the end of the script, he says, 'Great – good work, Maddy. I like the way you're thinking. I'm just going to let it sink in a bit and see if any of it's worth taking on board. You head downstairs and try not to disturb me. I need to concentrate. My car's coming at two.'

He settles himself at the ergonomically shaped desk with his back to me and doesn't look up while I get my stuff together. The wind has left my sails so fast I could have dried my hair with it. I hesitate, trying to come up with a way of asking if this work will be ongoing, but his back is to me now and he's tapping away.

'Let me know if you need anything,' I offer meekly as I head down to the basement and the usual pile of paperwork. But I regain a bit of a bounce in my step thinking how helpful I've been. My role with Casper is evolving – that must be good.

From Jess:
Have you heard? Casper's in trouble!
Production have called him in for crisis talks

Jess has a friend who works for someone high up at the production company and I'm guessing this is how she has such hot-off-the-press information. We have an unspoken pact to look out for each other's clients. It's annoying when people bring you gossip, but, from a trusted ally, it's more of a head's up in case we need to do damage limitation or be prepared for stormy waters. In this case, I'm confused. Is this the extra production meeting he mentioned today?

Downing tools and leaning back in my chair, the penny starts to drop – the time pressure and his jitteriness.

To Jess:
Thanks hon, I'm at his place
now. Speak later Mx

I'm tempted to say he is working on rewrites, but think this is the moment to support my boss rather than join in with a possible three-way gossip involving the PA at the production company.

> **From Jess:**
> **Sure, they're freaking out, ratings**
> **through the floor and he's**
> **refused to work with anyone.**

The penny dropping turns into one of those amusement arcade games where a single coin can cause an avalanche of other coins. Casper is being called in for emergency talks about improving ratings, probably for a roasting by the head of the production company, and he wants to take them something fresh. It's not unusual for teams of writers to work on a project, but Casper has always worked alone and been really insistent about it. Having me bounce ideas with him is surely a sign that he is worried, but he hasn't let on. At least not to me. I'm happy to help, it's my job, but I don't think he's being straight with me. Pride, I guess.

I'm done down here, but not sure whether to hang around or clear off. I had been planning to try a yoga class at the gym, part of my self-improvement drive, but also to keep my mind off the lack of communication from Ed. Casper clearly said not to disturb him, so I pack my stuff and head upstairs, pause outside his study and can't resist giving a chirpy, 'See you next week.'

No reply.

'Thanks for your help,' would have been nice.

Chapter 8

From Ed, 9am:
Hey. How're you doing? Ex

No idea what to do with this. Five days of absolute silence following his dramatic exit and now he wonders how I am doing. I was hoping for an apology, especially after I'd acknowledged my part in the row, and 'Ex'? What is that? 'E' with a kiss or is he signing off as my 'Ex'? Hang on, does he think we broke up? We definitely didn't break up. Did we? I honestly have no idea how to respond so I decide not to. It means metaphorically sitting on my hands or, at the very least, keeping them busy in order not to dash off a reply. I need time to consider this.

He's not the only one who thinks I am too beholden to my clients. Ella has made it crystal clear she feels the same. My clients couldn't care less about my personal life, that's a given, but if I don't take my role seriously, what am I doing with my life? I have a right to be annoyed with him, too – for being so dramatic and the skiing thing, and the Mimi thing and, oh, it seems all sorts of things, but...

But I can't stay angry with him. The way I feel when he wraps his arms around me, the way his eye catches mine across a room, or a table full of people, and we don't need words to know what the other is thinking. How much we laugh together at silly things, just watching telly, or stories from our day at work. I'm sure he feels the same; he just needs to realise it. He'd been single for ages before we met; his last girlfriend was a clingy nightmare by all accounts. Maybe he's just a bit freaked out about getting serious. Being stroppy isn't going to sort things out, especially not with Mimi sharking around. Best to give him some space.

Today's client is not one of my favourite assignments, Needy Steve, the author. I burrow into the depths of the under-stair office to find his bag – a fake Burberry satchel off the market. I only go to his house once a fortnight. I wouldn't accept a job like this now, but when I was starting out, I had to take whatever regular gigs I could get. I just send up a silent prayer that Bridget, his wife, isn't around.

Needy Steve's biggest plus point is that he really is local. He describes where he lives as Highgate, but it's still Muswell Hill as far as I'm concerned, and I don't even need the car. It's a walk through Highgate Woods, always a pleasure, and even though there is a major road running alongside me, I can temporarily lose myself in a life-affirming amount of plants budding, woods bursting with greenery and even hear a woodpecker making much more racket than its size would lead you to believe possible. I think I may be forest bathing – whatever, I feel calmer. Realising this is a perfect Instagram moment rather interrupts my Zen moment, but this little bit of headspace has clarified the two conflicting thoughts vying for my attention.

Firstly, just how much I enjoyed the work I did with Casper, even with him putting the pressure on. The next episode goes out tonight and I can't wait to see if any of my suggestions make it onto the screen. The other, of course, is Ed and how to get back on track because it feels like things are going a bit pear-shaped. Focus on the positive: the writing. I wonder if I might have a word with Steve about how he broke into writing. He'd love that.

The front door of the tall Victorian semi is opening as I come through the front gate. Bridget must have been keeping an eye out for me. She has her long, curly hair wrapped up on top of her head in an African print scarf and large colourful earrings swinging almost to her shoulders. I think she is going for a Hampstead Bohemian look, but looks more like someone who runs poetry workshops in the community centre. I don't think she's heard of cultural appropriation.

'Maddy, thank goodness you're here. It's all so overwhelming. Come in, come in, Steven's expecting you.' Definite whiff of ylang-ylang.

'Hi Bridget, how are you?' She's heading towards the kitchen; my aim is to slip straight up the stairs to Steve's study.

'Oh, you know, busy, busy, busy.'

She's not.

'Sigmund is such a handful; he's been identified as gifted and talented, which is a blessing and a burden.'

Sigmund is two.

She's stopped, just before the staircase. 'Maddy, before you go up to see Steven, I wanted to enlist your help in tracking down a particular Danish cot bed for Sigmund to transition into.' Here we go.

'Um, OK, I can find where it's stocked for you.'

'Actually, Maddy, I want you to find me one on eBay or Gumtree or something – they cost a fortune, and if the design is so classic, who needs a brand-new one, am I right?' She's barring the way to the stairs.

'Well, trawling eBay and bidding and everything can take quite a while, and then you need to get it collected and—'

'Exactly why I'm asking you to do it – I'm rushed off my feet and I thought this would be just the kind of little job that would be perfect for you.' She pulls a face meant to convey encouragement, but looks very much like patronising.

Summoning up my earlier bit of Zen, I take a deep breath. 'I'd better see what Steven needs first, I think.' I need to find a polite way of letting her know I am not here to do her household chores.

'Well, alright, but do make sure you take Coco out before you go – poor thing hasn't had a proper walk for days.'

At the mention of her name, Coco the toffee-coloured cockapoo comes skittering down the hallway, her whole body wagging with joy. Coco is my favourite member of this household by a long chalk and I would quite happily take her for a walk, but it's a bloody cheek of Bridget. I need boundaries.

Fortunately, Sigmund lets out a squawk that sends her rushing back to the kitchen, where he is tethered in his Tripp Trapp highchair – God forbid he might be choking on an organic freeze-dried blueberry.

I stomp up the stairs with Coco at my heels, framing snippy responses to Bridget that I will never deliver, wreaking a tiny bit of revenge by nudging several of the framed photos of the child genius that is baby Sigmund, so they hang askew. I know this will annoy Bridget. Passive aggressive? Me?

She was right about one thing: Steven is expecting me. I know this because as I tap and enter the study, he is sitting at his big antique desk gazing furrow-browed at his computer screen, notebook open in front of him, pen held firmly between his greying teeth, chin resting on a closed fist. Quite the portrait of a tortured writer.

'Ah, Madeleine, you are here to save me from this tsunami of the mundane.' He's definitely been rehearsing that line.

'Hi, Steven. How're you doing? I'm sure we have lots to catch up on. I thought we could start with the accountant – it's that time of year, I'm afraid.'

I gently push Coco outside the door with my foot as I shut it behind me. She is most certainly not allowed into the hallowed writer's sanctum.

'Indeed, indeed, but before we do, I wanted to talk you through my thoughts for publicising my forthcoming book. I've got some marvellous ideas.' Hmm.

'Happy to bounce ideas, Steven, but you know the publisher takes care of that side of things.'

'Technically, yes, but I rather fear their resources are overstretched. I've been suggesting a meeting with the publicity department for weeks and it never seems to happen. Time is pressing and I don't want some excellent opportunities to be missed.'

'Publication isn't until September, Steve; has that changed?' This isn't really my area of responsibility. I'm trying to draw boundaries.

'September it is, but the glossy magazines have a lead time of up to six months, Madeleine. I thought you would be aware of this fact.' His tone is mighty condescending.

'I am aware and I have no doubt the press office will have made sure proofs are there in good time for the reviewers.'

'I'm talking about editorial cover, Madeleine. A feature or – and this is the exciting idea I want to enlist your help with – a cover!' On this bombshell, he throws himself back in his chair, crossing his hands over his expanding stomach, wearing an expression somewhere between smug and exultant.

I'm speechless, although his optimism is to be admired.

'I was thinking *GQ*,' he goes on.

Optimistic? Change that to delusional.

'Gosh, Steven, that's quite a—' I hesitate and thank God

he interrupts, as I don't know how I would have finished that sentence.

'Hear me out, I've been doing some research and they haven't had an author on the cover for at least two years. High time they had one, I'd say, wouldn't you?'

Where to start? Surely during this 'research', he noticed something that all the GQ cover models have in common – devilishly good looks – quite apart from worldwide recognition. How can I diplomatically point out that it's not so much that he's an author as much as the fact that he is losing his hair, has long lost his jawline and appears to have lost his mind.

'Wow, you have given this some real thought,' is all I can manage.

'The publisher is organising new headshots for me and I thought once they were done, you could pop a couple over to the editor of GQ and take it from there.'

'Thing is, Steven, I'm not your publicist; you should put this to the publicity department of the publishers.' I want no part of this.

'Hmm... let's just say, from past experience, their plans are less than ambitious.'

In other words, he has already suggested it and has been turned down flat. Obviously, GQ would never go for it, but I reckon the publishers don't want to look stupid by even suggesting it. Full marks for honesty, but he is not going to take no for an answer. I don't want the weight of this vain man resting on my shoulders and have a lightbulb moment.

'Have you thought about hiring your own publicist? I'm sure I could find you a couple of names. It's such a specific skill and all about the contacts, which I don't have.'

I know he is tempted, but I can also predict his next question.

'How much do you think it would cost?'

'I really don't know, but you would pay for their time, not results. I could put feelers out to my network and get some idea for you?'

I mentally cross my fingers that I have diverted his attention.

'Well, if you're not up to the job, perhaps that is the way to go.' I'll suck that jibe up.

'Good call, Steven. I'll do it once we're done here and I've done all Bridget's jobs—' I know exactly what I'm doing.

'Bridget's jobs?' He's alarmed.

'Researching and sourcing a cot bed, walking the dog – not sure what else, we got interrupted.' He's doing some mental calculations.

'Has she made a separate arrangement with you, Madeleine?'

'No, she just asked me at the door. It will all take a while, of course, but I can make the time.'

'Does she know I pay you by the hour? Because unless she is offering to pay you herself, that is not happening. Your rates for dog walking? I'll be having a word, that's for sure.'

Job done.

Chapter 9

To Ed, 9.15am:
I'm ok. You? Mx

I congratulate myself on managing to wait the full twenty-four hours before responding and for keeping it pretty neutral – quite a feat for me. Ella was at Drippy Tom's when I got home, so I didn't even have to pretend to be civilised. I ate tortilla chips and houmous in bed for supper, did six episodes of a box set in bed and conked out, with my laptop and a few tortilla crumbs still on my stomach.

Have responded in kind, but am feeling anxious regarding our relationship status. Just when I think we should take things to the next level, I feel him pulling back. I really don't want this relationship to end – I've invested so much time and energy and I know we have tonnes of potential. I'd love to talk it through with Ella; things for her and Tom seem to be progressing so smoothly, but I have a feeling I know what she'll say. Talk to him about it. Be honest.

I'm aware I am overthinking, trying to read between lines and second-guess, and that is not how a healthy relationship works. A call would be awkward, but I could suggest meeting up for a chat.

Somewhere deep down, I know this is right. I'll be brave and do it. In the meantime – Casper's show! In my self-pitying state last night, I completely forgot the latest episode aired. Fortunately, I have time to watch it, if I forgo the HIIT class I'd booked. Consider it done. Making a big mug of tea, I settle down at the kitchen table with my laptop and hit play.

I see it all quite differently now, having spent time with the script and thought about the characters in depth, and even allowing for some bias, I think it's pretty good. My cheeks flush with pleasure when I recognise a tweak I suggested and there is no doubt that a couple of my dialogue suggestions have been incorporated. As the credits roll, I push back in my chair and feel a glow of pride. It's a totally different feeling to watching in view of making a complimentary comment to Casper. I was part of that bloody process. I have a quick check of Twitter and see that the fans were out in force and the messages are, for the most part, very supportive.

I think it might be time for a valedictory debrief. I address an imaginary audience: 'So, you see, my job is not all admin and paperwork. I *am* part of the creative process. You may not know of me, but I have the satisfaction of being a great help to my client at a time of dire need.' I manage to say this with about sixty-five per cent conviction.

'Thankless task, I'd say.' Imaginary heckler? Might have a point; I didn't hear a peep from Casper after his meeting. I don't even know if it went well or really, really badly. I can't exactly ask him outright, but I wonder what the ratings were like and how the production company are feeling. I'm not due to see him until later in the week, so unless he calls me about something else, chances are we won't speak in the natural run of things.

Remembering I still need to put the call out for a freelance publicist for Steven gives me the answer. Jess – my CHAMPS chum. I will use the network as the god of networking intended.

Logging on to the member's forum, I am sucked in to browsing the last few days' worth of desperate pleas for contacts at top restaurants who can pull a table for six out of the hat at five minutes' notice and masseuses who will visit a house in Knightsbridge after working hours. There's a request for a kids' tutor prepared to join the family on a yacht round the Med for two weeks to make sure the kiddies keep up with their schoolwork. Almost tempting, apart for the teaching part.

I phrase my request carefully: 'Can anyone a recommend a young, enthusiastic publicist who could run a campaign for a literary author with a book out in September?'

For 'young' read 'cheap'.

For 'enthusiastic' read 'pushy'.

That pretty much covers it, but decide to add 'Limited

budget' just to keep the response realistic. I don't want to have to humiliate myself in front of some A-lister's PR who has a bit of time for a side project, but expects megabucks.

And then I ping a direct message to Jess.

Any updates from Production?

Apart from popping by to check on Dani's place, I don't have any client meetings today. My choices are:

Go to the gym.

Watch another episode (or three) of my current box set.

My decision-making is cut short by a text from the dame.

Darling, could you pick me up some of that divine scent, gift-wrapped, for my director?

Don't be fooled by the 'Darling' – that's easier than remembering my name. I'm probably listed in her contacts as 'skivvy'. I know exactly the fragrance she means; they only stock it at Liberty. My guess is she's been rude or argumentative and wants to get back in the director's good books. I quite fancy a jaunt up to town and can't ignore the fact that Ed's office is so close that it really could be the heavens encouraging me to make contact. Someone has to break the Mexican stand-off we seem to be in, so here goes:

To Ed:
In town for work. Shall we
grab lunch – 1ish? Mx

Delete. Rewrite. Hesitate. Send.

I deliberately leave my phone in the kitchen while I go and get ready, so I don't obsess over how long it takes him to reply. Truth is, I only have about twenty minutes to make myself presentable, so no time to lose, and probably just as well I don't have time to get worked up over what to wear or do to my hair. It's going to be weekday casual and a slick of make-up on the tube. Doesn't mean I don't run back to the kitchen the second I hear a *ping*.

From Ed:
Great. Sushi place – 1.15? Ex

The analytics run as follows:
Isn't just ignoring me – good.
He wants to see me – good.
Could be to break up with me – bad.
Maybe wants to just get it over with – bad.
Choice of sushi place – good (happy memories).
Not going to make it on time – bad.

Text to Ed:
On way. Order my usual.
Mx

I dash out the front door to stride as fast as slightly too tight boots will allow. The tube journey is ideal for catching up on social media and I have a giggle at Jess's feed. I'm not sure where or why, but she is posting selfies wearing the most incredible designer handbags and even more unbelievable shoes – Balenciaga, Manolo's, Chanel. I'm sure I'd know if she had a new job; maybe she's backstage at fashion week? Whatever, her captions are hilarious. Hope she gets back to me soon with the gossip from Top Notch.

Heading into Soho to make up, to break up or to pretend nothing has happened. I decide to take control and not let that happen, even if I have to force the issue. I can't let things drift along as if all is well when it is feels very clear they're not. And break up is not on the table as far as I am concerned.

Squeezing past the queue at the Sushi bar, I'm only five minutes' late – respectable – and I spot the familiar dark mop of hair, head bent, looking at his phone. My heart manages to leap and stomach clench at the same time, not an altogether pleasant experience. At that instant, he looks up and spots me, his lopsided grin gets me in the guts every time and my knees feel a little melty as I approach the table. Leaning down for a double-cheek kiss, resting my hand on his shoulder, I'd like to freeze-frame this moment. Things feel right. We fit together; he must feel it, too.

'Hey, you. I've ordered, shouldn't be too long.' He seems a bit on edge.

'Great, I'm so glad we could do this—' I start as I squish onto the bench seat opposite.

'Yeah, look, I can see I was a bit pissy the other night and maybe I shouldn't have left like that, but the way you run around after these people—'

'My clients, you mean – my job.'

'Maddy, you're more than that. You had plans, ambitions – what happened to your screenwriting dreams?'

Ouch.

'I'm good at what I do,' I bristle, 'but as it happens, things have taken a bit of a turn. I've been helping Casper with his scripts.' It feels good to say it and should shut him up.

'Helping how?' I've caught his interest and start to explain, but Ed interjects.

'So, you're on his writing team?'

'Not exactly; he doesn't have a team. He's never wanted to write with anyone. He writes it; I just make suggestions.' Out loud, it sounds a bit feeble.

'Here we go again, Maddy, he's using you,' he says with a note of exasperation.

I don't want to be having this same old argument, so I cut in.

'Ed, let's not go round this again. I wanted to have a bigger chat, about you and me, about us.' I hadn't meant to bring this up so quickly, but keen to change the subject. Frying pan/fire etc.

'Right, yeah,' he mutters. 'You go first.'

I launch in: 'OK. Thing is, we were so happy, then things seemed to derail and I don't know why. I'm the same, you're the same, we enjoy the same things, but –

I can't put my finger on it – it feels like that's not enough anymore. I'm not enough.' There's a silence before he replies.

'Wow. That's heavy.' There's a pregnant pause and I have to stop myself from jumping in. Eventually, he continues, 'Yeah, we were having fun and that's what I still want – a laugh, good times, not analysing and stressing about "Where is this going?"' The last questio is said in a whiny voice – I hope not intended to be me.

'I get that, Ed, but we aren't kids. Things don't just stay the same; they develop, move forward.' I can't help thinking of Ella and Tom.

He's not looking at me anymore He's pushed himself back in the banquette and is fiddling with his cuff. Not a good sign.

'Maddy, I really like you, but you're sucking the joy out of things. I don't want to break up, but...'

Whoa – he wants to break up. This escalated quickly.

'Is that the choice? Stay in the dating phase forever or break up?' My voice sounds panicky.

'Maybe we just need a bit of space to work things out.' He seems very calm.

'Or the opposite, maybe we should make the effort to spend some quality time together and see how it feels? Take some time off and go away. No phones, no work.' I still believe a cosy weekend could solve all these problems.

'Maybe, but not any time soon. I've booked the ski trip.' That's a punch to the gut, but I'm not about to give up that easily. I know in my heart we have potential.

'Well, I could come, too. Maybe it's just what we need, some time together, away from it all, having a laugh.' Not what I had in mind, but better than nothing?

He won't look at me.

'It's more like a work thing now.' He's still not making eye contact. 'Anyway, it's full. The rooms are allocated. Mimi's got it all sorted.'

I bet she bloody well has. Work thing, my arse. This is just too convenient. Do I turn the other cheek for another slap in the face? No way. In my guts, I know what I must do, even though I really don't want to. I don't know how we got to this point so quickly, but, annoyingly, it seems I do have some pride.

'Ed, I can't believe you made that decision without me – and that says it all. You don't treat me like a proper girlfriend and I deserve better.' I'm sounding very calm and together. It's taking every fibre of my being.

'Don't be so intense, Maddy. Maybe some space will be a good thing. A chance to get some perspective.' Now he looks up, with those big, green puppy-dog eyes.

I may be a romantic fool, but I do not believe in breaks. I need to say this out loud before I lose my nerve.

'That doesn't work for me, Ed.' And I absolutely mean it, but I'm also hoping he will realise that and change his mind. 'I'm calling time on this relationship, but I genuinely think it's a shame. I know we have something special and I know you feel it, too, but I can't make you commit – so go on your ski trip, have all the fun and all the laughs, but I honestly believe at some point, probably after you get home, you will miss me and what we have, and regret what you've just made me do.'

I grab my jacket and bag and start struggling to get out of the booth before the tears come. I know my cheeks and possibly my nose are bright red, and I'm desperate to leave with some dignity.

'Maddy, wait—' Ed catches my hand and as I turn to look back at him, I can see he is struggling.

'I... I don't...'

Come on, Ed. Say you don't want this. I lock eyes with him, willing him to backtrack.

'What?' I will give him this one chance to renege. I can hear a countdown clock in my head. He's got about another three seconds.

'Sorry.' He exhales with a sort of shrug.

So, he won't change his mind. He's off skiing with MooMoo and her mates. Free as a bird.

Wrenching my hand away and barging past the confused-looking waitress just arriving with our order, I have to do a walk of shame past the people still queuing to get in, who no doubt enjoyed watching the scene that just played out.

I need to find somewhere quiet to process the last ten minutes. I can't quite believe I just broke up with Ed. I thought I was going to meet him for a heart to heart, to pull things back together, only to find out he was all signed up for a jolly with a woman who has made her intentions clear. Is it me that's got it all wrong?

Oxford Circus at lunchtime is not the best place to find

yourself in need of sanctuary and I really need to take a minute. Liberty! My happy place. Head down, blinking hard to hold back the tears, I can get to the fourth-floor furniture department on autopilot. It's always quiet up there. I'll find a cosy chair to settle in to nurse my wounds. And even in the midst of this personal crisis, I am still aware that Dame Annette is waiting for her fragrance.

Chapter 10

Clawing my way back to consciousness after a fitful night, disentangling the duvet wrapped tightly round my arm, scenes from yesterday scud through my memory. Clouds of shame and humiliation as I recall being quietly moved on from the Arts and Crafts armchair by a staff member, hiccupping my way through asking for a bottle of gift-wrapped bottle of Molecule and a kind lady offering me a tissue on the Northern Line. The damp patch on my pillow confirmed my suspicions – I'd cried for twelve hours straight. A little ray of hope breaks through as I see my phone screen. A message. Maybe it's Ed, full of regret, changing his mind. But it's Jess.

Call me – I have intel!!! Jx

Obviously not what I was hoping for, but intriguing enough to stop my sniffles. I think I have to accept that yesterday wasn't just a bad dream. But the rest of the world doesn't know my heart is broken and I'm due to be see Casper today, so I'm keen to get any inside info I can. It's unusual, but I haven't heard a peep out of him since last week's drama, and I know from Twitter that the latest episode was considered a return to form.

Can I call in 10? Mx

I'm not quite up to Jess's three-exclamation-marks level of excitement before nine in the morning – especially after a night of weeping. A cup of strong sweet tea and a splash of cold water to the face are required. Heading to the kitchen, the flat feels empty. Even though Ella would have left for work by now, I can tell when she hasn't been home. No lukewarm teabag in the saucer by the kettle, no traces of steam on the bathroom mirror and no jaunty Post-it note on the kitchen table asking me to pick something up/drop something off or if I'm in for supper. Ella's life seems so ordered while mine feels out of control. My sadness is starting to press heavily on my chest again as I get back into bed with a cuppa by my side and a cold flannel on my forehead to make the call.

'Hey, Jess.'

I can hear background noise, somewhere busy and loud.

'Maddy? Hi. I can hardly hear you – I'm walking up Bond Street. Bloody rush hour.'

Decide to buck up and stop being feeble. 'Is this better? I can hear you fine. What are you doing on Bond Street so early?'

'It's a nightmare. Madame is determined to return some serum she was gifted. Cheeky cow wants me to get money or at least credit. I spoke to head office and they weren't having any of it, so she's decided if I go in person, I can strong-arm some poor shop assistant by giving the 'Do you know who I am?' routine. I daren't go back without a result. I'm going to lie in wait on the doorstep. Glamorous, non?' She sounds like she's enjoying her indignation.

'Oh, Jess, we have to find you a better job. Any luck on the CHAMPS website?'

'Not really, nothing fashion, but that's not why we need to talk. Hot gossip from my production pal – Casper has a secret writing partner! Do you know who it could be?' She's practically panting with excitement.

'What are you talking about?' How can I not know about this? But it could explain why he's gone so quiet.

'Production had him in for a meeting and they totally roasted him about the ratings; insisted he use a writing team. He refused – said he had someone in mind he would work with, but wouldn't say who. They gave him one more chance and things started turning around. They are desperate to know who this saviour is, but he won't breathe a word. I thought you might have an idea?' She's talking super-fast due to excitement.

'Not a clue. I'm seeing him later; maybe all will be revealed then.' I'm trying to tone her down while also processing this information.

'You have to let me know if you find out who this

mystery talent is!' If only Jess spent as much energy on finding a new job as she did on industry gossip.

'Of course.'

Of course not. This is all very strange, but I'm not letting any cats out of any bags. Casper doesn't really discuss his professional life with me, but I tend to pick up on what's going on by being around, opening the mail, chatting to his agent. Maybe this afternoon will clarify things if I keep my eyes and ears open. Bit of detective work – add that to my list of accomplishments.

A quick check of the CHAMPS forum shows quite a response to my request. Gotta love these folk. There are a dozen messages, ranging from CV and brief covering note to full-on PowerPoint presentation with photo and testimonials. I'll forward a selection to Needy Steve and try to keep out of it as much as possible.

To Ella, 9.30am:
You in tonight? I am. And
every night for the rest of my
life Mx

I need a shoulder to cry on, but, in the meantime, I need to get my act together. I amuse myself as I get dressed by imagining what Jess is reducing herself to for the sake of a few quid. This job, honestly, you couldn't make it up.

Next, I swing by Dani's to check all is well. I can't help having flashbacks to my haunted house experience last week, which leads me to churning over how that night ended. In an alternate universe, Ed and I could have laughed about me being scared out of my wits by shadows. He could have comforted me, but no – he had a hissy fit and stormed off to book himself on a jolly. I start working up an 'I'm-better-off-without-him' sweat while flicking though the mail, but it's not really happening. It feels like unfinished business and, as my clients would tell you, I always see a job through.

Ooh! Guest passes to a fancy pants gym. They expire before Dani gets back. Shame to let them go to waste. This is a perk of my job: cast-offs and hand-me-downs. I'll check Dani doesn't mind – though I know plenty of assistants wouldn't bother – but I'm already planning a mini spa day. I could take Ella as a thank you for being a good pal. We could have a swim, do a class, hit the salad bar and maybe even splash out on a treatment. Basically, abuse the facilities.

From Ella:
Yes! Catch-up overdue.
Sourdough pizzas on me! Ex

That's my girl, and I can bring these gym passes to the table. We'll have a proper debrief and decide whether I should go all out to win Ed back or just wait for him to realise what a gross error he has made. I'm starting to feel better already. Time to head to Casper's. I'm wondering about the mystery writing partner and nursing a suspicion that has been scratching away at the back of my mind since Jess called. It feels big-headed to even phrase the question, but I can't see how he had time to confer with anyone else before that production meeting last week. I didn't exactly write anything new, but I think that's how writers work together – bouncing ideas, trying things out for size. I wonder if he'll say something, make it official.

My reverie is interrupted – Needy Steve.

'Hi Nee… I mean, Steve. How're you?' *That was close.*

'Maddy, who *are* all these people? I don't know where to begin. They all seem qualified for the job; they all have great credentials. I thought you were getting me some recommendations, not an open casting call.' He sounds irritated. Bloody cheek – I did exactly what he asked. He may be talented, but this isn't rocket science.

'That *is* a selection. You need to pick someone who is a good fit for you, has done a similar campaign, or at least understands what your aims are. It's quite straightforward.' I didn't exactly select, but ultimately it's got to be his choice.

'Can't *you* choose?' He sounds like Sigmund might if he could talk, i.e. a big baby.

'Well, I could, but it is important to have someone you can get along with – who 'gets' you. And it would take a while.'

There's a pause while he takes this in.

'Well, can you help me at least?' he wheedles.

I'll offer a compromise. 'I suggest you start by drafting a brief of what you want to achieve and an idea of your budget, then send it to the ones you like the look of. Ask them to respond with a plan for going forwards.'

Needy by name, needy by nature. Even so, I'm letting my frustration show. I need to reel it in.

'Then shortlist two or three to meet. We can come up with some questions and interview them. Does that sound reasonable?' Do *I* sound reasonable?

'I suppose so. I'm busy on my final edit, but I'll let you know when I'm ready to proceed.' His nerves are soothed.

'I await your call.'

Honestly! He's the one wanting to be a cover boy, then making it sound like I'm pressuring him.

I still get a buzz using a permit to park right in front of Casper's des res, which means no tooling around. I'm just scratching the appropriate boxes when the front door is flung open and there is Casper on the top step. This is becoming a habit. 'Hurry up! Chop, chop,' he shouts and sets off down the hallway.

'Right, sure.' I'm still getting my Casper bag out the car and locking up, and he's already in his office.

'We need to fill out your health insurance renewal forms today. Have you had any doctor's visits or tests?' I ask from the doorway.

'Fuck that, I need you in here,' and we are heading for his lovely, airy and terribly white workspace.

So, last week wasn't a one-off.

Now I see him up close, something is off. Normally super-groomed, he looks a bit dishevelled, but it's hard to read expressions with that much Botox going on.

Given the slight whiff in the air, I'm not sure he's even had a shower. With Jess's words in the back of my mind, I play innocent.

'Ratings have improved, you must be relieved.' Maybe he'll take the bait and give me the info I'm dying to hear.

'You'd think – but production are being a pain in my arse.' He flings himself down into his desk chair.

'Oh, really? In what way?' Let's see what I can find out.

'They've got no bloody confidence, banging on about bringing in other writers. They should have some trust in me.' He's absentmindedly running his hand over his stubbly head.

'Right, and is that what's happened?' I'm holding my breath for the answer.

'No way.' He barks at me. 'I'm not having some pen-pushing exec tell me how to write *my* show.'

Well, that answers Jess's question, but not mine. This is my chance to ask what exactly is going on with me and my input, and admit I'm the mystery writer he's fobbed them off with. But what if he goes off on one, which is a definite possibility? I don't want these sessions to stop. Given my personal life is falling apart, they are all I've got to cling on to.

Casper has his back to me, getting something out of his Louis Vuitton man bag, so I cautiously phrase my question.

'I have a friend who works at Top Notch.' He freezes and, if I'm not imagining things, his shoulders tense, but he doesn't say anything, 'She said something about another writer on the show?'

Silence. I decide not to go any further. Probably the right decision as he explodes.

'Bunch of bloody gossips – nothing better to do! If I find out you're part of this witch hunt, just remember whose team you are on.' He spins round to face me, his face red and angry.

'Of course, Casper – I'm with you one hundred per cent!' With a conscious effort to reign himself in, he gestures for me to sit opposite him at the huge desk he imported from Italy at ridiculous expense, and while I am working out how to adjust the fully adjustable chair (arm rests, lumbar support, height, etc.), he slams a pile of loose pages down.

Casper is looking at me, intently, but I'm keeping shtum until I know what is required.

'Here you go – have a read.' He pushed the heap over. He's reverted to his normal colour.

I don't know what he wants from me, but I'm scared to ask questions in case he kicks off. I can't take the words in, plus I can feel his gaze directed squarely at the top of my head.

After a few minutes of looking at the words swimming on the page, I grasp the bull by the whatevers and look up to meet his stare. I'm going straight in there.

'Casper, it would help if you told me what you want from me – do you want my response, my suggestions or should I just blow smoke up your arse?'

Cannot actually believe I just said that, but I've had enough of pussy-footing around. This could go either way...

We lock eyes for a long moment and then he gives a short bark of a laugh.

'Definitely no smoke this time, Maddy. I want some more of those home truths you seem to have a knack for.' The fury has left the room.

With a sense of validation, I can read on and have the confidence to point out that Edie only ever responds to other characters, when surely she is strong enough to initiate her own exchanges. With a look of concentration, Casper swings his equally ergonomic chair to face his computer screen and starts tapping away.

'Good stuff, Maddy, my girl – keep it coming.'

Thinking about what I've just said about being passive strikes a chord for me, too, but I focus on the job in hand. I'll park this thought and revisit it later.

When I mention the dialogue in the third scene doesn't sit right, we read it out loud together, dividing the parts up between us, with me stopping the scene where I think it jars, and then we throw suggestions back and forth until Casper says, 'A fairy dies every time you say that,' which makes me laugh out loud. He quickly notes it down.

A couple of hours fly by and insurance renewals are forgotten, until Casper leans back in his chair, which gives a worryingly loud squeal, and says, 'Basta! We're done for today. Good work.'

I'm desperate to clarify what my role in this is, exactly, but there is a change in the atmosphere. Having spent a couple of hours on an equal footing, the balance of power has shifted back to boss/assistant and I lose my nerve. Again.

'Shall I head downstairs then?' I ask, predicting the answer.

'Yeah, sure. Knock yourself out.' His attention is already elsewhere, working up the notes he's been making during our session. He doesn't even raise his head as I slip out of the office.

'Shit. Damn. Bollocks.' I hiss an expletive for each step as I stamp my way down to the basement. Running out of options, I end on three loud 'Fucks', which is reassuringly satisfying. This isn't fantasy. This is really happening. What 'this' is being the million-dollar question. Thank God I have an evening with Ella booked in, because, along with my Ed situation, this is right up there on the agenda.

My usual duties are a drudge after the stimulation of the brainstorm upstair and my mood sinks as I open the mail. Taking a break to scroll on Instagram to cheer myself up shows Jess has posted more photos of herself with incredible shoes and bags. Her followers have gone shooting up and I wonder how she's doing it – maybe trying them on while she was in Bond Street this morning.

To Jess:
Living the dream! Mx

And my phone rings immediately.

If it wasn't for caller display telling me it was Jess, I'd have no idea, because all I can hear at the other end are wracking sobs.

'Jess – what's happened? Are you OK?' I hope it's nothing awful.

'Aria's fired me – and said really nasty things.' I can just about make out her words.

'Because you couldn't get a refund on the serum? She can't do that! Outrageous!'

'Noooo,' which comes out as a wail. 'Her shoes.'

'Because you couldn't return some shoes? I'm having the same with Dani, but it's hardly a sackable offence.' Jess can be a drama queen, but, even for her, this seems completely over the top.

'My Instagram – she followed me and saw me wearing them.'

Turns out it's Aria's shoes and bags that Jess has been posting pictures of – she's been raiding Aria's wardrobe while she's been away. Hardly the crime of the century, but probably does count as crossing the line.

'Oh, Jess – what did she say?' I would find this funny if Jess didn't sound so heartbroken.

'That I'm a thieving little bitch and she'll make sure I never work in the industry again.' Wow, Aria certainly doesn't mince her words.

'Honestly, hun, I wouldn't take it too seriously. You've lasted longer than most of her assistants, doesn't she usually switch up each season?'

Feeble attempt at fashion humour, but it causes a break in the wailing so I go on.

'And she probably doesn't even mean it. Wait till she's calmed down a bit, then apologise.' I know how diva behaviour works – all fireworks in the moment, but you suck it up and move on.

'Maddy, she was so mean. She said I was a fat cow who couldn't fit into her clothes, so I had to make do with her shoes. Which is actually true...'

I hear a bit of a twinkle of the old Jess.

'I guess if worst comes to worst, I could sell a story. I could call a Caroline or whatever their names were from CHAMPS.'

I know she's joking, because that is the one sure-fire way she would never get a job again.

'I'd say hold tight and she'll have forgotten by morning.' I adopt my keep-calm-and-carry-on default position, which doesn't solve things, but anything for a quiet life.

'I don't think I will, Maddy, not this time. She's a monster. I've been miserable for ages. This is my kick in the pants to find something better.' I don't know if she's really thought this through, but she sounds like she means it. I admire her bravery.

'Good on you, Jess. She'll miss you more that you'll miss her.' Jess's don't-care attitude had served her well, but it seems everyone has their limit.

'Yeah,' followed by a sniff.

'Hell yeah! But, hun, I'm at work right now so I'd better go. Let's speak tomorrow and hatch a plan.'

Leaving Casper's without so much as a wave from him, I head back to the flat, contemplating Jess's decision. Is it brave or stupid to walk away?

Chapter 11

From Ella, 6.30pm:
Trying to get out of here.
Back by 8 Ex

I've finished work and we are ordering in supper, which leaves me no excuse not to go to the gym. With not much energy after the last few nights, and a head spinning with questions, I think Body Pump might finish me off. Checking the schedule, there's a yoga class I could just make. I've been meaning to give yoga a go for ages.

Heading up the stairs, the receptionist calls out, 'Yoga's in the wellness studio, through the swing doors.'

I have never been through the swing doors and didn't even know there was such a thing as a wellness studio, but it sounds exactly what I need. Rushing down a carpeted corridor of treatment rooms, I arrive with seconds to spare and barge in, hoping to slip into a place at the back without anyone noticing.

I'm met by the sight of a woman sitting cross-legged on a cushion thing with her hands held in prayer position in front of her chest. It is completely silent. The rest of the class are sitting facing her, all cross-legged, eyes closed and apparently praying.

What on earth have I let myself in for? I should have just hopped on a cross trainer and listened to a podcast.

The teacher opens her eyes to say, 'Hello. Welcome to Iyengar Yoga. Do you have any injuries?'

Strange way to start and, if I wasn't stressed enough, I could now add a new level of anxiety.

'Um, no, I don't think so.' Does a stiff neck count as an injury?

'Are you on your period?'

Rude! What the hell is this class? I'm in an alternative universe.

'No,' I reply in a small voice, wondering if it is possible to just reverse out of the door and pretend this never happened. They've all got their eyes closed, so I could probably get away with it, but she continues, fixing me with her serene gaze.

'Grab a mat and a bolster and come and sit over here. We are just about to start by chanting Om,' as if that is the most natural thing in the world.

No escape. I'm already picturing describing this to Ella later – at the very least, it will be an amusing anecdote.

Doing as the teacher says, I copy her stance as she tells

us to breath in deeply and say 'Om' when we breath out. I feel ridiculous; it sounds raggedy, with everyone starting at different times and different tones, but by the third one, it sounds quite nice. The voices have come together.

The class continues with the teacher directing us, moving around the room to straighten an arm or adjust a shoulder. She shows us what to do first; she's incredibly flexible, even though she looks pretty old. The positions have weird names and I have no idea what she is on about, but the others seem to know what they are doing, so I just watch closely and copy the woman in front of me. The strange thing is that even though we are moving slowly and just sitting or standing in simple positions, it's really hard work. It seems to be a case of getting into an uncomfortable position, like sitting cross-legged, but bending forward as far as you can, and then just staying there for an impossibly long time, or my personal favourite: standing with your legs wide open and trying to put your head on the floor. I am ninety-nine per cent sure that I heard someone fart at that point, but despite my head involuntarily shooting up to see who it was, no one else seemed bothered, which I realise retrospectively probably made it look like it was me letting one off. The atmosphere in the studio is very calm, not at all what I am used to at the gym.

After a while, she tells us to lie down on our mats with a blanket over us. Glancing up at the clock, I can't believe an hour has passed. She lights some incense, probably to cover the farty smell, and does a guided meditation thing like I've tried on apps. My muscles feel nicely stretched and my head feels calm until there is a familiar buzzing. My eyes fly open and I'm lunging for my bag, which I chucked down at the back of the class.

'Please – no phones in the studio,' says the nice, calm teacher with a slightly tetchy note in her voice. Mortified, I grab my bag and dash out of the class, leaving the others stretched out and looking mellow despite my interruption.

I'm hoping it won't be a work emergency, and that it could be Ed, but it's Mum. I answer in a hissy whisper: 'Yes?'

'Hello, darling, just thought I'd check in – fancied a chat.'

'Not good timing, Mum. I'm at the gym.'

'The amount of running around you do; I'm surprised you bother with the gym.'

'Actually, It's a yoga class.'

'Ooh – don't go all weird on us.'

'Why would doing some stretches make me go weird, Mum?'

'Well, it's a religious thing, isn't it?'

'I don't think so; it's at the gym.'

'Watch out you don't get sucked into a cult – you're just the type.'

'Mum – do you wonder why you don't hear from me much?'

'I'm doing Friday night dinner next week, all of us. Will you come?'

Even though she's annoying, I can't resist Mum's roast chicken and potatoes. And I haven't seen my sister and Elijah for ages so I agree and we say our goodbyes.

I also have a reminder on my phone from Jess about a CHAMPS breakfast event and another from Dame Annette, reminding me about the charity tea. Neither fills my heart with joy, unlike the thought of a Margherita pizza with extra olives and mushrooms and a crust dipper on the side. I decide everything can wait until tomorrow and I'll stop at the pizza place on the way home to pick up our order.

Texting Ella to confirm her choice, which I know will be *quattro formaggi*, I pick a up a bottle of rosé and start to formulate an agenda:

1. Ed situation update (priority).
2. Casper situation.
3. Ed (action plan).
4. AOB (any other business) including an opportunity for Ella to bring up any topic she wishes to talk about.

Do not let it be said that I am not a considerate friend.

Feeling chilled from the class despite my stressy exit, the parking fairy is sitting on my shoulder as I pull into our road and I get a lovely spot just by the flat, meaning I can manage wine, gym bag, Dani bag and Casper bag all draped variously across my back and shoulders with the pizzas held out in front of me like a sacred offering. What I can't do, however, is actually open the door and I'm just about to balance the pizzas on the wheelie bin to get to my keys when I hear Ella yoo-hooing from the corner.

'Stop right there! I'm coming – do not even *think* about putting the pizzas on the bin!'

I freeze, hearing her smart boots clacking towards me.

'Eurgh! As if I would!' God, she knows me too well.

Relieving me of a couple of bags, Ella opens the door and leads the way upstairs, past my so-called office – I'm thinking hot desk may be a better description – and into the hallway where we simultaneously drop everything except the wine and pizza and tumble into the kitchen as she unbuttons her trench coat and hangs it on the back of the door.

Not bothering with plates, or even cutlery, she opens the wine and we settle down in our usual places at the table, open pizza boxes in front of us. I have almost forgotten how miserable I am, until Ella takes a mouthful of wine, sighs deeply as she leans back in her chair and looks me directly in the eye.

'So, what has been going on with you, Ms Maddy?'

Launching straight into the Ed situation as it stands, since the lunchtime break-up disaster, she makes me go back and I tell her about MooMoo's party, the alarm call. As I tell her, I'm closely monitoring the look on her face and notice it changes from sympathetic to me, to a slightly furrowed brow and pursed lip, which I interpret as sympathetic to him. This is during the alarm bit.

'But, Maddy, look at it from his point of view; you've had a lovely dinner and evening together, he's introducing you to his work friends, back here for a romantic encounter, and next thing you're bolting off into the night like a vigilante security guard.'

'Don't you dare take his side – it's my job!' How dare she take his side?

'What would you have done if there *were* intruders? I don't think it is your job.' She's using a calm, reasonable voice, but it doesn't work.

'Shit, Ella, things are hard enough without you starting on me! Ed, my parents, now you – everyone thinks my job is shit, but people rely on me.' This isn't even what I want to be discussing with her.

'Maddy, take a breath, I'm not having a go at you. I know better than anyone how hard you work, the pressure you're under, but maybe it's time to take a step back – think about yourself a bit and not your ridiculously demanding clients. Draw boundaries.' Still calm and reasonable.

'These people aren't nine-to-fivers like in your world.' This came out sulkier than I meant it to.

'Excuse me? Nine to five? This is the first time I've been home at a reasonable hour for over a week.' Now she's rattled.

'No, I didn't mean that, Ella, I'm sorry. I don't even know what I meant, but the thing is – it led to us breaking up and I really, *really* didn't want that. I love Ed.' That's the truth and there's not much I can do about it.

'I know you do, hon, but he's always been a tough one to pin down.'

'Sorry? Since when is that a known fact?' Not what I was expecting at all.

'Well, you always seem to be waiting – waiting to hear

from him, waiting to see him, waiting to see if he'll go away for the weekend, waiting...'

'I get the drift, Ella.' This is so harsh.

'I thought he was going to suggest you moved in with him. I'm delighted to have you here, I really am, but...'

That is a body blow and it must have shown.

'Shit, Maddy, I'm sorry, I'm not trying to upset you. I didn't say anything because you seemed OK with it, but seeing how miserable you've been lately, and now you've split up, I thought it was time to be honest.' If this is her attempt at being comforting, I am not impressed.

Tears are now inevitable and I struggle to get my words out. 'But I don't want to split up, we have so much potential.'

Sometimes you just want a pal to say what you want to hear, but Ella is not that kind of pal. She's looking at me, with an expression that could be described as pitying, and then she's off again.

'And this ski trip, that doesn't sound good. He'd decided to go without you before you even broke up.' Thanks for the clarification.

'It's that bloody cow's fault. Things were fine till she came along.' Is that really true? I'm not even sure anymore.

'Maddy, come on, you know Ed doesn't do anything unless he wants to,' she says like it's commonly acknowledged.

'Why don't you just get a knife and stick it in my heart, Ella?'

'Because you are a great girl and I love you, and you deserve to be with someone who is crazy about you.'

I really want to get angry with her, want to kick off, but in my gut I know she hasn't said anything contentious. I also know she is my good and true friend and wouldn't be mean for the sake of it, so I just weep.

The pizza is getting cold and the wine is getting warm. Ella puts one in the oven and the other in the fridge and then comes and gives me a big hug.

'I know we could be good together,' I snuffle into her shoulder.

'Maybe, but he's not ready. You have to step back. Chasing after him is not the answer.'

'When did you get so bloody wise and clever?'

'Probably at law school. People pay a lot for my advice these days.'

I manage a watery smile, but don't want to raise the topic of Casper. I'm not strong enough for another telling-off, so instead I ask her how things are with her and she gets a bit dreamy talking about Drippy Tom, except I can't remember why I called him that, because actually he just sounds nice and kind and straightforward. I half tune out of listening to how lovely he is, until Ella mentions his friends and I know where she is going.

'I'm not interested. Ed is going to realise what a mistake he's made and come crawling back.'

Ella shrugs. 'Well, in the meantime, you could spread your wings a bit. There's a picnic on Saturday. I was going to ask you along anyway.'

I don't feel very sociable right now, so I change the subject, rescue the pizza from the oven, crack into the wine and before long I am doing an impression of the 'omming' from the yoga class and we are crying with laughter.

It's a good cover because I could very easily tip over into actual crying. Ella hasn't pulled any punches and I know she means well, but she doesn't know what it's like when me and Ed are getting on. She hasn't seen the way he looks at me the instant before we kiss or how he seeks me out when something happens only we'll find funny. I can see things don't look great right now, but I won't accept there's no hope.

We tidy up the kitchen in companionable silence, both shattered, and I give her a big hug goodnight to show no hard feelings.

'So you'll come to the picnic on Saturday?'

Accepting I have absolutely no other plans on the horizon and no boyfriend to just hang out with, I give a sort of scrunched-up face shrug as a reply.

'I'll take that as a yes,' Ella says as she heads into her room. 'It'll be fun, you'll see,' and she closes the door before I have a chance to backtrack.

Chapter 12

Pulling on a soft jersey Vivienne Westwood dress I picked up in the Liberty sale years ago, standing in front of the full-length mirror in the hallway, I bless Dame Viv's good design and wonder what she'd be like to work for? Probably best not to meet your heroes, plus fashion is so much more high-octane than light entertainment, which reminds me – Jess! If she really is walking away from her job with Aria, what on earth is she going to do? Much as I admire her screw-you attitude, I don't think I'd have the balls to just leave. smoothing my curls with the Frizz Ease serum that changed my life as a fuzzy-haired teenager, the germ of an idea starts to formulate – an idea that could help me, Needy Steve and Jess out, all in one fell swoop.

I tweet something quasi-motivational about making connections and head off, no client bag weighing me down, to get the bus. The route takes me past the fancy auction house the dame sent me to a while back, convinced if she went it would drive the price up, so off I went with a strict limit on what to spend.

Registering at the bidders' desk, I was given a numbered paddle and sat on a flimsy gilt chair in the front row, in among all sorts, from designer-dressed men with fancy glasses to elderly ladies with bulging shoulder bags and silk headscarves. Who were the serious buyers and who just came for a day out? I didn't dare lose concentration for a second as the auction began and they rattled through the items. I was aware of a bank of auction house employees with phone headsets standing behind a raised counter and, as the auctioneer banged his gavel sharply on his lectern, I felt like I was in court, he was a judge and I inexplicably started to feel guilty.

My nerves were quivering as the lot numbers jumped and Dame Annette's painting was up next. Equally terrified that either I would freeze and not raise my paddle or that my arm would shoot up involuntarily at the wrong time, I stared at the auctioneer as he gave a brief description of the painting and then opened the bidding. Silence. Now? My hand twitched. The auctioneer took a breath and we were off. Figures pinged around; he glanced between the phone bank and the room, then it slowed down and I made my move, raised my paddle. It felt like an eternity, but a curt nod from the phones and we were off again, the increments bigger, edging to my limit. I was buzzing. It would be so easy to get carried away, but a vision of the dame's face if I overspent kept me grounded – as did the vision of her face if we didn't get it. The room went silent. It was with me, the gavel was raised and... yes! I'd got it. Bang on budget. Air punch! Shit! I'd used my paddle hand, so I let out an involuntary 'Sorry – not bidding', though as the next item hadn't started, the auctioneer just gave me a withering look.

This wander down memory lane has brought me to my stop.

I join the flow of bodies and adjust my pace to avoid making physical contact with anyone – hard when the person in front slows down to consult their phone map, and the one behind is on a mission to break the UK power-walking record. To get myself in the networking/sympathising zone and to stop from mulling over Ella's comments about Ed, I listen to some old disco, which lifts my spirits and makes me strut.

The beat still in my ears, I arrive and make myself known to the smiley young woman behind reception who points me in the direction of a hubbub of voices. Most people are clustered around a table laden with bagels and fruit platters – my favourite kind of breakfast – but I don't see Jess's shock of silver hair. Then I spot her, sitting in a low, battered leather chair looking glum, mournfully chewing on a croissant. Grabbing a couple of freshly squeezed juices and ignoring the Buck's Fizz – because this is a) work-related and b) *breakfast*, for God's sake – I head over and plonk down beside her.

'Hey, Jess, how're you doing?' I say in my best upbeat voice.

'Unemployed and unemployable according to Aria,' she replied gloomily. She's not dressed to her usual flamboyant standards and her silver hair has lost its sheen.

'You haven't sorted things out?' I'd hoped it might have blown over.

'Are you kidding? It just gets worse! Because of my 'gross misconduct', I don't get any notice or reference or anything.'

'Seriously? Wearing someone else's shoes is a bit revolting, but that seems harsh.' Truth is, you would never catch me doing something like that, but Jess always takes things that bit further, plus she doesn't tend to hold her clients in very high regard.

'I signed a non-disclosure agreement, standard, and she says this is an invasion of privacy, so I haven't got a leg to stand on. I wouldn't go back now, anyway, but I was hoping for a bit of cash to tide me over. I tried threatening her with a tell-all story, but she got her lawyers to write me a cease-and-desist letter, so it's just not worth it. I'm practically broke. Rent's due in a week; I'm screwed. I have a Plan B but I don't really want to go there...' Trying to pull it together, she asks, 'How are things with you?'

Hoping it will cheer her up, I can't wait to tell her my master plan. 'I've had an idea for you, not permanent, but a bit of work for right now.' I can see it's not the time to be whinging about Ed.

'Oh my God – amazing – tell me more.' I launch in quick because she looks a bit too excited.

'Am I right you've done some PR along the way?' Please say she has.

'Haven't we all?' This is bit of a universal truth as we PAs often have to turn our hand to all sorts of things. Jess has visibly perked up now, forgotten the croissant and is looking at me expectantly, flaky crumbs round her mouth.

'Good. So, I have this author, Steve, and he's not satisfied with the coverage his publishers are getting and wants to hire a PR for his next book, starting now, to hit the long-lead magazines and get some mainstream attention. I put a note out on CHAMPS.'

'How did I miss that?' Probably too busy messing around in Aria's walk-in wardrobe.

'Doesn't matter, it's not too late. I'm sure you could handle it. Price yourself low and I could put you at the top of the pile. I'll help you with the interview and stuff; I know what he wants – GQ cover, no less!' She hasn't seen Steve, so she doesn't realise what a big ask this is.

'Maddy, that sounds fab. It would give me an excuse to brush up my contacts, you darling. Let's do it.'

She is morphing back into the jolly Jess I know and love, croissant now completely abandoned, starting to fizz with ideas.

'Just promise me one thing, Jess.' I look at her seriously.

'Anything.' She looks a bit anxious.

'Don't be trying on his shoes…'

Collapsing noisily into giggles brings the attention of some Caroline or another, the one who commandeered the steering committee and is self-appointed head of CHAMPS.

'Madeleine, Jessica, how are we? Having a good time, it seems.' Her body language shows her disdain for us, her face a rictus smile.

'Yeah, we just love networking at the crack of dawn, don't you?' Jess throws back at her.

'My point exactly, ladies. We're about to have the presentation from our hosts, so please use this time to introduce yourselves to some of the new members and show them how friendly CHAMPS are.'

Who made her the boss of us? She's hovering, all prim and proper in her nude heels.

'Absolutely, Caroline, as friendly as you.' Jess is fearless.

'Indeed, Jessica, and a little bird told me you are no longer supporting Aria,' Caroline says, smugly.

'Good news travels fast, doesn't it?' Honestly, if looks could kill, they'd both be dead – then Caroline delivers what she thinks will be her fatal blow.

'Please don't forget your membership is dependent on working for a high-profile or high-net-worth individual.' This is what she's been waiting to say.

Concerned that Jess might actually go for her, I diplomatically launch in, 'Jess and I were just discussing her new role, weren't we, Jess?'

I can almost see Caroline's nose go out of joint, torn between wanting to know more and wanting to see the back of Jess.

'Congratulations. Who's the client?' Curiosity wins over Ms Catty.

'Too hush-hush to discuss, still negotiating. Come on,

Jess, let's network the shit out of this event.' And I grab her hand and pull her out of the chair as I stand up, leaving Caroline standing there with a fixed smile and a whiff of fury.

Waiting in line for coffee would be the perfect time to ask Jess if she has any more info about what is happening with Casper and Top Notch Productions, but, rejuvenated, she is working the room, hoping someone will have a lead about a maternity cover or a friend leaving their job. As we know only too well, it's not what you know.

Coffee in hand, I head over to introduce myself to one of the hosts from Workspace, a smart young woman in a structural black shirt dress that looked like it would need a *lot* of ironing, ideally by an ironing expert. I explain that I have a roster of clients but that as my home office (ahem) is a bit out of the way, I'd be interested in knowing the rates for using the space on a casual basis. My face must have given me away when she told me. I couldn't even pretend it was going to be possible for me to afford, but I promised I'd mention it to all my clients.

'Madeleine, you are just the type of contact we need while we're getting established. How about we have an unofficial arrangement? You call me if you need some space and, if we aren't busy, you can pop in and use the facilities, as long as you spread the word?'

What a fabulous offer – total result.

'Seriously? Of course, I'll spread the word anyway, but is it OK with your boss?' I didn't want to be caught out blagging it and get marched off the premises.

She looked a bit surprised and then laughed, 'I am the boss, deal with me direct. Here's my card.' Taken aback, I'd have guessed she was younger than me.

'Brilliant – thank you so much...' Glancing down at the card to read her name, I am flummoxed. The card reads 'L-a'.

'Leyah...?' I try in an unconfident tone.

'It's pronounced Ledasha.' She's smiling. 'My mum learnt English as a second language and loved to play around with it. I hated it as a kid, but now I embrace it. I think it gave me inner strength.'

'L-a, you are a...' and I make a heart sign with my hands.

She gets it and laughs. 'I hope we'll be seeing you here soon, Madeleine.'

'Please, call me, Maddy. My friends do. And yes – see you soon.'

I can't help feeling my day is going incredibly well, especially given that it is not yet 10am. Maybe there is something in this networking malarkey, not just free grub and a goody bag. I'm quite chuffed L-a was interested in me, Maddy, and not just as a conduit to my clients, but also a little envious that she was so high powered.

I wave to get Jess's attention. She's in animated conversation with some edgily dressed fashion types and make the 'I'll call you' signal, even though phones don't look like that anymore. She responds with a thumbs up. The others turn round; one looks familiar and smiles straight at me. Having no idea who she is, I vaguely smile back, having probably seen her at another CHAMPS do.

Back onto High Holborn, I spy a sale sign in my favourite clothes shop. OK, *one* of my favourite clothes shops. I do love my clothes and I do love a bargain, so double temptation. I feel the pull of the sale rail deep in my guts and am about to press the button on the pedestrian crossing to head over there when I feel that familiar buzz.

From Dame Annette:
I need you at tea this afternoon.

Chapter 13

Having set up office in a coffee shop, I start assessing the PR applications for Needy Steve. I hadn't realised so many people worked like me, piecing it together here and there, as well as those with full-time roles looking for a side hustle. Catty Caroline being one of the latter. As I read her impressive and, no doubt, exaggerated CV. I'm faced with a dilemma: dismiss her out of hand, just because I can, or give her an interview and have the pleasure of being the one in control? My evil side wins. I'm pleased to see that Jess uploaded her CV and application straight after the event. Less experience than the others, but this is reflected in her rates, plus she is hungry for the work, so where's the harm in putting her on the shortlist? I suggest some dates to run interviews and was debating a bit of social media stalking (I'd discovered Mimi's Insta handle is @MeMeMe – classic), when I noticed a message in my CHAMPS inbox – unusual.

Lauren Argon
Hello! Don't think you recognised
me with my clothes on.

What the...? I click back to double-check the name, but it means nothing. I hit the CHAMPS members' page to see who this person is and there is a photo of a smiling woman with dark, shoulder-length hair, but it's titchy and could be any number of people. She does look vaguely familiar, but who doesn't these days? Am I losing my memory? I'm utterly befuddled as to how to reply when another message pings in:

Saw you at yoga this week –
maybe we're neighbours?

That's it! The woman who smiled at me when I was leaving, she was in the never-to-be-repeated yoga class. I was in such a state of high anxiety for the entire class, I barely noticed the other people, except as a tangle of arm and legs, and we were bent over double for most of it.

Hi! Yes, first time, probably
last tbh. I live in Muswell Hill.

Why? I love it. Game changer.
Bet you slept well. I'm in
Crouch End.

Thinking back, I did sleep well that night – first time for ages – but it was probably coincidence. She must work in the same field if she's a CHAMPS member and could be one of the HNWI crew, so I decide to keep a professional distance.

**Small world! Got to dash,
take care, Maddy**

Bit curt, but she might be a hippy-dippy yoga nut and I can't be dealing with one of those right now. I've got a bloody tea party to referee this afternoon. My checklist goes: dame for timings; venue for private room set-up; car service for logistics; charity rep for dietary requirements, guest attendance and – most importantly – that she is coming along to mind her guests and, as the dame has made achingly clear, pick up the tab.

I have a dangerously late-in-the-day cortado to pep me up and wait for responses from all of the above. The venue and charity lady are good as gold about getting back to me, then my phone goes. Dame Annette. She probably can't be bothered to put her glasses on to text.

'I will arrive at 4pm prompt. Meet me at the entrance. I will leave at 4.45pm. Have the car waiting.' Charming as ever.

'Got it and, just to warn you, they're bringing some theatre programmes to sign. I've got a Sharpie.' It's best to warn her before an ambush.

'The cheek – it's never enough. If I agree, they will want something else, you mark my words.' Gracious, as well.

'They're huge fans, Dame Annette, and it will be such a marvellous reminder of the afternoon for them,' is what I say. However, what I *think* is that given they probably paid ten grand or more for this privilege, forty-five minutes in her presence and a few signed programmes is not what I would call value for money – but, of course, it's for charity and that makes everything alright.

With my admin sorted and time to kill, knowing I look pretty good, it's tempting to sashay past Ed's office. The only small issue is that I would be leaving my dignity bundled up in a small carrier bag in the gutter, never to be retrieved. I can hear Ella's voice telling me not to be a complete idiot, when I am saved, sort of:

From Dame Annette, 2.50pm:
Make-up girl says she can't do
me. Sort something out

I'm secretly quite pleased to have this mini drama to deal with as it may well have stopped me making a fool of myself. The make-up girl from the theatre has made a powerful enemy, but I have several freelancers in my contacts, so I sit back down and get to work.

Lucky this is happening in central London as the lovely Rachel can come and bail us out. We meet at the stage door; I've already briefed her that the dame is in stage make-up and will need to go back on stage for the evening, so just to tone things down and smooth over the cracks. That is not the technical term for what Rachel is going to do.

Heading to her dressing room, we pass the hunky up-and-coming actor playing the grandson. I manage a friendly smile, but can see Rachel seems keen to stop for a chat – maybe she knows him. I remind her we are in emergency mode. He can't squeeze past her enormous wheelie suitcase and it all gets a bit awkward. I think she was blushing and wonder if there's history.

The dame is all charm and smiles for Rachel – she wants to look her best, plays down how vain she is, but watches the proceedings in her mirror like a hawk, attempting to boss Rachel around. Rachel is used to dealing with the most neurotic models and the most powerful players in telly, so she just carries on doing her thing, cool, calm and collected. After an hour of furious brushing, blending and buffing, she steps back and says, 'See what you think.' The dame looks absolutely lovely. I'm used to seeing her all caked-up for the stage or bare-faced at home, but Rachel has made her look twinkly and soft round the edges. The dame is admiring herself from all angles, and when Rachel gives her the lipstick she used to freshen herself up if she needs to, she looks fit to burst with joy. This experience has cheered her up no end. Of course, I am worrying about how she will react to Rachel's bill – probably charge it to the charity – but that's not a problem for now. I want to get her to the tea while she's still in such a good mood.

'Dame Annette, let's get this show on the road.'

Pulling up outside The Wolseley, we have just the reception she wanted – a posse of people waiting at the door and a smiling maître d' giving the back of her hand a theatrical kiss as he bows low. Everyone in the restaurant, or 'the cheap seats' as the dame calls them, is craning to see who has arrived and they are rewarded with a regal procession through the restaurant. The middle-aged couple who bought the prize are dressed up to the nines. The woman is wearing a pastel skirt suit and a fascinator, which strikes me as a little OTT; he is in a suit and tie. And they are so overwhelmed by her presence, I think they are about to bow or curtsey, which is, of course, just how she likes it. She reaches out an imperious hand to shake and winces slightly as the mister grasps it and exclaims what a huge fan he is.

Nice charity lady has done a seating plan, with the dame in between Mr and Mrs Donor, which is only fair. I know the dame is wondering if she can switch me in, but to give her credit she decides to sparkle for a good twenty minutes and reminisces about when she went to Hollywood and met all the greats, and how much fun she had with Dame Joan Collins in St Tropez, name-dropping enough to impress the couple from the home counties and even giving them a juicy titbit of gossip about a chat-show host's drinking problem that they can repeat to their chums at the golf club.

Acutely aware of her emotions at all times, I see her smile freeze when Mr Donor asks for a selfie and, without waiting for an affirmative, pulls his chair alongside hers and flings his arm around her shoulders. Amusing as it would be for me to watch this scene play out, I intervene, suggest I take a nice photo of all of them, standing behind her. I still see her flinch as Mrs puts a friendly hand on her shoulder, but crisis averted. She has done her bit and rises to leave, ahead of schedule. Mr reaches under the table for his bag – the theatre programmes – but he'll have to be fast if he's going to catch her. As I had agreed it, I rush over with the sharpie, open the page ready for her, and she barely breaks stride as she scrawls her signature. Reaching the door, she turns back, briefly, gives a royal wave and says how utterly divine it has been to meet them all and what marvellous work the charity does, taking care of those poor, sick children. A moment of concern as this is actually a mental health charity, but it's all in a good cause.

As if she is hitting her mark on the stage, the dame leaves the restaurant just as the Mercedes draws up to collect her and the driver is out and opening the door for her almost before the car has fully stopped. I'm surprised to see her pause before she gets in, but she's seen people with camera phones recognising her, and as she is looking great, outside a fancy restaurant *and* doing a good deed, she is quite happy for them to grab a quick snap or two before she slides into the back seat. 'Make sure the palace know I was here' are her last words to me as she drives off, leaving me to make nice with Mr and Mrs Donor and the rest.

Once I am sure everyone is happy, it occurs to me that I am shattered – it's been a long day. As I walk back to the tube station, I think of Ed because usually I'd have told him the story of the tea and played it for laughs. I am so close to his office, I feel drawn towards it – isn't there some fact about criminals being inexorably drawn back to the scene of their crime? Or maybe I saw that on telly.

Instead, I walk through our old stamping ground wondering what I'd imagined could happen. It's along the lines of he's on the other side of the road, spots me and his face lights up – he runs across the four lanes of Oxford Street, more if you count the bus and cycle lanes, and sweeps me up and off my feet, saying, 'I've missed you so much – never leave my side again.' It appears I have a pretty specific idea of what I want to happen. Maybe I could transpose that into a scene for *Just Between Us*, the imaginary version.

I can't look as I pass the restaurant where we had that awful showdown. I didn't behave well. Was it a bit hasty to break things off completely? It all happened so fast – maybe I frightened him off. What I want more than anything right now is to be folded into that broad chest of his and feel his arms wrapped tightly round me. That's the place I feel happiest and safest. I try and think of other things that can make me as happy. Not the fabulous top I bought at a seventy per cent reduction this morning, nor making sure everything went smoothly for the tea this afternoon, not even scoring free use of the luxurious Workspace. But there is one thing: the feeling I had working on the scripts with Casper. A different sort of happiness, true – buzzy and stimulated. I'm going to focus on chasing more of that feeling.

Chapter 14

From Casper, 8.30am:
Left you a script to get started.
Back by noon.

This is an early start for him – he would never schedule a meeting or even a personal trainer before 10am by choice. Next thought; excitement at having another session bouncing ideas with him later. Heading to the kitchen, I see Ella's left me a note on the table reminding me about the picnic on Saturday.

Bring the fun! Ex

Keen to get to Casper's and get stuck in, I have a quick wash and brush up and set off. Davina is straight on my case.

'Well, Madeleine, is seems this writing project has really taken off.' My enthusiasm is infectious.

'Yes, it's exciting – a new chapter, as it were.' Wry smile to camera – camera being the rear-view mirror.

'And will you get a credit?' That's the kicker.

'Much as I would love to feature in the credits, I am satisfied to be supporting a client who appreciates my efforts.' That's the official version, but am I? And does he?

Not sure if Davina said that or me. And as Davina is a figment of my imagination, I think the answer is evident. It is one thing not getting any recognition from the outside world for what I'm contributing, but, truth is, Casper hasn't given me any recognition either, apart from a few extra hours' pay and, frankly, that is no skin off his expensively sculpted nose. It's eating away at me that my efforts are being taken for granted. It's like Ed and Ella have been saying: the more I do for a client, the more they expect.

Hoping Jess has some inside track, I use the excuse of scheduling interviews with Needy Steve to call.

'Hey, Jess, heads up, we're doing interviews on Monday and guess what? You made the shortlist.' I sing-song at her.

'Brilliant, Maddy, you're a star. I really need this, cashflow is about to become a big problem.' She does sound relieved.

'Any luck with finding something more permanent?'

'A few possibilities – I actually met someone useful at that CHAMPs thing. Lauren Argon? She said she saw you in a yoga class. You kept that one quiet.'

'Not really; I tried it and it was weird. I couldn't work out where I knew her from. What's her story?'

'She works for Django, the photographer who does all the stuff for *Love and Dazed* magazines. I would kill for her job, but, second best, I will befriend her and hope something comes up. Maybe I should take up yoga, too.'

I'm thinking this is not a very concrete career plan, but decide now is not the time to knock Jess's confidence. Niceties over, I make my move.

'Have you spoken to anyone at Top Notch recently? I'm just on my way to Casper's.'

'I told you about the mystery writer, didn't I? Even under pressure, he won't say who it is. They are majorly on his case, calling him in for extra meetings, script changes before every recording. He does seem to be turning things around, so whatever it is he's doing, it's working. Come on, Maddy, you must have an idea of who he's using – stop being so bloody discreet with me.'

I'd love to share my suspicions with her, but until I'm sure… 'If I knew, I'd tell you, Jess,' I lie. 'I'll do some snooping. In the meantime, why don't you get on with some ideas to present to Steve?'

In this game, knowledge can be used as currency. Maybe I can find out who he's meeting this morning. I'll check the desk diary when I get there – fortunately, he still does things on paper.

'Good plan. Can I run things by you before the interview?'

I've got her off my back. 'No problemo – and keep me posted if you hear anything more about Casper.'

'Deal – speak soon.'

I don't relish asking someone to gather info on one of my clients, but having a strong inkling that I am the writing partner being kept under wraps is starting to really rankle. Today could be the day to talk to Casper about it, depending on what kind of mood he's in after this meeting. I remind myself that I am a strong, independent woman and, as if on cue, Mum calls.

'Hello, darling, it's Mum.'

'I know, Mum, it comes up on caller display.'

'How clever! Are you driving? Don't talk to me.'

'It's all on Bluetooth, Mum, it's fine.'

'Just a reminder about Friday night – your sister's coming, with Elijah. Isn't that nice?'

'Lovely.' I hope I sound convincing. 'Is Jeremy coming?'

'No – he's on a business trip. She told me where, but I can't remember. Not back until Monday, so she's staying over. You could, too, Maddy. It would be like old times.'

And that is exactly why I will not be staying and playing along with this charade of happy families. My big sister likes nothing better than to flaunt her picture-perfect family life, and mum and dad can't get enough of hearing about her successful husband, her incredibly advanced toddler, and her highly responsible job at a huge management consultancy. I don't envy her life, but she has this sense of purpose about her that makes me feel inadequate. I thought I'd made positive choices about my career, but, with hindsight, maybe I just reacted to my circumstances. I want to be proactive, starting with

Casper and this writing gig. The more I think about it, the more I think this could be my big break.

'Thanks, Mum, dinner will be lovely, but I won't stay – busy weekend.'

'Plans with that nice Ed? Bring him for dinner.'

I find it hard to tell a barefaced lie to my mum, so I fudge it, 'Got to go, Mum. I'm outside Casper's.'

'Ooh, tell Casper hello and how much I'm enjoying this series. Could you get us tickets to a recording?'

'Sure, Mum. See you Friday – let me know what to bring.'

With mixed feelings, I run up the stairs to the front door. Excited at the prospect of another script to work on – I've had a few ideas since watching the last episode go out – but super nervous at the reality of talking to Casper about the writing credit. I am adamant that I must seize the day.

It's there, printed and spiral-bound, with a Post-it on the front, saying 'Maddy'. Grabbing it eagerly, I settle down in the lap-of-luxury upstairs living room, forgetting all about checking the desk diary for who he's meeting. I measure my days out by the hour when I'm working, but today time stops mattering as I lose myself in the script – an improvement on the ones I'd worked on previously. Casper was addressing the key issues I had brought to his attention and I felt a bit annoyed. The script was better for it, but did that leave less for me to contribute?

I will dig deeper and offer more nuance. I know I can. Having read through, I go back to the start and focus right in on every little detail, every pause, every word and try and come up with a better way. This is serious work and I'm concentrating so intensely, I startle when Casper arrives home, kicking the front door shut behind him.

He bursts into the room and I see him take a beat to compute the fact that I am sitting there curled up on his extremely cream modular seating system.

'Casper, hi, I thought I'd concentrate better up here with no distractions – you know, the post and paperwork…' I'm blabbering and I know it. I see a frown gathering. Shit. This is not good for my strong, independent woman situation, so I stop, take a breath and look him straight in the eye, not budging from my spot. I have to believe in my right to be sitting here.

The cloud passes. 'Makes sense,' he says. 'And how's it going? Ready to talk it through?'

He's more chilled than he has been for a while. He seems to respond better the bolder I am.

'No, not yet. I'm going back over it, specifically looking at the exchanges between Edie and Ben. They used to crackle with tension, but it's slipped into everyday banter,' I reply, calmly.

Get me! I hadn't even planned that, but it is what I was thinking. I'm acutely aware that there could be an explosion of fury, but it's too late to take it back.

His expression relaxes and he comes to sit on the same module as me and says, 'Interesting, I'll take a look. Anything else?'

'I've marked up a few initial comments, but I was going over it more carefully now I've got the general idea.'

He does a snorty laugh and suggests I should attend to the admin downstairs.

Seeing my chance slipping away, I launch in. 'Casper, before I do, I wanted to have a word with you about this work I'm doing for you, with you – I don't know exactly how to describe what we're doing, but I really like doing it, and I'd like to do more, but I'd also like to be recognised for doing it.' Not how it sounded in my head.

'That's a shit sentence. What are you on about?' He's flicking through my marked-up script, not even looking at me.

'I'd like it to be official that I'm helping you. I want to be validated.' I sound like a self-help book.

Sitting back in his chair, he regards me suspiciously as he crosses his arms. 'I'll give you a bonus, for extra services rendered.'

His expression is closed; I'm not getting through to him. Also, I think that 'services rendered' sounds a bit dodge.

'Of course, a bonus would be handy, but what I'd really like is for Top Notch to know I helped you with the script.' I can't leave it.

'I see. And how would that make me look, do you think? An award-winning writer being 'helped', as you so sweetly put it, by a complete nobody? I have a world-class reputation. I have a fucking responsibility; people's livelihoods are at stake. You've tweaked a bit of dialogue – maybe put a bit of shine on what was already there. Let's keep this in perspective, Maddy.' With a patronising smile, he turns back to his screen.

I snatch up my bag, frustrated, and rush downstairs, slamming the basement office door behind me. *Why on earth did I think I could have a sensible conversation with Casper?* A boiling anger starts to build in my belly. I know I have been at least part of the reason for the improvement in viewing figures, even if there is some truth in what he said. He's been bloody relying on me; having clean scripts ready, getting me in early and using my suggestions – and, on top of all of that, it's become the most satisfying part of my job. The part I think about when I'm doing other stuff. The part I want to be doing when I'm doing other stuff.

Catching sight of my surprisingly hideous crying face in the mirror, which is helpfully surrounded by showbiz-style light bulbs, I decide to have a word with myself, because, when push comes to shove, I have the trump card – I just won't do it anymore. I see my own reaction to this revelation. My chin stops wobbling and I look myself straight in the eye. I am not powerless. I'm not powerful either, but I do have a choice. As soon as the blotchiness has settled down, I will calmly get on with my daily grind. If Casper asks me to do any more script work, I will tell him I'm sorry, but I have to go to my next client.

I pull an open-mouthed, eyebrow-raised 'Get me' face to myself in the mirror. He will absolutely hate that. He doesn't like to think I have other clients at the best of times – none of them do – but I seem to have uncovered a trace of self-confidence and I am going to stick with it. I have a plan and I always feel better when I have a plan.

Later, ploughing through the usual mound of invoices

and requests, I remember to check the desk diary for this morning's meeting. As I suspected, it was not with the mystery writer, but with Top Notch productions. I know in my guts that it's my efforts that have been helping him and I'm the writer he won't tell them about. I am going to stand firm and see how this plays out.

From Steve, 1.30pm:
Thanks for CVs. Happy to meet
all 4. Do confirm for Monday.
Not at my house, can you sort
suitable venue? Cheers.

Well, that's progress. I did include Caroline in the shortlist; it was too good an opportunity to pass up – the chance to take her superiority complex down a peg or two. I'll think of some really tricky questions to make her squirm. On this cheery thought, I start to pack my stuff up and nip to the loo.

It's a Japanese toilet – Casper had it imported. The kind that gives you a wash and dry rather than use loo paper, and I haven't quite got the hang of it. Last time I used it, I stood up too soon and got a squirt of water right in the face. The time before, I ended up having the back of my jeans rinsed, so this time I decide to stay put on it until everything has stopped happening. Turns out, this is quite a while.

When I head back, there is an envelope on top of my pile of post. 'Maddy – thanks for the extra help' is scrawled on the front in Casper's terrible handwriting. It's not sealed and I can immediately see that the contents are bank notes. Tipping the envelope onto the table, a wedge of fifty-pound notes slides out and elegantly fans itself onto the post pile. I can count the number of times I have even seen a £50 note, let alone held one. Pretty sure I've never actually owned one. That's not true, actually; Uncle Adam gave me one for my twenty-first and I didn't want to spend it – until I did.

Back to the matter in hand, or should I say the twenty matters in hand, because a quick tally has revealed that's how many notes he has bunged me. *A thousand pounds*! As well as the immediate euphoria, I am also aware that there is something a bit grubby about this transaction. Or am I getting caught up in the 'services rendered' conversation again? I'm confused and excited. If I accept, am I agreeing to the current situation – no recognition? Though it seems he isn't about to give me any credit anyway, so I might as well enjoy the windfall. I need to talk this through with someone sensible and before I have time to question how wise it is:

Text to Ed, 3pm:
Hey! Had a windfall. Mx

Chapter 15

I'm doing my absolute best not to think about the fact that Ed didn't respond to my stupid, stupid text. Ella isn't home, so instead of wallowing in a huge billowy cloud of misery, I decide to take myself off to the gym. My mind spinning with the day's events, a spinning class is the last thing I need. My choice is to work out in the gym on my own (which never quite goes as intended) or to do a different kind of yoga class. Yoga wins. And I remember to put my phone on silent before I go in.

I immediately recognise the CHAMPS woman, Lauren, even though she is lying on her back with her legs in the air. She gives me a big upside-down grin and gestures at the space next to her, so I roll out a mat and fetch the same bits of equipment she has piled up by her side, even though I have no clue what any of it is for.

'Glad to see you're giving it another go,' she says as I plonk myself down next to her.

'You were right about the good night's sleep and I've had one of those days, so it won out over spin.' I'd rather have been anonymous, but she's so friendly.

'Good call. We could grab a smoothie after and you can tell me all about it, if you aren't rushing off.' So friendly.

The teacher arrives and we all sit to cross-legged attention. This teacher is less stern, but she still asks the period question and two women put their hands up. I'm intrigued to see what will happen to them – maybe they'll have to perform some ancient fertility rite – but it turns out it just means they don't do handstands and headstands. I don't either, for the record. Lauren did. She was really good and knew what the teacher meant when she said the funny names of things, before the English version. But mainly I just listen to the teacher and try my best to follow. Being next to Lauren helps; I copy her but in a good way. At one point, she mouths, 'Other direction,' at me and I realise I am facing the wrong way. My cheeks flush but no one else takes any notice and, by the end of the class, when we are all sat facing the teacher again, there is a very mellow vibe in the room. It didn't even feel weird to put my hands in prayer position and bow my head. I don't think it was religious, just sort of respectful.

We put the blocks and blankets away and I notice Lauren has her own yoga mat, in a rather snazzy bag decorated with ethnic-looking symbols. I feel a pang of accessory envy and, when she suggests we go to the juice bar, I thought, *Why not?*

148

We already know we live pretty close and so we start off by keeping it safe and chatting about local stuff, then move on to CHAMPS and how we'd come across it – she knew one of the founding members – and, of course, we talk a bit about work. Her job sounds pretty great – full-time, holiday, sick pay and allowed to work from home if she isn't needed on site. She even gets time in lieu if she works crazy hours, which – being in fashion – she often does. It does make me wonder about my hand-to-mouth freelance existence, especially as she really is having the working-closely-with-a-creative-genius experience that I claim makes my career worthwhile. We move on to Jess. Lauren knows Aria's reputation, so doesn't think badly of her for getting the boot. When I tell her about the Instagram incident, she says Jess has gone up in her estimation and we have a good laugh about it. I am incredibly discreet and don't mention the high-net-worth crew, but then she says something about a Caroline rubbing her up the wrong way, and even though I wasn't sure *which* Caroline she means, I know we could be real friends.

Just as we are getting up and gathering our stuff, the inevitable happens.

From Dani, 7.45pm:
Hey Stranger! How's London?
Missing me?? Weekend off
coming up – might head home.
Will confirm. Dx

Lauren recognises the furrow of my brow and raises an eyebrow.

'Working the crazy shift?' It was such a relief to be with someone who totally gets it.

'Client coming into town,' I shrug and, unusually for me, continue, 'Dani Nicholls – she's been in New York, working.'

'Of course, she's acting, right?' Lauren looks interested, but not in a gossip-gathering way.

'She is – theatre's a new thing for her, bit of a career change.' Lauren hasn't done the usual slag-off-my-client thing, so I am sharing more than I usually would.

'And going well from what I hear on the grapevine. Django was talking about her, about maybe inviting her into the studio when she is back in London.'

'Oh my God, seriously? She would *love* that; she's working really hard to move away from her old image.' I know Dani would be over the moon to have a session with Django, even if it wasn't for a magazine commission, but just to be moving in the trendy arty world rather than the sidebar of shame universe. 'Can I mention it?'

'Let me run it by Django. I'll tell him we know each other and that we could work it through the back door, no agents and stuff. I'm sure he'll go for it.'

And I'd get massive brownie points from Dani. I bloody love networking. And I am liking Lauren, too; no bullshit. She's just really straightforward.

'I'd better run, but I've really enjoyed this,' I say as I pull my jacket on to leave.

'This smoothie? This yoga? This chat?' she's laughing.

Smiling, I reply, 'All of the above!'

'Well, let's do it again, same time next week?'

Without hesitating, I reply, 'Sounds like a plan,' give her an awkward hug and leave the juice bar having completely forgotten not only my woes, but also the wedge of cash sitting in the glove compartment of my car.

✦

Back at the flat, I'm ambivalent about even taking the cash indoors, but it's obvious madness to leave it in the car – so in it comes. I leave it sitting plumply on the kitchen table while I make myself a superfood salad involving broccoli and feta and then can't resist a thickly buttered piece of toast on the side. I sit at the table looking at it, chewing thoughtfully while I try and work out my feelings.

It is a form of recognition, but not the sort I want. I want to be acknowledged as a writer. Casper is clear – I am not a writer and he may well have a point. I don't want to lose my job. I don't want to stop 'helping' him with the scripts. So, I accept the money, shut up and everything stays the same. Reliable Maddy hovering in the background, always the support act. I've made a career out of it. I've never pushed on through when the going gets tough. Now there is a twinkle of ability for writing and I'm about to do my usual thing, walk away before someone tells me I'm not good enough.

While I'm going down this route, I reach for my phone and check Instagram – certain to make me feel inadequate.

More inadequate. No mindless scrolling; straight to Ed's account. He's not usually very active, but there are a couple of blurry bar shots from last weekend. So, he's out and about, having a good time – liked by bloody @MeMeMe. And it gets better: she's commented, all in emojis – hearty-eyed, laughy tears, sodding clappy hands. Now I'll have to check her feed, like a creepy sad stalker.

'Maddy? You're here!' I look up, guiltily.

'Whatcha doing?' Ella's back from work, looking slightly dishevelled, but still pretty smart. Her glossy bob never has a hair out of place.

'Sticking red-hot pins in my eyes.' *Bitter, me?*

She looks bemused and, with a sigh, I explain, 'I had a weird day at work, then a good time at yoga, but came home and fell down a black hole of social media. I'm not proud of myself. Can I make you a cup of tea?' I could really do with her take on things.

'Sounds like tea is the very least we need. I'm knackered, but also fascinated. Make mine a peppermint and tell me all about it.' She slumps down opposite me, simultaneously kicking off her shoes and shrugging off her jacket. *How does she keep her shirts so white?*

'All?' All friendships have their limits. 'How long have you got?'

'Highlights... and what the hell is this?' She's picked up the envelope of shame and her expression changes as she sees the contents. 'Maddy, seriously, what are you into?'

The anxious look on her face makes me smile and I launch into the saga of the mystery writing assistant who happens to be the very real personal assistant sitting right here.

As I finish my tale of woe, she sighs and says, 'Pleased as I am you aren't running a side hustle in drug dealing, I do think we have cause for concern. It doesn't have to be all or nothing. Why don't you take some control?'

But before we can take this intriguing conversation any further, my phone rings and I see it is Jess. Assuming she wants to run through the brief for the interview with Steve, I send it to voicemail and turn back to Ella, who is now checking her emails, but before I can get her attention, my phone goes again. It's Jess, not getting the message. Then, a text:

**The shit has hit. Need help,
URGENT!!!!**

All I want is a major session with Ella, but Jess is not giving up. I manage to ignore voicenotes as we sip our tea, but it's distracting. Expecting the usual melodrama, I tap to listen and, to be fair, she does sound frantic.

'Maddy, I'm in trouble, real trouble. I think I need a lawyer. Can I talk to your flatmate?'

This doesn't sound like the usual I've-just-said-something-stupid/lost-my-temper/kissed-someone-I-shouldn't-have type of drama, so I nudge Ella's foot with mine. She looks up and, without explaining, I play out Jess's message.

'She's a fellow PA,' I explain. 'Was with that supermodel,

Aria, until last week. They fell out, big time. She was sacked and I genuinely have no idea what this is about. Shall I say you're not around?' I want to give Ella a way out. She's had a much longer day than me and looks shattered.

'Aria sounds like a nightmare; I've seen the stories. Let's call her.' Ella can't ignore someone in distress.

As soon as she answers the phone, Jess is babbling hysterically about being treated unfairly, calling Aria every name under the sun.

Ella cuts in very calmly, 'Jess, this is Ella. Can you just hold on and listen to me?'

'Oh, thank you, thank you so much. It's not good—' Jess's voice cracks and we can hear her short, shallow breaths trying to hold back tears. 'I think I need a lawyer, but I'm totally skint.'

'Start at the beginning. Tell me what's happened.' My phone is on speaker and Ella leans back with a look of concentration.

'I've had an email from Aria's lawyers. It's really scary. They're talking about taking action against me – police, everything.'

Her voice is quavering, so I butt in, 'For trying on her shoes and taking some photos? Has she lost it completely?'

Ella looks across at me, quizzically. I'm trying to give her a heads-up about Jess's misdemeanour, but Jess continues, 'It's not just that; it's her credit card. I was so desperate. I didn't think she'd notice a few hundred pounds. I was going to pay it back, but I had to pay rent. I was skint and—'

Ella interrupts, 'This sounds a bit more serious, Jess, but let's not panic. It's not exactly my area, but I'll help you as much as I can.' This is the first I've heard about a credit card and it sounds much more worrying. *What was she thinking?* There's no coming back from fraud – her reputation would be ruined and reputation is everything.

Jess starts to sob down the phone and I look at Ella, my friend, who is so clever and so kind and try to show through my expression how grateful I am. She clearly gets the message because she mouths, 'Make me some food,' and then tells Jess to hang up, forward her the email, have a drink of water and calm down until she calls her back.

While I start scrambling eggs, Ella gets her laptop out and is soon hunched over it, making notes on a pad at her side. Once the toast has popped and been buttered, I sit back down with mugs of tea for us both and quickly fill her in about the Instagram debacle and how Jess had been with Aria for longer than most and that having a sense of humour had probably been her saving grace.

'Well,' Ella started, 'it's not as bad as it sounds. This is a Letter Before Claim, so they haven't actually reported her to the police – yet. It is very wrong of Jess to have used the credit card, but I think they are using scare tactics. Aria has form for abusing employees. I'd need to double-check, but, in my opinion, Jess should have had some notice period or a formal warning, and we could use that as a bargaining tool to get them to back off. I'd better call her. She's probably doing her pieces, expecting the police at her door.' All this wisdom has been imparted through mouthfuls of scrambled egg on toast. She takes a big swig of tea and calls Jess.

Ella calmly explains what she needs: the employment contract Jess had with Aria, the NDA, a statement saying she was working under tremendous stress and a promise to pay the money back within the month. Jess sounds much calmer; she can't stop thanking Ella and making all kinds of promises of how she will pay her back, be forever in her debt etc.

Ella, ever sensible, stops her, 'It's not a done deal, Jess, but we have something to work with. I'll get back to you with a response you can send tomorrow. In the meantime, let's all get some sleep.'

There aren't really words, so I just give Ella a big hug and head off towards my room.

'We will resume our earlier conversation,' Ella says to my back. My shoulders slightly sag as I know I will be taken to task about my uselessness. 'At the picnic.'

How does she expect me to 'bring the fun' when it sounds like I'm in for a telling-off? But what she has done for Jess tonight has been brilliant and I am deeply in her debt. She said I should take control and I did try. It just didn't go according to plan.

'Of course – looking forward to it.' Can you hear gritted teeth through the back of someone's head?

Chapter 16

From Ed, 9.05 am:
You, Me and some après ski.
Can't wait x

Sitting bolt upright in bed, staring at my phone in disbelief, I re-read the message to make double sure I can be certain of what I am seeing, because this is my actual dream come true. Telling him about my windfall wasn't a terrible mistake after all. It was exactly the right thing to do; spontaneous and fun, just like we used to be. He's been a dick and I will find the right moment to address that, but he's come to his senses. There will be a full and frank discussion about his behaviour, and then we will spend four glorious days wrapped in cosy yet sensible outerwear, laughing as I gracefully pirouette into a fall while he teaches me to ski, which I'll pick up remarkably quickly and soon join him on blue or possibly black runs.

Nights will be spent rekindling our passion, possibly under a pile of furs, definitely in the soft glow of firelight. I'm picturing a fur rug in front of a roaring wood fire, with a champagne bucket in the background – every cliché you like. He will be murmuring in my ear, something along the lines of: 'I can't explain how much I have missed you. Never leave my side again...'

I haven't forgotten that this is a group trip and that I will have Mimi to contend with, but faced with Ed and me so deeply in love, she will be powerless. I will be gracious in my victory, perhaps a little disdainful, but certainly the bigger person.

I type back:

'Fantastic!
Call me!!
Beyond excited!!!
Mxxxxxxxxxxxxxxxxxxxxxxx'

Then I head off to the bathroom, starting a mental list of what I need to beg, borrow or steal in terms of ski kit, and how and when to tell my clients I am off for a romantic mini-break with my boyfriend. It will be short notice – but maybe that's best, so they can't work themselves up. I'm not sure of the exact dates, but I reckon I have a least a week, so plenty of time to get sorted. Plus I'll only be away four or five days, and over a weekend, so it really shouldn't cause any problems.

I wonder if my sister has ski gear? It's just the sort

of upwardly mobile holiday they would take and we're similar sizes. Well, we were before she had Elijah. Not that we were the sort of sisters who shared clothes; even as youngsters, our styles were completely different. She was more Mango, while I went Beyond Retro.

After a long, luxurious shower filled with thoughts as steamy as I've made the bathroom, I give myself a thorough assessment in the mirror. Not too bad – perhaps a spray tan is needed. Rachel introduced me to a mobile spray tanner, who offered me a free trial. I will dig her number out and see if she'll do a home visit. Oh, yes, things are certainly falling into place.

Next stop: the kitchen. Humming a happy tune as I fill the kettle, Ella emerges from her room, looking really sleepy.

Before I can tell her my good news, she leans a hip against the counter by the window and, looking out over the rooftops, says, 'I went through Jess's contract and I think she has a good case for unfair dismissal. I would argue it wasn't gross misconduct, that the credit card use was against her notice period. I drafted something for her to send – not an official lawyer's letter, but enough to make them realise she's taken advice. I don't think they'll want a fuss…' She trails off.

Glad to hear it all sounds under control, I'm unable to hold it in any longer. I pass her a mug of tea, blurt out, 'I'm going skiing!' and look at her expectantly.

Instead of sharing my excitement, she puts her head to one side and says, 'What are you talking about?'

'He texted! This morning. I messaged him last night and he's replied, very romantically, obviously delighted. I told you he'd realise he's made a terrible mistake eventually.'

There is a pause and she regards me coolly. 'Maddy, you astound me. I have been up half the night, after a long and shitty week at work, sorting out the issues of a friend of yours that I have never even met. Instead of being interested or – dare I suggest – grateful, Ed clicks his fingers and, as usual, you jump.'

Ella's directness is one of the things I most admire about her. She's right about the Jess thing, of course she is, but she's never understood how things are with me and Ed. She likes steady and reliable; I'm drawn to passionate and fiery.

'Sorry, sorry. What you have done for Jess is amazing. She thought she was going to jail and you've turned it around. Let me make you a special breakfast as a thank you.' I'm fully contrite.

'No, thanks. I'm meeting Tom for brunch on the Broadway, then we'll do the shopping for the picnic.' Her manner is distinctly cool.

Ah yes, the picnic. I have about a thousand things I would rather be doing now I have a mini-break to prepare for, but there's no backing out. There's so much to sort out and Dani could be coming to town, which will require all sorts of prep. I'm making mental lists while my bagel is toasting.

Then, Ella adds, 'Hang on, is it the bonus you got from Casper that's paying for this stupid trip?' Her eyes have

160

narrowed and she is looking straight at me. I have no choice but to brazen this out.

'Exactly! It's perfect. I couldn't afford to go and now I can!' but I'm keeping my back to her while grating cheese.

'Maddy, you are rewriting history. It wasn't just the money; you and Ed had bigger issues, like how he was treating you and how you were feeling about it. We sat at this very table while you cried your eyes out.'

'Ella, chill. We had a falling out – it happens. It gave us a chance to recalibrate. He's obviously been missing me, like I knew he would, and this windfall has come at the perfect time. People can make mistakes; I believe in second chances.' As I say these words, they sound perfectly feasible. I'm not going to over-analyse; I am living in the moment.

I feel her steely gaze fixed on me as she continues, 'That money could have been a chance to make a difference.'

'You sound like a charity appeal.' I'm trying to lighten the tone. Turning to face her, I shrug, 'It's £1000, Ella. It's not going to buy me a flat.'

Ella gives me a different sort of look, a hard-to-read look, but my breakfast is ready and I have a tonne of stuff to do, so I tell her I'll catch up with her later for picnic prep. Grabbing my plate with my mug of tea balanced precariously on the side, I head for my room, defiantly humming a cheery tune.

I can see the text alert on my phone from the door, probably Ed with some practical details about booking my flights. Fortunately, I have a jpeg of my passport I can send straight over, so, setting my breakfast carefully down on the chest of drawers, I grab my phone and simultaneously read the text.

From Jess, 10.23am:
Hey M, Ella is my hero. Please
thank her again, I owe her big
time. Can we chat through
Monday's interview? Jess x

She's right, Ella really came through. I just wish she could do the same when it comes to me and Ed. Maybe at the picnic, when the dust has settled, we can talk it over and she'll understand that Ed and I are a work in progress. It's not all smooth sailing with us.

From Steve, 11.03am:
Ceremony tonight is black tie.
Can you pick one up and drop
it round?

Not even a please or thank you.

From Steve, 11.04am:
By 2pm

It's just some crappy book awards ceremony and I very much doubt he has won anything, but none of this matters – he doesn't care that it's the weekend. I'll just have to get on with it. Fortunately, there is a Moss Bros in Muswell Hill. I call ahead with his measurements. I have all my client's vital statistics stored in their personal files. It makes life much easier in a situation like this, as long as they're the right measurements. We had a catastrophe with Dame Annette a while back, when she asked me to pull in a selection of frocks for a first night. I used the measurements she had given me and, without going into detail, let's just say it was not a pretty sight. Not one of the dresses even came close to fitting her. I recall lots of swearing and letting out of seams, and I think some Velcro may have been involved round the back. Now I make a point of taking my own measurements. Even Steve's inside leg. I don't know who felt more awkward: me or Steve.

I'd rather walk up to the Broadway and get some fresh air, but as I will be carrying a man's suit and all the trimmings back, I decide to take Betty the banger. There she is – nestled between the standard Muswell Hill four by four and an electric car charging through the letterbox. Hopping into the driver's seat, I swipe my arm across the windscreen to clear the condensation and try to ignore the smell of damp.

*

From Ed, 12.20pm:
Sorry. Sent to wrong person.

Wait, what? A cold prickle of sweat breaks out across my top lip. My stomach drops away as my chest tightens. I've misunderstood. Eyes locked to the screen, I scroll back to see if I have missed any other interim messages that make this one make sense. Nothing since the 'you, me, blah blah blah' from before. Still clutching my phone, I make it to the bed and slump down, never taking my eyes off the screen, trying to fit the pieces of the story together in a way that doesn't mean the very worst. But I can't, because I've done it myself, pinged off a quick text and then realised it has gone to the wrong person. Maddy, Mimi; we're probably next to each other in his damn contacts – and I know, without knowing how I know, that this is who the text is meant for.

The hand clutching my phone drops to my lap. There's a pressure in my chest and I hear my own short, sharp breaths as the panic subsides and sadness takes hold. How is it possible to go from such joy to such misery so breathtakingly fast? I am a fool. I shut my eyes to try and hold in tears of humiliation. I have to accept that things really are over with Ed – try as I might to convince myself otherwise. He has moved on with obscene speed. That text reveals so much in so few words that even I, the queen of optimism, and possibly delusion, cannot deny the intentions it conveys. And I genuinely thought they were aimed at me.

I fling myself face first into my pillow, revving up for a big, fat, ugly crying session. There is no hope of a reconciliation with Ed left for me to cling to – no coming back from this. All the frustration and longing and dashed hopes for a future together combine for a full-on sob fest.

Tears and free-flowing snot are all permitted. I can hear Ella is in the shower, so I don't hold back, because that's another thing to weep about. I've made an absolute idiot of myself in front of her and I don't think her opinion of me is very high at the moment, anyway, so I can't go crying on her shoulder. In fact, I owe her an apology for being a self-centred cow. And then more and more misery just comes piling in.

I thought Jess was a mess, but she's left her miserable job and is sorting herself out. I thought Ella and Drippy Tom were boring, but they're just happy. It's me. I'm the mess, I'm miserable and I've got a headache from crying. My relationship is dead in the water; my career has stalled. I come back to Ella's 'making a difference' comment. That hit a nerve because, recently, I've been feeling that my professional life could do with a shake-up. Running around for Steve today compounded it. My current role feels like a dead end. I want to find a way to make writing part of my future, but Casper is not inclined to help. It's on me to find a way forward.

Crying subsiding, I vow to stop procrastinating and sign up to that creative writing course. If this is rock bottom, then it's time things got better. I just need to figure out how to make some changes.

The 1000£ *is* a good start. It could be a new car – well, a newer car. It could be a safety net if I dumped a client. Tempting as diamond earrings or a personal trainer are, I resolve to take the make-a-difference route.

Chapter 17

The picnic is fun, considering I am an emotional wreck. About fifteen people gather on the field in Highgate Woods and there is enough food for twice as many. We are at the age where a tube of Pringles and a bottle of cider is not considered a suitable offering. Instead, nearly everyone made an Ottolenghi salad or baked something delicious, yet gluten-free. Ella and Drippy Tom splashed out on fancy cheese from the specialist cheese shop and I made a load of ironic white-bread cucumber sandwiches with the crusts cut off. I enjoyed the peeling, slicing and buttering – quite therapeutic given my state of mind. Also, they suited my restricted budget.

I'm not feeling super sociable but can't let Ella down, so I pull it together. And I'd try anything that might take my mind off the humiliation coursing through my veins. There are some familiar faces, including Maya and Stella, so I join them on their blanket. Stella tells me a dramatic story about a client's dog shooting out the front door when she went to collect it and running into the road, but I can't really concentrate on the intricacies of the chase. It turned out fine in the end, but she doesn't know if she should confess. I suggest the owner leave the dog in the kitchen on days Stella was picking him up. She thinks this is an excellent suggestion and congratulates me on my practicality. My forte.

Maya seems to know about Jess's situation – I guess Ella asked her advice about the criminal bit. I thought it would be OK to show them the Instagram posts and they have a good laugh. I fill in some colour about quite how awful Aria can be and they are suitably horrified. After a bit, I lay back to watch the clouds float by and let the chatter flow around me, riding the waves of mortification that wash over me intermittently. *What must Ed be thinking?*

'Are you in a cheese coma?' The voice is close and it startles me. I may have nodded off. I have to squint into the light to see who is talking. He looks familiar, but I can't put a name to the face. 'Mind if I squeeze on the end here?' he says, already settling down just by my shoulder. 'I think I've eaten my bodyweight in Stinking Bishop.'

There is an awkward silence. My face must have shown what I was thinking because he carries on, 'I'm Dominic. We met at Ella's – I mean, yours and Ella's – flat a couple of weeks back…' He is trailing off uncertainly.

My dormant social skills suddenly kick in and I try to rescue the situation. Sitting up, I manage, 'Of course! I knew that. Dominic! Dripp… I mean, Tom's friend.' I'm still a bit dozy and possibly a bit tiddly on Prosecco.

I rush on, 'You're not a lawyer.' Then, realising this is a weird thing to say, I shut up.

'Yes, that's me, the not-lawyer – in good company with you, I seem to recall. You offer down-the-line emergency services?' It's coming back to me and, with a sense of relief, I can confidently respond, 'You're a student.'

He looks a little crestfallen and clarifies, 'I'm writing a PhD and lecturing at Kings.'

Knowing how it feels to have people underestimate your job, I start to gush by way of compensating. 'You must be super brainy. I was a rubbish student, hated my course and spent all my time hanging out with the drama society. It's a shame looking back really. I regret not studying something I was interested in.' I'd never articulated it that clearly before.

The look on his face shows he is taking me seriously, 'It's not too late.'

'To go back to university? I think it is! I'd be ancient, plus I've got enough of a loan weighing me down with no prospect of paying it back any time soon.' What a weird thing to suggest, but Dominic looks so earnest I curb my instinct to move away from him.

'Isn't there something you've become interested in that you weren't aware of when you chose your degree?' Other people in our group are laughing and messing around, but this Dominic is leaning in to talk to me, giving me his full attention. Peering through his glasses, he continues, 'At my school, we were just encouraged to continue with whatever we were doing best in at A Level – striking out in a new direction was not encouraged.' This does sound totally familiar.

'Exactly! I wanted to be a writer, so I studied English Lit, which turned out to mean speed-reading through tonnes of books a week – or not, in my case. Honestly, it ruined my love of reading.'

He nods, leaning back. He's proved his point, but continues, 'You don't have to do a degree. There are loads of great places in London to study informally.'

I'm just about to ask if he has any particular recommendations, when Ella appears with a bottle of fizz, filling up paper cups and checking everyone is alright. She doesn't make eye contact with me and I know she is still annoyed at my behaviour this morning. Little does she know that my world has come crashing down since I was flying high just a few hours ago. She's crouching down to give Dominic a refill and he has turned his laser beam attention to her.

'Has Maddy told you she's living the jet-set life these days, flying off for a weekend of skiing with Ed, the invisible boyfriend. Alright for some, isn't it?'

I freeze, pleased she has moved on to the next group, because my lip has gone very wobbly. Ella speaks her mind, but I've never known her be sarky like that. I must have really annoyed her. Also, since when does she get to give people nicknames? That's *my* thing.

'Maddeeeeeee! Tell us some funny work stories!' Maya is now pissed and throws an arm round my shoulders, almost knocking me over. I give Dominic a look that I hope portrays the fact that I would rather continue our chat, but he's struck up a conversation with someone else. Making a massive effort, mainly to show Ella I am trying, I launch into an anecdote about having to rehome two teacup pigs that turned out to be – well – just pigs, which goes down a treat.

As the sun starts to go down and there's a bit of a chill, Ella suggests moving back to the flat. The combination of crying, day drinking and shouty people has given me a thumping headache, so I offer to stay back and clear up, hoping this will earn me some brownie points. Tom gratefully hands me some bin bags and, as everyone else starts gathering up their stuff, I set about collecting empty cans and bottles, dirty paper plates and tinfoil. I note Ella giving me an approving look as they head off and she calls out, 'Don't be too long,' as they leave. Progress.

As well as the fresh air, I need some peace and quiet – time to process a few things. Once the rubbish is dumped, I decide that rather than head home, I'll take a walk in the woody bit away from the field of revellers and kids having kickabouts. I don't often crave solitude and silence, but the last twenty-four hours have been an emotional overload and I haven't had a minute to let things sink in.

Foremost in my mind is Ed, the very thing I have least control over. The facts are: we fell out, we broke up, he moved on and I humiliated myself. He's probably cosied up with MooMoo somewhere, huddled over his phone and laughing at me. Playing this scene out in my imagination is not helpful. I must just accept we are done.

This brings me neatly to the reason I could make that stupid offer – the money from Casper. I need to work out why I'm not delighted by the extra funds. I'm frustrated at the lack of recognition, but Casper is not going to credit me. He is using me as a sounding board; I am voluntarily making constructive suggestions and he is paying me for the extra time. Generously.

Coming to the end of the woodland path and popping out at the back of the field, it seems I have not been ambling through the woods, rather stomping furiously head down through nature, completely ignoring it, and that is when the seed of an idea germinates. The money is an acknowledgement of sorts.

Ella said I could make a difference. Dominic suggested further education. I blame Casper for my current situation, but it is up to me to take charge of my own destiny. I half expect an orchestra to start playing soaring music and a flock of butterflies to surround me, because I decide, in that instant, I *am* going to be a TV writer like Casper. I can do it; this is the creative calling I have been waiting for. I will use the Casper cash to pay for a course that covers the nuts and bolts of screen writing. Thoroughly excited by my personal revelation, I want to tell Ella my plan. I know this is something she will approve of, but stop short. Ella is the other reason for my lonely trudge. I have pissed her off, big time. We never really fall out, just a bit of gentle bickering about who finished the peanut butter or whose turn it is to put the bins out, but nothing like the cold shoulder she was giving me this afternoon.

My overwhelming urge is to rush back to the flat and apologise, properly, for not appreciating her, to agree that the ski trip idea was a nonsense, to tell her I accept things are over with Ed and then to announce my big revelation. However, she has the gang over. They will be several hours into a proper session at an age when the booze won't run out any time soon and they have the comfort of the flat to enjoy it in. The scene will not play out as I would like it. I think I need to let the dust settle, so I'm at a bit of a loose end with nowhere to go. The sun is nearly down and it's chilly.

Thinking maybe I'll sit in a coffee shop, I go all old school and make my way to the Muswell Hill Library – a building I have walked and driven past a thousand times but never been inside. It's been somewhat modernised and, looking past the entrance lobby, I can see a bank of clunky PCs with a few slightly sad-looking types sitting at them bathed in the gentle blue light of the screens. Undeterred, I make my way round, settle into a grubby swivel chair and log on. I am going to research courses and book myself on to one starting ASAP. I am striking while the iron is hot.

Twenty minutes later, I am overwhelmed by the choice. A spreadsheet is required so I can compare cost, geographical desirability, convenient timing, etc.

From Jess, 5.49pm:
Howdy! When's a good time
to chat through Steve stuff? Jx

From me, 5.50pm:
No time like the present.
Fancy meeting me for a coffee?

From Jess:
No! but I'll meet you for a
drink Jx

So that's settled and, a few texts later, certainly not looking my best but pleased to have a diversion, I am on my way to The Flask in Highgate. We arrive at the same time and the sight of her, in her pink fluffy fake fur jacket and bold floral-print palazzo pants, instantly raises my spirits. The fact that I am greeted with a huge and fragrant bear hug cheers me up even more and we bundle into the pub, arms linked. I get the first round and we settle into a cosy nook.

We chat about the interviews on Monday. I tip her off about Needy Steve's lofty aspirations regarding his profile – being a cover boy, an appearance on Graham Norton or Jonathan Ross – and even though we both know he is batting way above his station, she will make the suggestions he is dreaming of, but also try for 'My Cultural Life' or a 'This Much I Know' feature in the *Guardian*. This is bound to land her the job and, as Jess says, you can but ask. I come clean with her about having shortlisted Caroline. We cook up a plan where I tell Caroline that he is very low-key and just hopes for a mention in the Waterstone's newsletter and a local bookshop event, so she goes in way off the mark.

We have such a laugh imagining it that I forget my cares and decide not to tell Jess about Ed. It will ruin the mood and it's still a bit raw. I can't talk to her about the Casper situation because she has all those contacts at Top Notch. I wonder whether now is the time to talk to her about my new career aspirations, but as it's such a baby seed of an idea I decide not tonight.

She insists on buying more drinks to thank me and, by extension, decides it is more economical to buy a bottle than glasses of wine. It's kind of amazing how she doesn't let things get her down and I'm thinking I need to be a bit more like Jess and stop getting so worked up and upset about everything. Soon she is telling me how she will be kicked out of her flat if she can't make the rent, but is hopeful that the letter she drafted with Ella will buy her some breathing space in the form of a severance pay out. We drank a(nother) toast to that.

Things become a bit unclear as the evening wears on. We are now on the second bottle and she is telling me about her idea of offering celebrity house-sitting as a niche add-on to the usual PA duties. She offers to stay at Dani's for nothing, but I laugh it off. Especially as she is the girl who has just been fired for invasion of privacy – Jess doesn't seem to do irony!

Suddenly, she shrieks, 'Shit! What's the time? I'm meant to be at a thing in Shoreditch.' By the time I look at my watch, she has shrugged and her jacket is back on; her lipstick is redone with one hand without looking, while texting frantically with the other. 'Babe, you are a lifesaver. See you Monday.' With that, she is gone in a puff of Jo Malone's Red Roses perfume.

I stay sitting for a minute, a bit dazed, trying to work out where the last three hours have gone. On the plus side, I'm probably in a better mood for joining the after-party at my flat. Getting up to leave, I sway a bit – some fresh air is a good idea. Showing my maturity by not completely finishing the glass of wine in front of me, I make sure I have all my belongings and head out into the night air.

From Jess, 9.48pm:
What would I do without
you? You can give me keys on
Monday. Jx

I spend most of the walk home trying to decipher the meaning of the second sentence. She must mean keys to Steve's place, which seems a bit previous. I do admire her self-confidence.

Chapter 18

Most people have left by the time I get back. I can hear murmuring voices in the kitchen and pause to listen out for Dominic, keen to tell him about the courses, but I am reluctant to intrude. There are days when I'm very aware that this is Ella's flat and today is one of them. I tiptoe past, not wanting to alert them to my presence, choose to forgo using the bathroom, lay on my bed fully dressed, stare at the ceiling and think about all the creative writing options I researched in the library. I make a mental shortlist, promising myself I will make a decision in the morning and sign up by the end of the week. Satisfied, I snuggle into bed to watch *Dirty Dancing* for the billionth time.

From Dani, 4.10am (11.10pm New York time): I'm coming! Can you look into flights – Sunday am, back Weds night? Dx

Classic start to a Sunday morning, if you can even call it morning.

I can picture the scene; she'll have finished the sell-out Saturday evening performance and be high on adrenaline. Director says she can have a couple of days off and, without a thought, she's pinged me a text. Dani knows I always have my phone on. Would she have considered the time difference? Of course not.

Try as I might to put it out of my mind, I can't get back to sleep. Sitting up, it becomes instantly clear that my head is pretty fuggy after last night's wine consumption. If I shower, it will wake Ella and presumably Drippy Tom, so I creep along the corridor to the kitchen to get a big glass of water. A very big glass of water. It's carnage in there: cans, bottles and glasses on most surfaces. I can see sticky patches on the table and feel them under my bare feet. The food is mostly eaten, but the containers are strewn everywhere. I sigh deeply, wash up a pint glass, fill it, knock it back and refill immediately. I'm not going to clear this up now. Apart from the racket it would make, I want Ella to see how bad it is, then I will offer to help as part of my penance.

Fully awake now, I might as well check out some flight times. I'd rather have a travel agent do it, but, lest we forget, it's Sunday. And it's about 4.30am, so World Wide Web it is. Sitting in bed on my laptop, I can barely focus, so I put on my panda onesie and go and sit in my cubby hole office. The draught blowing in round the edges of the front door gives me goosebumps but helps clear my head.

Notepad to hand, I start scanning the websites. She'll be in London for about thirty-six hours and it will cost a packet, but I've learnt not to question. Not my job.

When I have several viable options, I put them in an easy-to-read table and email it to Dani, highlighting the one I think makes the most sense, economically and time-wise. By now, she may well be tucked up in bed, but I can't resist the chance to show her how on top of things I am – even at 5am on a Sunday morning. My eyelids are heavy and I think I could sleep now, cosied up in my warm nest of a bed. Heading back up, avoiding the creaky stair, I swallow a precautionary pair of paracetamol with the last of the water.

Yawning so wide I could swallow my head, I burrow down into my pile of pillows. My hip vibrates. Well, the pocket of my onesie that contains my phone vibrates.

From Dani, 5.35am:
Sort me an upgrade Babe, free
of charge preferable. Dx

I'm done. What strings does she think I can pull at this time? Even I have my limits. I fire back a holding text:

I'll see what I can do. No
promises. Mx

I will email the PRs and press offices of the airlines, but not right now. They won't be checking their phones;

there's only one idiot doing that. I scrunch my eyes shut and do my best breathing exercises, determined to get back to sleep.

I do, but have a vivid nightmare where a knight in full armour is banging on my door trying to get in and I am pushing back against it with all my might, trying to keep him out. I wake with a start, the loud clanking noises are real and coming from the kitchen. Ella must be doing angry clearing up, maybe with the intention of waking me? I hate to think there's a bad atmosphere between us and I fully acknowledge it is me that is in the wrong, so I haul myself out of bed to go and offer to help. Those couple of hours sleep have really helped – no sign of a headache.

Presenting myself in the kitchen, Ella is standing at the sink with her back to me, sploshing soapy water around. A couple of bin bags full of cans and bottles are lined up by the door, along with some bags of general rubbish.

'Shall I take these downstairs and then make a start on the floor?' I offer, doing my best to sound chirpy.

'What the fuck!' Ella spins round, clutching a wet sponge to her chest. 'Oh, it's you. Did I wake you? Sorry. I didn't realise you were here. Tom's at football. I thought I was home alone.'

'Where else would I be?' I answer with a shrug.

'I assumed you'd bailed out and gone to Ed's. You didn't seem interested in hanging out with my friends.' She is still a bit cross and fair enough. I cringe when I think of how I carried on like a dope yesterday.

'Ella, I'm really sorry I was such a tit. You've missed

several episodes of my miserable life. Ed is the last person I would've seen, but, you're right, I wasn't in the party mood. Can we have a tea break and I'll fill you in?' I plop down onto a chair.

She seems quite happy to abandon her sponge. 'OK. These glasses could do with a soak. I'll stick the kettle on.'

Soon we are settled in our usual positions at the table and she reacts appropriately to my tale of woe about the mis-sent text, letting out an involuntary gasp and clapping her hand over her mouth when we get to the second text. When I tell her that I am done with Ed for good, she softens completely and gives me a big hug. 'I'm sorry that happened to you, Maddy, but maybe that's what it took to get you to see through him? And you still came to the picnic! No wonder you weren't the life and soul.'

Her sympathy releases something and, leaning over the empty mugs on the table, I have a cry into her towelling robed shoulder. Trust Ella to be wearing the right attire for a sobbing session. There are also some tears of relief that she's not angry with me anymore. When I've calmed down a bit and mopped myself up, I tell her about the writing course I plan to sign up to using the Casper money and that I am going to concentrate on work and self-development. I don't tell her I was up at 4.30am, looking into flights for Dani.

She says that all sounds great, good for me, but then adds that in the spirit of full and frank disclosure, she wants me to know that Drippy Tom has suggested moving in together. Nothing immediate, but she wants me to be aware, so it doesn't come as a shock. I'm such a dummy it does come as a shock, but it shouldn't. They are solid.

'Your place or his?' I ask, trying not to sound too forlorn.

'Honestly, Maddy, it's just an idea right now. Maybe we'd both sell up and start afresh. I promise I'll give you plenty of warning – don't worry about it.'

Easy for her to say, I'm the one being threatened with losing my home, but I manage a mature reply. 'I'm happy that things are going so well for you guys.' And I mean it. We spend the next hour companionably clearing up the mess, singing along to her awful 'Easy Sunday Vibes' playlist.

In the spirit of my new can-do attitude to life, I send out Dani's upgrade enquiries, decide which course to sign up for, then run through the interview questions for Steve and reward myself with a trip to the gym. Happy Sunday to me. Checking the timetable, I don't have the energy for the circuit class, but see that there is a yoga class. If I combine it with a swim, I can justify it as exercise. I get dressed in my swimming costume under my clothes to avoid awkward changing room scenes. I still haven't recovered from being butt-naked opposite my GP, who greeted me by name while I desperately tried to be invisible.

Breast-stroking up and down the pool, I give my myself a bit of light relief thinking through the interview questions for Needy Steve, managing to come up with a few curveballs for Caroline. I want to put her on the spot and watch her wriggle. Maybe: 'Which luxury brands would you suggest as the perfect match for Steven?' or 'Would you recommend media training?' Completely over the top and pitching it all wrong. Or go the other way and ask which regional radio stations she'd approach.

I have 'suggested' to Jess that she prepare a wish-list of interviews and features that are achievable for a man of his public profile (i.e. not much of one) with a budget (within his reach) and tell him who her media contacts are. That should seal the deal.

Pleasantly quiet on a Sunday afternoon, with a lane of the pool to myself, I settle into a rhythmic crawl – just the thing to clear my head. All the questions and thoughts pinging round my brain start to recede and I imagine I am somewhere hot and exotic, swimming though calm seas with the sun warm on my back. I get so carried away I forget to count my lengths and a glance at the clock shows I just have time for a quick shower before donning gym gear and heading to the yoga studio. Funny that a couple of weeks ago, I wasn't even aware it existed.

Entering the studio, there is a different atmosphere in this class, noticeably younger with a scattering of men. I self-consciously note the basicness of my high-street running leggings and vest. This lot are dressed in pastels with complicated strappy bra tops making macramé patterns across their toned backs, midriffs on show. Some of the guys are bare-chested. Actually, only one incredibly sculpted guy, bending down in a way that shows the muscles working across his broad shoulders, chatting to a lithe young woman sitting with her legs twisted like a pretzel, but looking like it's the most natural thing in the world. Straightening up, he strides to the front of the room, turns, closes his eyes standing stock-still, takes a deep breath and bows deeply. It looks like he's the teacher, but before I can digest this information, he's off, arms up, bending down, not talking nor explaining anything. Incredibly, the rest of the class seem to know what to do. Trying to keep up, I can't begin to imagine what I look like flapping around like a great kipper.

Once my initial panic passes, I focus on the woman in front of me and realise that they are repeating the same sequence and I start to get it. It's certainly more of a workout than the other classes. I'm hot and sweaty and panting when I feel a hand on my lower back as I am bending forward. 'Let your breath follow your movements,' a voice murmurs in my ear. The teacher is going round the room giving comments, but I feel a distinct tingle where he laid his hand. Fortunately, my blushes are covered by my sweatiness. As the class goes on, I catch him looking at me, and a couple of times we make eye contact. He's probably keeping a close eye because I'm new.

We do the relaxation thing at the end, lots of talk about softening your belly and relaxing every muscle from your toes up. I must have conked out somewhere round the hip area because next thing I know my eyes fly open and I just know I have snored. Looking from side to side to see if anyone has noticed, I catch eyes with the instructor. He's smiling, benignly, and puts his finger to his lips, shushing me, but managing to look pretty sexy. I close my eyes again, flustered, and can't relax at all – very un-yogic thoughts are going through my mind.

At the end, I keep my head down in case anyone is giving me dirty looks for snorting like a hog during the relaxation, and fiddle about rolling up the mat and folding the blanket. When it's quietened down, I dare to look up and there is the instructor, chatting to a woman who looks like she could be a ballerina. Making my way to the door via the equipment cupboard, he calls out, 'Hey, Miss Piggy, hold on a sec.' I freeze. *Oh my God, did he really just call me Miss Piggy? Am I about to be banned from yoga classes for life?*

Turning around, blushing, he is grinning in a very twinkly way. 'Your first time?' he enquires.

'First time in this class,' I manage, tailing off as I take in the mystical eastern tattoo on his incredibly defined bicep.

'I love popping people's ashtanga cherry,' he says.

No mistaking the tone of this conversation, but I'm caught so off my guard that all I manage to come back with is a weird, strangulated kind of laugh, then gather myself just enough to say, 'Sorry about that, I had a terrible night.'

Looking concerned, he lays a hand on my shoulder, 'I'm sure I can help with that.' *Oh my God – is that a chat-up line?* 'I bet you sleep well tonight. Practice the breathing cycle as you drop off and a deep sleep is guaranteed.'

Maybe I'm misreading the signs. He's just a caring yoga kind of person. But then he gives my shoulder a bit of a squeeze and says, 'I really hope I'll be seeing more of you. I'm Raj, by the way.'

'Um, yes, maybe. I'm Maddy,' at which point the next class start to file in and, confused by my feelings, make a dash for it.

'Come again!' I hear from Raj as I head for the turnstile.

I don't turn around, but I do feel a little flutter somewhere in my chest. Could be indigestion, but there's no denying he was cute. 'Maybe,' I call back, hoping he heard, because, for the first time in ages, I was feeling a teensy bit flirty.

I'm delighted to find Virgin have come up trumps for Dani. A free upgrade if the plane isn't full, access to their VIP Clubhouse and use of the chauffeur service, so that's a result. I feel a glow of satisfaction as I send her the good news.

Davina is there with her mic, looking impressed. Turning Betty on, I smoothly say: 'Value added, Davina, I'm value added.'

Chapter 19

Text to L-A, 9.00am:
Morning! Just confirming
interviews start midday. I'll be
there 11.30. Maddy

Kiss or no kiss? Never quite sure with work stuff.

I'm meeting Steve in town, so I've got time to go via Dani's and make sure the house is ready for her arrival. I arranged for her cleaner to go in and freshen up first thing, had her favourite flowers – Stargazer lilies – delivered and arranged an Ocado delivery so she can have breakfast.

Letting myself in, I can immediately tell the flowers have arrived – I hate the smell of lilies and they are everywhere. I turn the heating up, make sure the beds are freshly made, check the contents of the fridge and then nearly jump out my skin when the doorbell goes. *What the...?* It's too early to be Dani. I am tracking her flight and she has at least another hour before landing. Perhaps she's been ordering stuff online.

'Jess? What are you doing here? The interview's at Workspace and not for hours?' She's certainly not looking interview smart, quite the opposite.

'I know, but I checked you on Find my Friends and saw you heading here, so thought I'd come and drop some stuff.' I see she has a rucksack and a wheelie case by her side.

'I've got no idea what you're talking about. I'm here because Dani's arriving in a couple of hours. Why are you here?' I know I sound impatient, but I could really do without complications today. I'm on a tight enough schedule as it is.

'But we agreed!' I have absolutely no idea what she means and it must show because she continues, 'On Saturday night, you said Dani was staying in New York for a while.'

We are looking as confused as each other. There's an uncomfortable silence.

She continues, 'I've got to move out. I told you about my celebrity house-sitting idea. I offered to stay here.'

Now, I know I drank too much, but even so there is no way I would have agreed to this. 'Jess – there has been some colossal misunderstanding. Even if I did agree, which I really don't think I did, that was before Dani decided to come home. Today. So, no way are you moving in here.' We stare at each other in a Mexican stand-off.

'Maddy, you said you'd give me the keys at the interview

today. I'm just here early so I don't have to haul my cases to town.' How does Jess get herself into these situations?

'Jess, are you not listening? Dani is landing as we speak; she's home for a couple of days to relax. There's been some massive miscommunication.' I'm rattled, not least because I can't see what part of our conversation led to this ridiculous state of affairs. I can tell Jess is thinking it through, but instead of backing off, as I'd expect, she responds with, 'How long is Dani in London? I can stay at yours until she goes back.'

'No! I mean, I don't know. It's Ella's flat, I'd need to ask. And I don't think Dani would go for it anyway, Jess. I'm sorry for the confusion, but I've got a tonne on today. You'll have to sort something else out. I'm due at Steve's interviews, I've got to go. Want a lift somewhere?'

She lashes out, 'Really? Or is that just another empty offer, Maddy? You have no idea the amount of stress I'm under. I'm homeless as of tomorrow morning.' She grabs the handle of her case and turns to leave.

'Jess – I'll ask Ella and tell you at the interview. I'm sure you can stay for a night or two.' I call after her, but she carries on marching down the road. The set of her back is furious, but what more can I do? I'm starting to wonder if Jess actually is the drama.

It's a fuck-up, but I can't see that it's my fuck-up. I've got a busy day ahead and need to get my head back in the game. Hopefully she's a shoo-in for the job with Steve and we can take it from there.

Satisfied Dani's flat looks welcoming, I leave a Post-it

on the mirror. 'Welcome home! Call me later, Mx' and head back to my car, fretting about Jess and the way she stormed off. She's third on my list of four interviews, which I hope will be enough time for her to calm down and get herself sorted.

L-a is there to greet me and shows me into a private room with a couple of mid-century armchairs reupholstered in olive-green tweed and a teak work table with a fake (I assume) Eames office chair and an industrial desk light. It's very hipster, if a little predictable, but the main thing is it's free and makes us look very professional. They get to post that a respected author is in the house and everyone's happy.

'Brilliant, L-a, this is perfect. I've arranged it so the interviewees shouldn't cross over, but if they do, can reception seat them at a polite distance from each other?' I don't want Jess and Caroline getting into one.

'We'll do better than that, we'll offer them coffee and, of course, you're welcome to order drinks on the house. If Steven wanted to post something on Instagram about us, it would be much appreciated.' She's such a professional.

'Seems like a good deal to me, but Steve's not on social media. It's one of the things these potential PRs should investigate, so how about I set that as an on-the-spot challenge for them?'

L-a laughs and says she knew I was savvy, which I like.

From Dani, 11.45am:
Good to be home! Knackered.
Talk later but can you book me
an area for drinks somewhere
cool tomorrow night? Dx

Reckon I just about have time to send out a few enquiries to the usual suspects before Steve gets here. Dani is hot property now the show is doing well, so it shouldn't be a problem. Once her mates know she's in town for one night only, they'll all want to see her. Wonder if the press has caught a sniff of her presence? Knowing Dani, she may even have tipped them off herself.

Looking up after some fleet-fingered texting to bar contacts, I see Steve hovering outside the smoked glass frontage, wearing corduroy and looking daunted. I nip out to rescue him.

'Steve – hi! All set? We've got a lovely room ready and time for a quick coffee before the first candidate.' Ushering him in, his tweedy jacket and leather briefcase are somehow in keeping with the retro look of Workspace. It's just his anxious expression that makes him look out of place. I go into reassuring mode. 'One of the directors is going to come and say hello. They're very pleased to be hosting you today.' I see his chest swell with pride a little.

L-a approaches, hand extended. I'm not sure if it's my imagination or did he flinch a little? She is dressed in an asymmetric draped dress, with chunky studded biker boots and massive swinging earrings. Steve thinks he is urbane and worldly, but the poor man is so far out of his comfort zone, he needs oxygen. He'd better grow a pair before meeting these PRs.

We settle into the interview room. First up is a young woman with lots of social media experience, who can build a website in her sleep and has plenty of contacts in the tech world. I set her the Workspace challenge of setting up a temporary Instagram account for Steve and she takes it in her stride. The problem is this means nothing to Steve – all he wants is to be on the cover of a magazine and not a digital one. We will treat this as a warm-up.

Next up is a guy, very suave, dressed in a skinny-legged suit and rocking some carefully sculpted facial hair. Also, several piercings. Steve can't seem to see past the ring he has in his nose and can barely get a question out. To be fair, the guy doesn't seem to 'get' Steve either – and when he suggests an image makeover and that he knows one of the guys off *Queer Eye*, I worry that Steve is going to make a run for it.

I had Jess on third, but when I go outside to fetch her, there is no sign. This is not good. I check with reception who say there is a candidate waiting, but she's called Caroline. Of course she is. Caroline is sitting there, primly; an Anya Hindmarch handbag on her lap and *agnès b.* cashmere cardigan buttoned Chanel-style, hair swept up in a chignon. Does she think we're auditioning for *Breakfast at Tiffany's*? Fake smile on, I approach.

'Caroline! Hello. Would you like to come through and meet Steven?'

'Hello, Madeleine. My appointment isn't for forty minutes. I came early to compose myself and run through my proposal. Are you not running to schedule?' Her fake smile blows mine out of the water.

I grit my teeth. 'Unforeseeable circumstances. I thought you'd appreciate the opportunity to meet Steven while he's still fresh. If you'd rather wait and go later, that's fine. Do order yourself a coffee.' I predict this will do the trick and, as I turn away, I can practically hear her inner turmoil.

'Alright, but I need a moment to powder my nose.'

Christ almighty, can she not just go to the loo like a normal person? But I swallow it and say, 'Of course, come through when you're ready.'

Two minutes later, Caroline wafts in on a cloud of Miss Dior, strides past me straight to Steve, kisses him on both cheeks, before stepping back to look him in the eyes and says, 'Mr Bamford, such an honour to meet you. I have read and adored *all* your books.'

Good opener. He is charmed and a bit flustered. We all sit down and he starts fiddling with the CVs. *Bollocks*! He's got Jess's on top and asks Caroline a question about Aria.

She narrows her eyes, working out what's going on. Leaning down, she pulls a CV from her bag along with a very smart presentation folder. 'Steven, this is my CV. I think there is some confusion with your admin.' Sharp look in my direction. 'I have extensive contacts in high-end luxury and would absolutely *adore* to introduce you to some superb brands.' Standing directly in front of me, she leans over Steve and starts flipping through the proposal she has prepared, which might as well be a fairy tale. As if they'd be interested in him! I can hear her murmuring 'Rolex' and 'Burberry' in his ear. After a few minutes of this, she returns to her seat and primly crosses her legs. 'Please do ask me any questions you may have.'

How has she managed to take control of the situation so effectively? Steve is gazing at her with a look of utter wonderment. I have to pull this back before it's too late.

'Caroline, how would you pitch a British middle-aged author to these highly fashion-led, international brands?' They both look at me as though I've just told them there's no such thing as unicorns.

'Madeleine, you shouldn't underestimate the intellect of fashion people. I think they would leap at the chance of such an erudite association, plus it's all about inclusivity these days.' She has him in the palm of her hand. His eyes are shining and blinking behind his specs.

'Maddy, I think Caroline understands exactly what I'm after. We speak the same language!'

'Exactément!' she simpers in a stupid French accent, coyly looking at him from under her eyelashes.

'Indeed, well, thank you for your time, Caroline. We have other candidates to see, so we'll let you know by the end of the week,' I say, trying to be professional, while getting her out of the room ASAP.

'*Such* a pleasure to meet you.' She leans forward and takes both Steve's hands in hers. 'And I *dearly* hope we have the opportunity to work together on this exciting chapter in your career.'

He is dumbstruck.

I have one last line of attack. 'Oh, Caroline, have you included your rates in your proposal?' I have no doubt she is way out of his budget.

'I have, but this would be such a wonderful campaign to run, I'd be happy to come to some mutually agreed arrangement,' and she shoots Steve a look. Oh my God, is she actually flirting with him? I feel sick. She uses this opportunity to fire the killer shot. 'Oh, and if you were expecting Jessica today, I saw her getting on the Eurostar on my way here, but I'm sure you were well aware of that, Madeleine.'

Fuck. Jess is turning into a liability and making me look a fool in the process. I had bigged her up to Steve as the sensible option, but she doesn't appear to have a sensible bone in her body. Add to that the fact he can't see that Caroline is all talk and no trousers, and probably only wants this gig to annoy me. Steve is yammering on about how exciting this all is, caught up in his own importance. L-a pops in to say goodbye and that the Instagram experiment worked, encouraging Steve to keep it up, to which he glibly says, 'Oh, yes, my PR will be taking care of that.' I have no choice but to swallow my pride and go along with this madness. I don't have time to wonder if today could get any worse, which is lucky because it is just about to.

I hurry to usher the still flushed-with-delight Steve out of Workspace and steer him towards the tube, suggesting he sleep on it before making a decision. I can't even bear to mention Jess. I haven't heard a peep from her.

Making use of the private room, I call the dame back. She's heard rumours that the documentary crew are interviewing an actor she had fired. She wants to earn some brownie points with the director. As the director is a foodie, I suggest a rare truffle as the perfect offering. To add some pomp to the occasion, she wants it biked to the production office, ideally when as many people as possible are there to see it, but, worst case, by the end of the day. Of course. When L-a pops her head round the door to see if I am done, I am deep in conversation on speakerphone with a verbose Frenchman who runs a specialist shop in Notting Hill. I manage an eye roll in her direction. She waves; I respond with a grateful thumbs up and get back to Monsieur, who thinks he may be able to help, at a price.

**From Needy Steve, 4.45pm:
Caroline's the one!**

Chapter 20

From Dani, 5.50am
(she clearly has jetlag):
Come by for a catch-up –
LOADS to do! Dx

I will have to fit her in today, but after my now regular session with Casper – he emailed last night confirming my attendance first thing. I have gone over and over it in mymind and decided: I will continue to help him with the scripts and learn what I can; I will take the extra money and use it to make a difference; and I will start my script-writing class.

The benefits are I will be richer, I will get some experience and I will be ahead of the rest of the class. This is called focusing on the positive and making the most of what is available to me. I can only control so much.

No doubt Dani will be sleeping now, so I allow myself

the luxury of staying in bed and having a little wander round social media. Dani's night out has made it on to the *Daily Mail* sidebar of shame, but a quick read reveals nothing except that she's 'out on the town' and 'fresh from Broadway success' – nothing to worry about. Instagram brings a nasty shock: Mimi the Moo-Cow posting a photo of her wheelie case and skis and gushing about counting the days. It's happening. Try as I might to push all thoughts of their weekend away to the back of my mind, I was only too aware it was coming around. Ed rarely uses Instagram, so I can't stalk him even if I wanted, which I obviously would, but Mimi has helpfully tagged all the members of the party and it jolts me to see his name included. The depressing thought of the pictures to come propels me out of bed and into the bathroom. Major sessions with Casper and Dani mean no time to linger.

I remind myself that I am *Capable*, *Flexible* and *Competent* and I will dress to reflect this. Black Cos trousers always make me feel business-like, but I reject the white shirt as I'm in danger of looking like a waiter. Instead, I go for a lightweight cashmere sweater I bought at a sample sale in Shoreditch. I am going to be cool and professional with Casper, so I sling on a classic Whistles jacket I usually only wear to interviews. Hopefully, I look too smart for Dani to ask me to put the bins out like last time.

In the kitchen, I find a cute note from Ella stuck on the kettle: 'Don't let the bastards get you down! And don't take any CFC x'. She's right. With my KeepCup of tea in one hand, I scoop up my Dani and Casper bags, momentarily compare my set-up with the luxury office space I had the use of yesterday, remember to send a deeply grateful email to L-a and I'm off.

I put in another call to Jess on the way – no answer, but no international ringtone either. I sent texts yesterday that escalated from '**Are you on way?**' to '**Where the fuck are you???**' and I haven't heard a peep. This morning, I tried, '**Let's talk.**' Annoyed as I am, I am starting to worry, and what on earth was she doing on the Eurostar? Best-case scenario, she's got a job with a designer or model and has had to rush off to Paris. Worst-case? She's had a full-on meltdown.

Hoping it's the former, and that she's OK, I would still love to know what the chatter is at Top Notch and she's my way in. Just to add to it, all the traffic is terrible and I arrive at Casper's frazzled and unable to put my anxieties about Jess aside.

✦

'The ratings are on the rise, so give me a fucking break and let me get on with my job.'

Casper is on the phone and the study door is shut, but he's loud enough to hear clearly. I'm not going in while he's in that mood. The safety of the basement beckons. I bang the porch door to signal my arrival. He'll come and find me when he wants my help. This is the new me talking. Trying not to scuff the walls with my bulging work bags as I head down, I can still hear Casper's muffled voice, so turn the Sonos on to drown him out.

The dulcet tones of Radio 4 are soothing – a discussion on eighteenth-century philosophers, no less. I have no idea what they are on about, but having it on will add to my air of seriousness when Casper does make his appearance. I could murder a coffee, but I don't want to cross paths with him. I'll start with the post. There's an official-looking brown envelope on top of the pile. Please God, not an HMRC investigation.

Shit. Nearly as bad. A fixed penalty notice from a speed camera on the A21. The fine won't bother Casper in the least; the three points, however, will be a major cause of stress, because Casper already has nine points on his license. Anticipating his reaction has me debating a sneaky exit through the back door and over the garden fence. Seriously, because this means he is going to lose his license, and that will cause him to lose his shit, and I will have to deal with the fallout. Add this to the fact that his baseline mood these days is tetchy, to put it politely, and despite my resolve to have a positive attitude, I know today is going to get tough.

From Casper, 9.45 am:
Come on up. We need to get
cracking

Dilemma. Tell him about the points now, have the whole drama and then get on with the script work, or hold back and try to concentrate with this hanging over me, then tell him and make a quick exit. I've got about thirty seconds to decide, I reckon, and I'm finding it extremely hard to think rationally. I'll try a bit of yoga breathing; I close my eyes and breathe in for one, two, three…

'Must be something fascinating keeping you down here, but a read-through is the priority – Maddy?' I'd pushed my chair back and was sitting with my hands resting on my knees, my eyes closed. It must have looked a little unusual.

'Casper, yes, morning. I was just, um, composing myself. Getting my head in the right space…' The thick stair carpet must have muffled his steps.

'Have you been hanging out with hippies again?' Why did I ever tell him I'd been trying out yoga? 'Peace and love to all, but you're here to work, so come on.'

My eyes inadvertently dart towards the post pile, with the penalty charge letter on top. 'Looks ominous.' He strides over to the table and snatches the letter up. I look at the floor and count backwards. Three, two, one… and sure enough, we have blast off.

'What the *fuck*! I'm an excellent driver. I've never had an accident! What is the *matter* with these people?' Even after attending a speed awareness course, he still thinks he's the best judge of how fast is safe to go. 'How many points is that?' I'm going to have to break it to him.

'Twelve. In the last three years.' I can't bear to say it, so I bite my lip while he works it out.

'They only count the last two years, don't they?' he says, confidently. I checked this out last time and he's wrong, but I can buy a bit of time and hope he calms down.

'I'll look into it; see what the story is.' Cowardly, but

there's no harm in double-checking the facts and at least we can get on with the work today. I'll email him later, after I've gone.

'I can't think about this right now. We need to focus on the script, so leave it. Come on.' I follow him up the stairs, reminding myself it's not actually my fault.

He heads to the kitchen to make coffee after handing me the script, but I find it hard to settle.

From Steve, 10.03am:
Have you told Caroline? Let's
get this show on the road!

Ugh. I've got no comeback. Still no word from Jess and she's screwed it up anyway. She's really dropped me in it, not only making me look a fool yesterday, but now I'll have to work with Caroline, which was never the plan. Infuriatingly, her fees were not as high as I anticipated. Either she needs the work or dislikes me enough to drop her fees, just to be able to annoy me on a daily basis. I try not to dwell on the horrors ahead and maintain a positive attitude.

To Steve, 10.05am:
Sure! I'll get things set up
ASAP

Casper is back in the room, trying to hide his irritation about the speeding ticket with false jolliness.

'Maddy, Maddy, Maddy, what have you got for me today?' I find it kind of creepy. He's perched on the edge of the desk, attempting to look casual.

'I haven't read it right through yet.'

The façade drops. 'Well, get on with it. We've wasted enough of this morning already.' He stays where he is, glaring at me, as if that's going to make for a conducive atmosphere.

I turn away from him slightly and start to read, aware of his eyes drilling holes in the back of my head. *Calm, Flexible, Competent.* That's me. Let's do this.

These characters are so familiar to me, I can picture it all in my mind to the extent of knowing what they would be wearing and exactly how the actors would be delivering the lines I'm reading. And that's when I realise a major problem. It's all getting too familiar. Casper is sticking to what he does best, but at the risk of the show becoming boring and conforming to a formula. Do I tell him this? What's the worst that can happen? He stops using me. So be it. I'm done trying to second-guess his reactions.

I raise my head and look him straight in the eye. 'It's getting dull, Casper. You're playing it too safe.'

His eyes narrow and I prepare for a blast, but, without breaking his gaze, he says 'Go on.'

'Look, it's fine, but that's it, just fine, nothing special. We know these characters so well and that can be comforting, but the patterns of speech are always the same, the same people get the punchlines, the same people are the straight guys. Let's shake things up; grab some attention.'

He uncrosses his arms and leans forward; he would be furrowing his brow, but nothing above the eyebrows moves. 'What do you have in mind?' He is taking me seriously. My confidence seems to have changed the dynamic between us.

'Nothing specific, yet, but let's play with it. Throw everything up in the air and see where it lands.'

This is taking things to another level. We are not making minor tweaks here, but I know in my guts it's the right thing to do. And I know what else I need to do. He's settling himself in, script open in front of him, ready to get stuck right in. It's now or never.

'I'll help, Casper, but I want credit.' That's the jacket talking.

He doesn't even hesitate. 'We have been over this before and I am not wasting time on this conversation again. You get rewarded, but you are – read my lips – *not* a fucking writer.'

We stare at each other angrily. This is about the least creative atmosphere you could have.

'Come on, Maddy, work with me on this. You've got good ideas – well, some good ideas – and I like bouncing off you. But there is too much at stake to start rocking the boat. If you don't like the set-up, go back downstairs, file some shit and let me get on with what I do.'

He's called my bluff and he knows it.

Well, two can play at that game. I get up and head for the door.

'Wait!'

I stop, heart racing. This could be it.

'You do bring a different perspective, but it's to what I've already written. Come on, Maddy, we can work something out. We're a good team.'

I turn, waiting to see if there's more.

'How about I make you my official intern, like an apprentice?' he offers. 'I think that would be reasonable, don't you? We could take it from there.'

Infuriatingly, 'reasonable' is my middle name.

Recognising he's got me back on side, he goes on. 'Let's throw the rule book out – like you said, show me what you've got. Wow me. What's the most unlikely thing to happen?' He's looking at me expectantly.

Unable to resist the challenge, I suggest a scenario awfully close to home. The central couple – Edie and Jake – break up or at least one of them strays with someone wildly inappropriate. Maybe a colleague or, better still, their boss, which could lead to plenty of awkward situations. My imagination starts galloping, I'm about to suggest a same-sex liaison, but Casper hurries back behind his desk, scribbling hastily on a large notepad.

'OK – bold moves, but, above all, we need the funny. This could get sad.'

No need to tell me that relationships breaking down are sad, but also plenty of room for funny/embarrassing or funny/uncomfortable. Without thinking, I tell him about my mistakenly sent text from Ed as an example. It stirs his excitement – no room for empathy in this situation.

'I like it, I can work with this. You can carry on downstairs. I'll give you a shout if I need you.'

Disappointed at being done so soon, but appeased by my new internship, this works for my schedule. 'I have to leave at lunchtime.' I haven't heard from Dani, but I know she's expecting me.

No acknowledgement. Back to the daily grind.

A quick internet search reveals that Casper will certainly lose his license, probably for six months, but, even worse, he will also be summoned to court. I can just imagine the scene. A bit more searching gets me the details of the lawyer famous for getting celebrities off their driving offences. Not a route I approve of going down; he finds technical loopholes in the law and I can only imagine Ella's reaction. Next, I contact the household staff agency to make enquiries about hiring a driver. I'm getting my ducks in a row, as they say. At this stage, there's not much else I can do.

My phone is buzzing. Dani's agent, Stephanie, has a hundred and one requests now word is out that she's in town. It seems Dani didn't inform her she was coming and she's having to play catch-up. Next up, Caroline, who is 'delighted' to accept the job with Steve – of course she bloody is – and can't wait to get started. She's asking for headshots and cuttings and a whole lot else to start making approaches for press coverage. She's right, of course, but it seems hiring a PR is going to mean more work for me and, even worse, doing it for Caroline. I can't see this panning out well.

From Dani, 12.25pm:
Come! Bring Aspirin. Dx

So, she hasn't changed that much then.

From Dani, 12.26pm:
And a big Mac. X

That's my girl.

Chapter 21

Arriving at Dani's with a meal deal in one hand and my Dani bag in the other, I compartmentalise my anxieties about Casper's impending loss of license. I hope Dani isn't going to have too much for me to deal with. I think I've kept on top of everything pretty well and all I really want is to hear about her stateside adventures.

There is one lonely *paparazzo* lolling against the wall of the house opposite, hoping for someone interesting arriving or leaving. He glances in my direction, but I am clearly not someone interesting. He raises his camera as I knock on the door – the possibility of an unmade/worse-for-wear Dani is better than nothing – but I only knocked as a warning I'm letting myself in, so two fingers to him.

'It's me, Maddy!' I sing-song as I push the door shut behind me with my foot. 'Bearing a Big Mac.'

'Now you're talking,' her familiar husky voice comes

from the landing, followed by a galloping thump down the stairs. She grabs it and gives me a hug at the same time. 'I don't know what I've missed more – you or Maccy D's.'

I follow her as she heads to the kitchen, already unwrapping the burger, where she will make me a cup of tea much weaker and far milkier than I like, but it's the thought that counts.

'Paps still outside?' she asks. 'You won't believe the stunt they pulled this morning – put a parking ticket on my windscreen. They must've nicked it off some other poor bugger's car, hoping for a reaction shot.' Shaking her head, she joins me at the kitchen table. 'That is something I have not missed, *at all*. I come and go in New York without any hassle. Now, tell me some juicy gossip. What have I missed?'

I need to be careful. She's a terrible gossip herself, so anything I say will certainly go further. I decide the safest subject matter is me, so I tell her about Ed dumping me, omitting text-gate.

'Babe, I'm sorry. That is shit, but, if I'm honest...' – oh, here we go and I don't recall asking her to be honest – 'I didn't really take to him. At my birthday party, he was scoping the room and even gave me a little wink, if you know what I mean.'

If this is Dani being supportive, I can do without it. I don't believe Ed would do that. He was probably just starstruck. But no one seems sorry to see the back of him and I'm starting to wonder if I only saw what I wanted to see.

'I've got some exciting news to tell you, though.' Her eyes are literally shining.

So that's enough about me then! 'Go on, good news, I hope.' I wonder if it's on the romantic or professional front. She left for New York saying she was done with men and focusing on her career.

Leaning forward so close our foreheads are almost touching over the tea mugs, she hisses, theatrically, 'It hasn't been announced, but I'm being nominated for a Tony!' and sits up straight, positively glowing with excitement and scanning my face for a reaction.

Feeling genuinely delighted for her, I don't have to fake my congratulations. 'That's amazing, Dani! Well done you! How come you know about it?'

'They give your agent the date to make sure you'll attend. It means so much to me, Maddy, I can't tell you. It's a proper acting award, up against real actors. Honestly, I don't even care if I win or not, just to be recognised...' She's not fooling anyone.

Laughing, I chip in, 'Are you practising your acceptance speech on me? *I'd like to thank...*'

The smile drops and, looking serious, she goes on, 'I've been thinking about it and I want you to ask Casper to help me with a speech, in case I do win. This isn't some low-rent British telly award, it's the real thing. I don't want to look stupid.'

I'm not sure how to respond without letting on that Casper is permanently on the edge of a nervous breakdown these days, and certainly not that *Just Between Us* isn't

209

doing very well. Being out of the country, I assume she's unaware. She's looking so intently at me; I need to come up with some kind of response.

'Maybe it would be better if you asked him yourself?' I don't want to be asking Casper for anything right now, especially not a favour. However, I also don't want Dani to pick up on any tension – she'd be right on it, asking questions.

'But you're so good at handling him,' she continues, 'and I forgot to thank him for the hysterical gift he sent me on opening night – did he tell you about it?'

Do I shatter her illusion? That it wasn't, in fact, Casper who went to buy her a Jessica Rabbit, packaged it up and posted it? Time to deploy diplomatic skills. 'Hilarious, right? He loves to shock! But it's not too late; you've just landed. Why don't you thank him now, pave the way for the big ask?' Now I'm the one looking beseeching.

'You are so right, Maddy. I'll do it and be super gushy, then when you next talk to him, test the waters – but don't tell him what it's for. He's such a bigmouth.' Pot, kettle, etc.

'Good plan. Now, when is this ceremony? Do we need to think about borrowing clothes, and booking hair and make-up? Should I come over?' It would be stressful, but for a few days in New York, I'd cope, and it would take my mind of Ed and his stupid ski trip.

'Babe, you're so sweet. My US agent is taking care of all that. She's hired me a stylist, but come! We could totally hang out – it'd be super fun!'

Reading between the lines, this means the trip would be at my own expense, but I'd still be at her beck and call. Not so tempting, after all. 'Well, keep me posted and let's see nearer the time. Now, shall we slaughter some of this paperwork?'

The next hour is spent presenting her with various requests and marking them up yes or no. Mostly no, as usual. Stephanie, her agent, calls to say she's got her tickets for the absolute-must-see-but-totally-sold-out show this evening and then she's back on the plane first thing in the morning. I can see she's lost interest in our chores. Hoping she'll ask me to be her plus one for the evening, I suggest we wrap things up.

'Yeah, good idea. I don't know how you put up with all this boring shit, Maddy. I couldn't.'

I'm starting to wonder the same thing, but reply jauntily, 'Oh, it can be quite satisfying when we hit the bottom of the pile! Plus, I've got rent to pay.' Which reminds me, I really want to have a word with Ella about Casper's situation. As soon as Dani sweeps out the room to start her elaborate grooming routine, I text Ella:

You in for supper tonight? I'll cook Mx

I don't expect an immediate reply. She's probably busy with *Important Stuff*, so I set about tidying up, shredding, binning and taking what needs to get posted. The press have been known to go through Dani's bins. I'm just heading out the door when she calls down, 'Can you get a spray tanner round?' So I sit back down and get on it.

From Ella, 4.30pm:
Not tonight, going to Tom's.
Might need a quick chat if poss.
Everything OK?
With me, yes, work question.
I'll call when I can x

She's a pal. My phone vibrates and pings at the same time.

A nice St Tropez person can come in forty-five minutes and a reminder of the yoga class I said I'd see Lauren at this evening, which works out well as I don't relish the thought of an evening at home alone. Without Ella there to cook for, it would probably be peanut butter on toast and a Netflix binge in bed, followed by a social media vortex – but it's more than that. I really enjoyed hanging out with Lauren last week and the yoga wasn't bad either.

I nip up to tell Dani the tanner will be here shortly, hoping I can get away. She's lying in the bath, talking to a friend on speakerphone as I hover outside her room. Her feet are reflected in the mirrored wardrobes through the half-open door.

'Hang on, babes, my PA's here.' Dirty laugh. 'Not **right** here. At the door, silly.' Maybe more than just a friend.

'Tanner here in about half an hour. Shall I head off?' *Please, please, please.*

'Could you let them in and set up in the lounge? I want

a proper soak. And check if it's clear outside?' Without waiting for an answer, she goes back to her conversation, 'Not that kind of soaking, you cheeky sod.' Filthy giggle follows. I wonder who she's flirting with.

Sighing, I head back downstairs, pausing on the landing to peek through the shutters. All clear.

From Casper, 4.47pm:
What's the story with the points?

I reply honestly:

Just waiting to speak to a
lawyer. I'll let you know.

In the kitchen, I make a cup of tea the way I like it and peruse the notes and photos on the fridge while it's brewing. There seems to be a new guy around. Polaroids from New York show a tall, rangy man holding her hand in front of the Washington Square arch. He looks nice. The fact that he hasn't appeared on her social media means he must be a real person, rather than someone to be photographed with for publicity or attention. A deep sigh escapes just as my phone goes.

'Hi, Ella, thanks for calling me back.'

'Sounded serious, but I haven't got long. Is it about Jess? I can't get hold of her.' Ella is so kind; I'd almost forgotten about Jess and I'm still a bit cross with her.

'No – I've been trying too. She's gone AWOL. It's Casper.

He's hit twelve points on his driving license. Is there anything we can do?'

'Not unless he has a valid reason to appeal – valid in the eyes of the law, not just because he's well known and thinks normal rules don't apply.' Her tone is professional and brusque.

'OK, but will it be public knowledge?' I'm keeping it business-like, too.

'Yep – it'll go to the magistrate's court. He doesn't have to appear if he's not contesting it, but the press keep an eye out for well-known names in the public listings. Sorry I can't give you better news.' She doesn't sound sorry. She sounds a little pleased. Ella hates it when people think they should get special attention. 'If that's it, I'd best get on. Let me know when you track Jess down. I've got some good news for her – a counter offer, all tied in with non-disclosure agreements – so please tell her not to talk to *anyone* in the meantime.'

Keeping shtum is not Jess's strong point; I hope it's not too late. I make my farewells to Ella and fire off yet another text to Jess, asking her to please get in touch or, if she's sulking, with Ella. Maybe that'll break the impasse.

Now for the not insignificant matter of telling Casper. It's won't be pretty, so I decide to email him explaining it as calmly as I can. I don't know why I feel so guilty about it, but this often happens when I'm breaking bad news to clients. It feels like I've failed in my role.

Dani's still burbling away upstairs, so I shut the kitchen door and carefully word an email to Casper, explaining it all as simply and undramatically as I can. Trying not to overthink it, I hit send just as the doorbell goes – must be the spray tanner.

We greet each other warmly. I was one of his guinea pigs when he was training. There was a shout out from CHAMPS for volunteers and I was up for it, so we had a hilarious session in his salon. He managed to make me feel relatively relaxed wearing nothing but a paper thong, so I knew he'd be good at the personal side of the job. When he got me to lift my bum cheeks up to spray the crease underneath, I knew he was a perfectionist, so he made it into my contacts. Greetings over, I leave him setting up his pop-up booth in the living room and run up to the landing to tell Dani he's here, still planning to make it to yoga.

As I start the engine, Casper comes through the speakers, loud and very clear.

'What the actual fuck are you talking about? Fucking chauffeurs and wanker lawyers – no sodding way.' He sounds furious.

'Hi, Casper. You got my email.' I'd hoped for a little longer to gather my guts.

'Come on, Maddy, you can do better than this. There has to be a workaround. Think!' No point telling him I've thought of little else, but I can't work miracles despite my reputation.

'Honestly, Casper, I've done some research, spoken to a lawyer and wracked my brains. We knew this would happen if you got more points.' I'm doing my best not to feel personally responsible, but failing. Why do I let clients do this to me? I need a reflective shield to deflect all of the blame.

'Don't sound so smug about it – I haven't killed anyone; I haven't even had a fucking accident. It's a joke! You can drive as fast in you like in Germany.' He spits like it makes any difference at all.

I resist pointing out we are not in Germany. I resist saying anything at all because, in this mood, Casper is looking for someone to take it out on. Bitter experience has taught me that there isn't a right answer, so I just drive and let him rant, trying my best not to absorb his negativity.

I can't imagine what my reality show would make of this little scene. There would be a lot of bleeping for sure.

When he's run out of steam, I say, very quietly, 'I'll keep thinking Casper. Let's talk tomorrow.'

This seems to do the trick and I pull into the gym car park with just enough time to change. Relaxation exercises are just what I need.

Chapter 22

I felt quite at home heading to the studio and, for once, I wasn't last one in. I gathered up belts and blocks with an idea of what they were for and laid a mat out, keeping a spot for Lauren. I check the door every time it opens, like I watched the classroom door at school for my mates to come in, and so am staring expectantly when Raj arrives. I'm confused; he's not meant to be teaching this class. Of course, he catches my dopey look and grins at me as he heads to the front.

'Sorry to disappoint you, class. I know you were expecting Tessa, but she's been struck down with a lurgy, so you'll have to put up with me. I'll try and do things your way – bear with me.'

I'm digesting this information when Lauren slips in and settles down beside me.

'I thought you weren't coming,' I manage to whisper as he starts the class.

'I nearly didn't but couldn't let you down,' she manages from downward dog and that was the end of chatting as we concentrated on the class, which was a faster-paced version of the one we did before. I actively tried not to catch Raj's eye as he showed us what was next, but it was difficult as I really had to pay attention so as not to make an idiot of myself. He was so smiley and upbeat, it was hard to tell if any of it was directed at me. I kept telling myself it wasn't, but then thinking maybe it was. I was tying myself in knots, physically and mentally. Double tiring. Lauren and I managed a few eyebrow raises to each other and I'm sure she caught my appreciative look when he demonstrated how we should be engaging our shoulder blades by turning around and showing us his back muscles. I think the technical term is rippling.

Time flew and soon we were stretched out on our mats for the relaxation. I kept my eyes open so I didn't doze off and honk again. As we rolled our mats up, Lauren said, 'Smoothie?'

'You called?' came a voice behind my shoulder. Raj. I jumped. And blushed.

'Shut up, you idiot,' Lauren said, but with a smile. 'How come you're teaching an Iyengar class?'

'Tessa called in sick last-minute and I was in the building. I need all the work I can get, so, as *you* could no doubt tell, I bluffed my way through it.'

They clearly know each other.

'Lucky for you, most of this lot were so blinded by your biceps they didn't notice the difference.' Lauren fired back.

Quite well, it would seem.

'Now, what's that about a smoothie? I get a freebie for teaching – can I join you?' He is an actual smoothie, but I can't read Lauren at all. Fortunately, I don't seem to have to say anything in this exchange.

'Sure, this is my friend, Maddy. We're in the same line of work and she's getting into yoga.'

'I believe we've met across a crowded mat.' He's smiling right into my eyes as he says this and I am mesmerised, then realise they are both looking at me expectantly.

'Yes – I remember,' and recall that tingle where he touched my back. The next class are filing in, so I scramble about trying to pile up all the bits of kit surrounding me, while Lauren deftly zips her mat into its bag.

'Here, let me help.' As he leans across me to stack up some foam blocks, our arms touch and I pull back. He looks at me quizzically, but I can't maintain eye contact and scurry off to the store cupboard.

Lauren follows me. 'You OK? You seem on edge. We can skip the juice bar if you like.'

'No! I've been really looking forward to seeing you. I've just got a lot going on and feel a bit spaced out after the meditation.' Hope that covers my awkwardness.

'And Raj slinking around is enough to make anyone jumpy,' she murmurs in my ear as we head down the corridor. I look round guiltily, worried he might hear us.

'Is he a creep?' I don't want her to say yes.

'Not really, but he certainly takes advantage of being

219

in the minority, gender-wise, round here, as well in pretty peak physical condition.'

'I hadn't noticed,' I mumble and get a friendly shove from Lauren. 'Don't give me that – I saw those puppy dog eyes you were making at each other. Be careful, though, it's a small yoga world.' There's a note of concern in her voice.

'Christ, no, I've got a boyfriend. I mean, I had a boyfriend, until very recently. And I might have one again.' I'm stumbling over my words.

Lauren buts in, 'I should hope so, if that's what you want. Not my thing.' She's very direct and it's making me more flustered.

'It was just meant to be a break – it's complicated.'

We've arrived at the juice bar and Raj is already sitting at a corner table with a carrot juice ring around his mouth.

'I've saved you a place,' he calls out unselfconsciously, clearly right at home in the gym environment.

'You go and sit,' Lauren insists. 'I'll get the drinks.' I'm left with no choice in the matter.

'Your yoga is really coming along,' Raj opens with. 'Lauren's a good influence.'

'Really? Thanks. It's funny – we met at a work thing and then met here by chance. She's really encouraged me.' Safe territory.

'Yoga's like that. We can get a bit evangelical. There's a great workshop coming up, you should come. Give me your number and I'll ping you the details.'

As I get my phone out, my heart sinks. The screen is a patchwork of notifications, missed calls and texts. I deflate and the lovely straight back I had after class slumps. Something major must have kicked off. Raj notices. 'Impressive – you must be very important.'

'The opposite. I work *for* people who are very important—'

'Or think they are!' Lauren interrupts as she puts some very healthy-looking green drinks down.

'Maddy does a similar job to me – fixer – but her work life balance is out of whack.'

4 missed calls from Casper and a text saying: **CALL ME.**

Missed call from Jess but no message.

Text from Caroline: **We need to touch base with you.**

Missed call from Mum – answerphone message.

Reaching for the green juice, I start to get up, 'Sorry, guys, I need to deal with this stuff.'

'Really?' Lauren looks dubious. 'It's gone 9 o'clock. What can you do that can't wait until tomorrow?'

'You know how it is...' I trail off. I thought she got it.

'Not really – you're entitled to a personal life.'

I seem to be having the same conversation with everyone. Raj is looking studiously at his phone, keeping out of it. 'There's a legal thing kicking off. My client's really cut up about it.'

'I only went to this joker's class cos we said we'd hang out after. I've done my bit!' She shrugs and looks at me while slurping her smoothie.

Raj looks up. 'How about we get her to sign up to the workshop to make it up to you?'

Lauren laughs. 'Make it up to you, more like! OK, Maddy, it's a deal, but we go for a curry after – no arguments.'

This seems like a good compromise, so I happily agree. 'Deal. Tell me when and where and I'll be there.'

✦

I hit dial as I'm walking towards Betty.

'Maddy! At last.' Casper sounds less angry, more like his old self. 'I've got the solution! We're sorted.'

'Great – let's hear it.' Relieved I'm not getting a bollocking, I just hope it's not that nightmare loophole lawyer. Ella would never forgive me.

'*You* take the points! It's so simple. I don't know why you didn't think of it.' He sounds really chuffed with himself.

'Wait, what?' I'm caught completely off guard by this development.

'You're on my insurance. You could have been out doing an errand for me.'

'But I wasn't, I don't understand...' I genuinely don't. I have driven his car in the past, but I hate it. It's big and flash and electric and not like Betty at all.

'I'm assuming you have a clean licence?'

'Yes, I do.' This is something I'm quite proud of.

'So, we say you were driving at the time of the offence. Why would anyone question it? We fill out the form, send it back, I pay the fine and you take the points. No biggie.' His tone is very upbeat. My mouth is open, but no words are coming out. I'm still processing.

It's perfect. No biggie. He thinks it's a done deal.

'Hang on, Casper. It's not right.' I have to stop this. 'Apart from anything, my insurance would go up.' I know this isn't the worst of it, but that's what came to mind.

'Fine – if that's your concern, how about I pay your premium, as a thank you?' He couldn't care less about the money. Or my integrity, it seems.

'But, Casper, I'm sure that's illegal.' I sound really whiny. I should be angry.

'Come on, it's a victimless crime.'

He's making light of it and making me feel prissy. I can't organise my thoughts; the pressure is building up behind my eyes. I feel panicky; my breath is catching, but I don't want to sound feeble.

'I'll have to think this through, Casper,' I manage, sounding stronger than I feel. 'Let me sleep on it.'

'Stop being so uptight, Maddy. Live dangerously. Tell you what, I'll pay your car insurance for the whole three years the points are on your license. That's a generous offer – you should be biting my hand off.' He just doesn't get why I'm not agreeing and I'm not doing a particularly good job of explaining it.

'I'll call you tomorrow, Casper. I have to go.' I cut him off. It's good I hadn't set off because my eyes are a blur of hot, frustrated tears. My head is whirring with questions I can't answer and thoughts that all lead to the same dead end. I know it's wrong, but I can't phrase it in a way that Casper will accept. I lean back against the headrest. I've got a thumping headache and I'm in no state to drive.

A tap on the passenger window makes me gasp, which becomes a sob and ends up in a choke. The windows have steamed up, but I can make out a shadowy face peering in at the window. I got a fright but I'm in a private car park and under a spotlight, so I cautiously open the window a crack.

'Are you OK?' It's Raj. I can't see his expression in the gloom, but I recognise his voice.

'Yeah. Fine,' is what I mean to say, but it comes out as a strangulated croak.

'What's happened?' His voice is full of concern. I take a breath and try to compose myself. 'It's just a work thing.' I swipe at my face with my sleeve. 'It's been one of those days – I'm just having a moment.' I'm trying to sound bright, but also need to sniff, urgently.

'As long as it wasn't my class that's left you crying in the car park?' I've opened the window fully and he leans in. 'Shall I get in and sit with you? You could tell me about it. Problem shared and all that.' I'm tempted; I would love to talk it through and I know Ella would be hard-line. Ed's not an option. Jess's got her own shit going on. I'm going home to an empty flat, so I hit unlock and he slips into the passenger seat. It's been ages since anyone except imaginary Davina has been in my car. Now it feels awkward. Plus, my face is puffy.

Tactfully, he looks straight ahead. 'What's got you so upset?'

Not having to look at each other makes it easier. After taking a deep but jagged breath, I start to explain.

It sounds a bit silly saying it out loud, but if you don't know Casper and don't understand the precariousness of being freelance, it probably doesn't make much sense anyway. Talking about it does calm me down, though, and Raj *is* freelance, so he gets not being able to just walk away. He doesn't say anything while I'm talking, and when I come to a natural end and turn to see his reaction, he opens his incredibly well-defined arms and says, 'I think you need a hug.'

With a slightly awkward twist past the steering wheel and sucking my tummy in to avoid the handbrake, I lean gratefully into what is a really top-end hug. Starting out rigid and formal as I start to relax, we fit more naturally and it feels *so* good. My phone goes but I don't care. Even knowing a drip is forming at the end of my nose isn't going to get me to budge. For this brief moment, I feel safe and I'm not going to give that up in a hurry.

It's Raj who pulls back slightly and extricates himself. Holding me by the shoulders, he tries to look me in the eyes, but I'm hanging my head in the hope it hides my ravaged face, as well as feeling like I might have rather just overshared with a comparative stranger.

'Maddy, you know the answer – and as much as I am enjoying the cuddle, I think you'll feel better if you just message him now and stop driving yourself mad.'

God, it sounds so simple. I look up but can't maintain eye contact. 'You're probably right,' I mutter into my coat collar.

'I'm definitely right – come on, let's do it now, together,

and you can give me a lift while I guard your phone from incoming attack.' Seeing it from someone else's perspective makes me realise how easily things get blown up. Or is it just that I let them?

'God, I'm sorry – I've held you up. Of course I can give you a lift. Where to?' I pull myself together, ready to drive.

'Not so fast, send the text and then you can take me wherever you like.' I catch his eye and the twinkle is unmistakable.

To Casper, 9.55pm:
I've given it a lot of thought
and I'm saying no. Sorry. M

Without a word, Raj takes my phone out of my hand and turns it off.

Chapter 23

Never mind yoga, turns out switching your phone off guarantees a great night's sleep.

Raj was a honey. There is no doubt that if he had made a move, I would have gone for it. We didn't talk much as we drove back here. I assumed he had intentions and was trying to work out how I would feel about that, but once we got back here, it was just mint tea in the kitchen. We chatted away and it was all very open and honest. He told me he'd wanted to be a sports journalist or commentator, that sport had always been his thing, but he couldn't get a break so qualified as a personal trainer to make ends meet. He'd tried yoga after reading an article about top athletes recommending it, but had become more and more interested in the philosophy behind it, so was trying to live a life more in the moment and making teaching yoga his main thing.

I was genuinely interested but unable to hide a few

massive yawns – it had been quite a day. He made me swear a solemn promise that I would go to bed without turning my phone on, just for one night, and I said I would if I could have another of his awesome hugs. By then, I was rather hoping it would turn into something more. Would that count as living in the moment? But he didn't give me an opportunity – warm but friendly. On the upside, I don't have any regrets this morning. In fact, I think I will leave my phone until I'm showered and dressed. And Ed didn't even cross my mind.

When I do give in, Casper's messages go through the whole spectrum from angry to reasonable to apologetic and back to angry. He still thinks me taking his points is the ideal solution. The final text, received in the early hours:

Name your price

Classic buy-your-way-out-of-trouble attitude so common to those with money to throw at any situation they don't like. I'm managing to hold my nerve, but I'm worried that if I talk to Casper, he'll wear me down, so I don't respond. And I have work today, for the dame. The combination of a good night's sleep and the very grounding evening with Raj has given me some inner peace and I resolve to hang onto this feeling as long as I can.

Applying my morning routine of cleanser, serum and moisturiser as instructed by Rachel, I remember Caroline's text last night: 'We need to touch base'. Either she is using the royal 'we' – not impossible given her snooty manner – or she's palled up with Needy Steve and is setting up a me-versus-them situation. I won't rise to it; I won't have her lording it over me. I'm sure the novelty will wear off once she realises how needy he is. And poor Steve and I rub along pretty well – at least he doesn't shout or swear at me.

Idly, I wonder what Jess is getting up to in Paris. Her social media has been silent – unusual, but it could be that she's really busy, or maybe it's to do with the legals? I assume Ella got hold of her.

I need to get a shift on to be at the dame's on time. Her low-key relationship with technology is a blessing (no rambling emails or frantic texts), but the downside is arriving for our weekly meet-up with no idea what she may have up her sleeve – apart from the ragged tissue that lives there to dab at the drip that habitually forms at the end of her nose.

The dame likes things a little formal, so I dress appropriately – smartish wide-leg navy trousers and a cream fake silk blouse from Zara. Who buys an *actual* cream silk blouse? Just one look and it needs dry-cleaning. I add a navy cashmere cardigan the moths haven't discovered yet and clean white trainers and I reckon I'm good to go. I have a quick check of my Dame Annette bag, note the ermine looks a little grubby, pop a packet of tissues in for good measure and off I go, feeling surprisingly cheerful.

Which is lucky, as Davina and her bloody microphone are waiting in the passenger seat. I decide to practice taking control.

'Things are very busy at the moment, Davina. So sorry, but I can't chat just now.' That's telling her. I focus on the road ahead with a determined expression.

'You seem to be falling out with clients, colleagues and friends, Madd. What do you put that down to?' She thrusts the mic across and does that raised eyebrow expectant look.

This programme is meant to be an admiring look at my busy lifestyle, not a cross-examination. I give her a firm 'No comment' and give Jess a call back, fully expecting to hear an international ringtone. That scene at Dani's flat was very weird and even though it was a genuine misunderstanding, she really dropped me in it with Needy Steve. I want a fulsome apology, but so much has happened since then and I miss her. I also miss having a mole at Top Notch and I'm dying to know what's going on over there.

'Maddy? Thanks so much for calling back. I thought you might be blanking me.' Jess does not sound her usual bubbly self.

'Well, you certainly have some explaining to do. How's Paris?' It's good to hear her voice, but I'm keeping it tight-lipped till I get a proper explanation.

There's silence, punctuated by some muffled noises. 'Jess? Are you there?' Maybe she's dropped her phone. I'd wonder if she's tipsy, but it's too early, even with the time difference.

'Oh, Maddy,' her jagged breathing sounds like she's been running, 'what do you mean, Paris? I'm in Kent, at my mum's. I had a total meltdown after I saw you and made

230

such an idiot of myself. I literally had nowhere else to go. Mum is my last resort.' She sounds so flat and defeated, and she's crying. 'Yesterday was the first day I could even think about talking to anyone and I wanted to apologise to you for the way I carried on. I've mucked everything up. I'm so sorry.'

'Jess, sweetheart, what is going on? Caroline said she saw you getting on the Eurostar.' Why on earth did I believe Caroline? It's impossible to stay angry with someone who is clearly so deeply miserable.

'I *was* at St Pancras, in a total state, but I was getting the train to Mum's. It's lucky I didn't see her. I might have punched that smug face.' That sounds more like my Jess. 'How come you spoke to Caroline anyway? There wasn't a CHAMPS do was there?'

'God, Jess, you don't know the half of it. She came to interview for Steve. I thought it was my chance to take her down a peg or two, but she turned the charm on full beam and he went for it. Blinded by poshness. You didn't show up and she got the job.' I don't want to make her feel any worse, so leave it at that.

'Shit. I've really fucked up, I am *so, so* sorry, Maddy, but the thing with Aria was the start of a chain of events that ended with me having to get off the train having a panic attack, and Mum having to drive all the way from Deal to get me. I spent the next two days in bed crying, the next two sleeping. Mum was so worried and, honestly, I was, too. She thinks I'm depressed. I might be, but I have started to feel a bit better and I need to put things right.

Starting with you. I can't face talking to Ella yet.' She sounds so subdued. It's hard to picture Jess not being the loudest, the funniest, the naughtiest in the room.

'Listen, lovely, I've arrived at the dame's. I've got to go, but it's so good to hear your voice and I'm glad you're OK-ish. We need a proper catch-up – don't think you're the only one having a shit time.' I hear a familiar chuckle at the other end. 'Can I call you back on my way home?'

'Hold on while I check my very busy calendar – of course. I'm completely around and would love to hear about someone else's misery. Have fun with her majesty.'

'And you should call Ella. She's got good news for you.'

'I don't deserve you. Thanks, babe.' And she's gone. I do a precarious manoeuvre to park in the narrow Hampstead street that has ostentatiously large 4 by 4s parked both sides and take a moment to digest my conversation with Jess. I thought she just shrugged stress off, but seems everyone has their limits. Maybe her don't-give-a-shit attitude is just a front. Things with Aria did deteriorate pretty quickly. She's never mentioned depression or panic attacks before. I wonder if I could have done something more, seen some signs.

The dame likes me to buzz the intercom and responds with a highly enunciated, 'I've been expecting you.' Does she think we're in an old movie? A horror movie? I push the heavy wooden door that theatrically creaks and enter the gloomy hall, unable to avoid her stare from studio shots and film stills that cover every inch of the walls. They must be at least forty years old and the shrine to herself continues all the way up several flights of stairs, aging as you go higher. Her haughty tilt of the chin was there right from the start, but fair play to the old bird – no sign of any cosmetic procedures.

'Hi – I'm in,' I call out. There is more formality here than with any other clients. I'm expected to wait in the hall for instructions.

'Drawing room,' she sing-songs.

Drawing room, my arse. It's the lounge, sitting room – whatever, it's the room right by me so I head in.

Seated at a small table, back erect, with the light from the window behind her, I can't make out her expression. 'Shall I sit here?' I indicate the squashy old sofa. 'Is there much post?'

'Yes, sit, but the post can wait. I have a far more interesting project to discuss.' She smooths her tweedy skirt over her knees before going on, 'There's going to be a documentary. About me.' There's a pause, for my reaction, and I know exactly what is required.

'Dame Annette, what wonderful news and long overdue.' Slight bow of the head for emphasis. I lived through her annoyance at not being invited on Desert Island Discs. Her agent, Charles, had to make a not-too-subtle request. I have made the correct response because she softens and comes to sit next to me on the sofa.

'I was absolutely shocked, but it's the BBC, you know, so reluctantly I agreed. I've turned down all sorts of requests over the years. I would only do it with someone one can trust.' It's clear she is absolutely delighted at the prospect. 'It's going to focus on my fifty years in theatre, with a nod to film and television, of course.' She has always been a theatre snob, so they pitched it exactly right, as well as calling it an anniversary and not a retrospective. Very clever production team, I'd say.

'Sounds perfect! When will they start?' I'm wondering how this will impact on me. TV production companies are second only to feature films for thinking their project is the most important thing happening in the universe and that everyone should drop everything to do as they ask, but it would be fun to get my teeth into something more challenging than filing paperwork. It could be fun to be on the right side of the crew.

'I believe researchers have already started work. Obviously, my agent will be involved, but I've given them your details as a main point of contact.' Here we go. Nice to be asked – not. As it's not a paid gig, Charles, her agent, won't be very invested. No fee, no ten per cent. 'There'll be filming at various theatres. I've said I don't want them here – too intrusive. Could you suggest a hotel suite or, better still, a private members' club? Perhaps the RAC for my interview?' I see where this is going; she wants to be seen to be living in the lap of luxury. Not that her house isn't lovely, but it is very old school and country cottage chic can easily come over as, well, shabby. Clearly, I am going to be the buffer between her and the production company, and if my own experience is anything to go by, she will start out being charming and accommodating, and become more challenging and demanding as it goes on.

On the upside, it should keep her in a good mood as her national treasure status will be confirmed.

We carry on discussing the practicalities and I make some notes, after which she loses interest and goes off to 'check something in my script', which I believe is a euphemism for 'have a little lie-down'. The post is in a pile on the table.

From Dani, 12.45pm:
Will you ask Casper about the
speech ASAP?

I've been studiously avoiding even thinking about Casper – and decide to carry on doing so.

Once my work is done and I'm back in Betty, I call Jess back. She's been on my mind the whole morning. She sounded in such a bad way. She answered immediately, seeming a bit brighter.

'Sorry again, Maddy, for everything and thanks for not hating me. I've left a message for Ella, but she's in a meeting. I'm getting my shit together. Now, what have I been missing in the cut-and-thrust world of British celebrity?'

It wasn't at all planned, but I ended up spilling my guts about Casper and his driving points. Work dramas are something I have always been able to share with Jess. No matter how crazy they might sound to anyone else, she has probably encountered something along the same lines, or heard of someone else who has. Right on cue, 'Yeah, it's a thing. I know a nanny that did it for a new car.' She doesn't sound fazed at all. 'That's the kind of stakes we are talking, Maddy, not a few extra quid. This is a chance in a lifetime.' Not the response I was expecting at all.

'Jess – I'm not even contemplating doing it and taking money would make me feel even worse.' Maybe she's still a bit unstable.

'Maddy, I've had a lot of time to think this past week and – correct me if I'm wrong – I've put two and two together and come up with a theory. About you and Casper.' She leaves a pause – for me to fill, I guess – but I'm not sure how to play it, so don't say anything. She goes on, 'The mystery writing assistant. It's you, isn't it?'

I feel like I've been caught out, but, really, what have I done wrong? Falteringly, I confess. And once I've started, it's hard to know where to stop. When I eventually do, there is a brief silence on the other end and then she says, matter-of-factly, 'That's it, then. He said to name your price. Ask for the writing credit you deserve.'

Chapter 24

A small bubble of excitement keeps rising up in my chest, only to be swiftly pushed down by the weight of anxiety. Try as I might to put Jess's ridiculous suggestion out of my mind, it keeps slipping in round the edges.

As I will do almost anything to divert my attention from the absolutely ludicrous idea of selling out for a writing credit, I respond to Caroline:

**Sure. Let me know what
you need from me. Maddy**
(deliberate no kiss)

I keep it vague and arm's distancey. I've got my regular meet-up with Steve tomorrow, anyway, and I've already had some non-urgent urgent requests from Bridget: a mindfulness class for toddlers in Primrose Hill that several celebrity offspring attend, which she wants me to get

Sigmund into. I'm going to give it my best shot, mainly because the thought of Sigmund in a mindfulness class has such potential hilarity, and the thought of Bridget trying to wrangle him in front of a Spice Girl delights my dark side. Which brings me straight back to Jess's not-so-throwaway comment. It's tickling my temptation. Casper is desperate – that much is clear. 'Name your price' is offering me whatever my heart desires, isn't it?

To Dani, 4.30pm:
Will do! Mx

I'll have to be in touch with him soon, but what am I going to say? Jess has changed everything. First off, I didn't know that taking points was a thing. Am I so naïve? Secondly, she's hit a nerve, because although I absolutely wouldn't do it for money, competitive doesn't even begin to cover the job market for TV writers. If I can't be ruthless about breaking in, how do I think I can make it in that world? I could do courses and workshops and enter bloody competitions and never get a chance like this again. I made a commitment to becoming a writer. My driving license is clean, but would three points be such a big deal?

Right on cue, my phone goes.

'Maddy? You there?' Casper is sounding quite chilled, friendly even.

'Yeah, hi, just driving.' I'm trying to sound casual while my heart is hopping around in my chest.

'I was beginning to think you were avoiding me.' He does a little laugh to show things are still amicable.

'Just busy – other clients and stuff.' Bright and breezy, and reminding him he's not the only fish I have to fry. 'Actually, I have a question for you from Dani.' I'm playing for time. 'A special request.'

'I can hardly wait. Let's hear it.' Bit of tension in his voice. I wonder what he's expecting.

'It's all hush-hush for now, but she's been nominated for a Tony.'

He lets out a genuine laugh. 'You have *got* to be kidding! It's true what they say about an English accent opening doors then!' And Casper is back in the room.

'She's nervous about winning—'

He cuts in, 'I wouldn't lose any sleep over that prospect.'

I push on, 'And if she did, she'd have to make a speech. You know, an acceptance speech.'

He pounces on my floundering, 'I know how awards ceremonies work, sweetheart. I do have experience in that sphere.'

As if I could forget his proudly displayed trophies. 'Of course, but she wants to do more than just "thank my agent blah blah blah", she wants something clever and funny.' I leave that hanging, appeal to his vanity.

'She wants a massive fucking favour, you mean.'

'Well, yes, she's asking you, as a friend, if you'd help her out to make sure she comes across as smart and witty.'

He explodes with a honk. 'It would take more than a few lines from me to do that! Tell her I'm too busy, which I am, and that brings me neatly to the reason I keep calling. This driving thing is messing with my concentration and I've got serious amounts of work to do. I need an answer from you, Maddy, and I need it to be the right answer.'

Here we go, I've practised saying this in my head, so it comes out sounding quite calm and reasonable.

'I've given it a lot of thought, Casper, and I don't want your money.' I can hear him sigh at the other end, so I rush on before he kicks off, 'But you said I could name my price.' I pause to gather my guts. 'And there *is* something I want from you: proper recognition for the work I've been doing.' I'm determined to shut up now, which is fortunate as I can hardly breath for anxiety.

After what seems like forever, he grunts, 'You won't let this go, will you? Let me make it clear, you are *not* getting a writing credit for a bit of brainstorming and a cute suggestion or two. You do not fucking deserve it. I made you my intern, didn't I?'

'You did – but what does that really mean? I want Top Notch to know about me.' There. I've said it.

There's a silence. I'm holding my breath.

'OK. I hear you. I'll have think about what I can do to make you shut the fuck up and actually help me instead of banging on and on about your tiny little contribution.'

Could have been worse. 'Good. Well, let me know what you decide and I'll tell you if I agree to taking the points.'

I hear him mutter, 'For fuck's sake,' under his breath and we both hang up.

Lightheaded with my own show of bravery, I don't know which answer from Casper I truly want. If he says no, he's the baddie but my honour is preserved, but if he agrees, I think that makes me the baddie. But he's also a baddie. He's usually the baddie. I would love to talk it through with someone, but the possibilities are limited. Jess is all gung-ho go for it and Ella would be horrified and must never know I even contemplated it. They are black and white; I need someone grey to talk to. But... honestly? I know the answer I want and if it makes me a baddie, well, so be it. Maddy the Baddie even has a certain ring to it. I will own it and be a badass.

Arriving back at the flat, I can tell by the stillness in the air that Ella hasn't been back. Best not to see her right now as I am generating enough nervous energy to power the microwave. I have plenty of work to be getting on with – enquiries from brands wanting collaborations with Dani and Steve's publisher trying to confirm a tour of independent bookshops located at all the furthest points of the country. As expected, someone from the production team on the dame's documentary wants to 'check in' and 'touch base', but I can't settle to any of it until I hear back from Casper. Only one thing for it in a situation like this. Burn it off. I decisively shut my laptop and grab my swimming bag – iridescent blue; resembling a mermaid, I like to think – and head back out the door less than twenty minutes after bursting through it.

I keep checking my phone every few seconds to the point where I can feel my face being pulled towards it like a magnet. Being underwater is the only way to give myself a break.

Mid-afternoon is the perfect time to hit the pool – the yummy mummies have left for the school run and the nine-to-fivers are still at work. Retired folk pace up and down the dedicated water therapy section, leaving three lanes free for swimmers. Slow, medium and fast. There is invariably a middle-aged man in the fast lane, kitted out with snorkel and flippers, ploughing up and down, stopping regularly to check his Fitbit and take sips of water. I'm happy to see the slow lane is empty and slide demurely off the side into the tepid water and start my sedate breaststroke to warm up, enjoying the sensation of the water slipping over my shoulders and stroking the length of my spine. I focus on making the biggest sweep of my arms as I can, pushing against the pressure of the water, feeling the muscles in my shoulders waking up.

I ease into a slow crawl. Gazing down at the cool blue of the mosaic floor has the desired effect of slowing my thoughts down. A childhood's worth of lessons means I count my strokes and regulate my breathing accordingly. My flowery swimming hat seals me off from outside distractions and I'm alone with my thoughts, which all revolve around Casper. Apart from my own issues with him, he didn't seem very amenable to Dani's request. As my jumble of thoughts slows down, It dawns on me that I may be neglecting my other clients, but until this is resolved I just can't focus on anything else. No, it's more than that. My wonderful job, which I created for myself and then found a like-minded community for, is feeling a little mundane. Maybe it's Ella's comments, or maybe it's just me, but I think I do have more to offer. Maybe I should offer to help Dani out with her speech. It can't be that difficult.

The slow lane is no longer my own. I'm approaching an elderly lady doing a very leisurely backstroke and my concentration is broken. Ducking under the divider into the medium lane, I am immediately part of a relay with three other speedo-clad women and having to keep pace with them stops my meandering thought processes. After a couple more lengths, I've had enough and make my exit.

It's a chilly dash from the pool to the changing rooms and straight into a shower cubicle. I make full use of the complimentary shower gel and shampoo, probably one and the same – they smell like washing-up liquid – but they get rid of the chlorine aroma and that's good enough for now. I'm jittery opening my locker.

From Caroline, 4.30pm:
We can discuss tomorrow.

She's not wasting any of her charm on me, that's for sure.

Notification from Instagram:
Your friend @EdandShoulders
has posted for the first time in
a while.

I have to look before I even put my underwear on. The photo itself isn't too illuminating; it's a repost of eight pairs of skis in a circle all pointing inwards. The snow is glittering, obviously reflecting bright sunlight. What's more intriguing are the people tagged in the photo, which leads to a hunched stalking session on the changing room bench. It's hard to identify people in ski goggles and helmets, but the wide grins are universal. There's a group shot where Ed has his arm linked with Mimi's, but his other arm is round an unknown woman. Could be innocent? I'm vaguely aware of people coming and going around me in the locker room, to the point where a middle-aged lady crouches down next to me wrapped only in her towel to ask if I'm alright. Pulled back to reality, I'm made horribly aware that crouching down wearing only a towel is not a good idea. I force a smile and say, 'Yes, thank you. It's a work thing.' Somehow, work things are a more acceptable excuse than heartbreak things. There wasn't anything too incriminating, but I can't help noticing Ed manages to make even salopettes look hot. I'm experiencing several shades of sad. Sad they all look so happy, sad Mimi looks so good in ski gear, but most of all sad that I'm not there with him.

Even though friends' recent comments have caused me to question how well I really knew him, Ed is still the person I would most like to talk this through with. The right mix of pragmatic and ambitious, he's the grey area I need.

Standing in front of the mirror, trying to make my hair do something socially acceptable, I wonder how things went from trundling along quite nicely to all this sadness and confusion and, above all, my growing sense of dissatisfaction with my life.

My eye lands on a poster advertising the workshop Lauren and Raj were on about. There's a strip of paper stuck on it saying, 'Last Few Places'. I don't want to spend the whole weekend tracking social media and obsessing over Ed and Mimi. I have slightly mixed feelings about Raj, a bit embarrassed about the state he saw me in, but I did promise Lauren I'd go. I resolve to book a place on my way out – at the very least, it takes care of a big chunk of Saturday.

To Ella, 5.15pm:
You around this weekend? I'd
love to catch up Mx

So strong is my resolve to keep busy, I even contemplate a Friday night dinner at Mum and Dad's. I've just about recovered from the last one where my sister hogged absolutely all their attention and we had to admire the achievements of a hyped-up toddler, the height of which was managing to do a poo in the toilet. You'd have thought he'd come up with a cure for cancer by the amount of praise heaped on him. On the bright side, all the toilet excitement meant there was no room for the usual dissection of my life, which suited me down to the ground, so I joined in the loo celebrations wholeheartedly and made a swift exit as soon as dessert was over. A chocolate log, no less.

My sister's become a baby bore. We used to have a laugh. Actually, she was a bride bore before that, so it's been a while since we were united in taking the piss out of Dad's fads and Mum's middle-class competitiveness. Now she's ticked all the boxes with her management consultancy job and professional husband, not to mention his royal highness, the grandson. When she had Elijah (I know – don't get me started), I fancied myself as a fun auntie, but she's such a control freak I couldn't even pick him up without her flapping around giving orders, so I backed off. Elijah is the same age as Sigmund; I could give her loads of intel on what's hot and what's not for toddlers, but she's got this active birth crew she met at pregnancy Pilates and it's all about what *they* say and do – apart from when she wants tickets or a signed photo to impress her new pals.

Weighing up Mum's roast chicken against another episode of *Drag Race* as I vaguely swipe moisturiser over my face, Casper messages.

Call me.

No kiss.

Chapter 25

Casper picked up straightaway and launched in without so much as a hello.

'Here is my offer. No discussion – take it or leave it. I will tell Top Notch I have taken you on as my writing assistant, but you will *not* get a writing credit. You will get paid the going rate and for that you will put in proper hours and maybe come to some – not all – production meetings, but you will be there to listen *only*. I'm the fucking showrunner and don't you forget that for one single minute. You take the driving points and the next three if I happen to get any more. You tell no one. If it gets out, the whole deal is off and your name will be trashed because it will be *you* who has leaked it. Do we have a deal? Yes or no?'

Wow. Not what I was expecting, but what was I expecting? Without much time to think it over, the writing part sounds like a fair deal. Realistically, a formal credit would be extraordinary, but everyone involved will know about me and I'd get a chance to make my voice heard. The extra points, however. I take a breath to object...

'No! I can hear you starting a sentence and there is no sentence required. Yes or no. You've got until first thing tomorrow morning to decide. Either you are here at 10am for a writing session or you can come to do the filing on Tuesday as usual. There is nothing more to discuss.' And he hangs up.

Dazed, I fill the kettle and switch it on. Think better of it and check the fridge for an open bottle of wine. Nada. A single bottle of Corona lurking behind the mayonnaise will have to do. I pop the cap while the kettle boils in the background and try to get a grip. I underestimated what a shit Casper can be and that's saying something. Agreeing to take these points is one thing, but signing up for the next lot? As well as having to make the decision about this tonight, there is the small matter of my regular meet with Needy Steve tomorrow. Usually, I wouldn't think twice about rearranging, but Caroline has made it clear that she is going to be there and she already thinks I'm flaky – and if I'm thinking along these lines, it means I'm planning to be at Casper's tomorrow.

Draining the beer, I send a text.

To Steve, 6.25pm:
Really sorry – urgent appt at
10. Can we rearrange? Thanks
Maddy x

I hope the kiss will swing it. I'm debating a run to the shops for more beer and maybe something for supper when I hear the front door bang.

'Hello, hello! I saw Betty outside. I come bearing supper,' Ella sing-songs up the stairs. This brings on a state of acute panic. I freeze. She breezes into the kitchen holding out a couple of carrier bags, ready for me to relieve her of them. 'What's up? You look stressed.' She dumps them on the floor by her feet and starts disentangling her work bag from over her shoulder, holding my flustered gaze.

'Um, nothing. I'm fine – just wasn't expecting you. Tonight, I mean.' I splutter. I need to pull it together. 'The kettle's just boiled. Tea?' Seems to do the trick.

'Sure. I'm so glad you're here. We are *well* overdue a catch-up. I spoke to Jess after she left me a cryptic message – I can fill you in. I got fresh pasta so easy peasy. Hungry?' She starts unpacking the shopping while I use making tea as an excuse to keep my back to her and concentrate on acting normal.

'Brilliant. That's really brilliant,' I try to sound cheery. 'Here's your tea.'

Turning to hand her the mug, she is resting against the counter looking straight into my soul. 'You sure everything's OK?'

'Ha! Of course! You just caught me having a sneaky beer.' I waggle the empty bottle. 'I'm really glad to see you. I think I've spent too much time on my own recently.' What would I do normally do? A great big info dump – omitting the one huge thing I really do need to work through. 'I got freaked because I saw Ed and Mimi the Moo-Cow having all the snowy fun, Steve is being needy – what's new? – and I have to rearrange him because Casper called me in for a writing session tomorrow and—'

'Whoah! Take a breath, Maddy. There's a lot to unpick there. I suggest we crack open this lovely bottle of Merlot I just happen to have right here and go through these topics one by one. Forget the tea, grab some glasses and let's sit down.' She is smiling now and it's such a relief. I can totally talk her through the Ed thing and even Steve, and then just skirt round Casper as much as possible. I also need to check in with how she is.

Washing up at the sink a good few hours later, I feel so much better. She understood about Ed, even joined in with analysing the photos online. She mentioned 'moving on' and advised keeping busy. All good advice. Then, she invited me to a brunch at Drippy Tom's on Sunday, so the weekend is shaping up. We had a good chat about Jess, who was massively relieved about her situation with Aria, but wasn't coming back to London yet – not until she had some work lined up and could draw a line under everything.

When I told her Casper was calling me his writing assistant and telling Top Notch about me, she jumped up and gave me a big hug, congratulating me on holding my ground and standing up to him. She said she knew I had talent and that Casper had seen it, too. That didn't feel so great. Nice as it was to hear she thinks I have talent, I changed the subject and told her about Dani's flying visit and the fake parking ticket, which I knew would get her worked up because of the injustice, but we were on safer ground.

When I asked about her, it turned out things were pretty stressy at work for her, too. She wanted to be made an associate so is under pressure to bring in new clients, as well as keep on top of her caseload. Listening to her talk made me realise that, for the first time in my career, I have ambitions, too. I joked about her picking up my waifs and strays, and she got all serious and said if any of my clients ever needed representation, I had to promise to let her know – which I would have done anyway. Drippy Tom is a year ahead of her and didn't make associate last year, so he's under even more pressure and they are sort of in competition, which is a bit of a thing between them, so they have promised not to talk about work outside the office. I pointed out that that would make Sunday brunch a whole lot more fun and we were back to giggling. She mentioned that Dominic would be there and probably Maya and Stella. She said she was relying on me to keep things jolly.

When I finish washing up, she makes me delete all of Ed's and Mimi's social media from my phone. Probably a sensible idea, as a deep dive into Instagram is exactly what I had planned. Like reading someone's diary, no good will come of it and, anyway, people only post the good stuff. Right? That was when I see the text.

From Caroline, 8.40pm:
We have scheduled a call with you
tomorrow at 9am. Regards Caroline

What the actual fuck? 'We'? A bit pally for my liking and using 'Regards' in a text is a bit formal. The tone and implications cause me to brush my teeth so furiously my gums bleed. I'm looking forward to hearing what madame has got to say tomorrow. She might have Steve wrapped round her little finger for now, but he and I go way back, and much as Bridget loves bossing me around, I'd love to see how far she gets trying that on with Caroline. Maybe I should just leave them all to it.

As my indignant fury recedes, the reality of my meeting with Casper hits. Why do I feel so anxious? I'm getting what I wanted from him. Well, a bit more than I wanted if you count the extra points. I'm comfortable about it, but sitting comfortably won't get me anywhere. I am hyper-aware that I didn't mention it to Ella, because I know in my heart it isn't right, but if I want to get ahead, I have to grab opportunities. Maybe a bit of early morning argy-bargy with Caroline will get me fired up in a good way. I'm almost looking forward it.

Hearing Ella padding along the corridor to the bathroom soothes me, her night-time routine as familiar to me as a bedtime story. She showers at night, very weird to me, and always uses the loo twice – both before and after her shower. Wondering what she knows about my toilet habits, I drift off.

Where's best for my zoom with Caroline and Steve?
I don't want to do it on the move, but I can't be late for
Casper. Logistics can be a bitch. I'm feeling up and at 'em
and I'm not going to take any shit. I decide to call from
here and cut them off after twenty minutes to leave for my
'appointment'. That's my plan.

Dress like a writer. This makes me pause because I
think of Needy Steve and he is pretty sloppy. Black. I will
wear all black. I quite fancy a polo neck for a serious look,
but putting it on will wreak havoc with my hair. A writer's
life is hard.

With a cup of strong sweet tea by my side, I settle myself
in my office under the stairs, with my Casper bag already
packed for a quick getaway. I'm just having a debate about
whether I join first when my laptop starts ringing with a
facetime call, which I was definitely not expecting, and
there is a bewildered-looking Steve with a very coiffed
Caroline by his side. I never noticed how bony her hands
are before. I'm about to give a friendly wave when she
launches straight in.

'Madeleine, thank you for making the time to meet
with us.' Super formal verging on sarcastic. 'We were
surprised at your late cancellation of this morning's
meeting, but this shouldn't take too long.' More sarcasm
followed by a dig. I'm not rising to it; I stay silent and
smile, trying to make eye contact with Steve, who is
studiously looking down, picking at his nails. 'Steven and

I have worked through his needs with a view to streamlining his operation.'

She is talking as if Needy Steve is a major corporation, but I hold my tongue to see where this is going. Steve still hasn't looked at me. His study door bursts open and Coco the cockapoo bursts in, but before she can cross the room, Caroline turns and barks, 'Get out!' so ferociously she freezes briefly before turning tail and scooting. Caroline gets up to slam the door and, in that moment, Steve looks at me with a sorrowful expression, not dissimilar to the dog when she's done something naughty. I smile encouragingly, but Caroline is back.

'I have put together a business plan for Steven's upcoming publication and it is abundantly clear that it is essential I have full control of his activities moving forward, so I will be taking over as his main point of contact.'

'Hang on,' I interrupt her flow, 'how are you suggesting this works? Because I have relationships with his publishers, his agent, the family – all of which go way back. Steve?' Matters are taking an unexpected turn here, but he still won't look at me.

Caroline gives me a tight smile. 'Well, that brings me to our proposal. I will be frontline; you continue to take care of the admin. Also, you mentioned the family, and I believe Bridget would like to delegate some aspects of the running of their daily lives to you. There will be a decrease in your hours, but Steven and I agree that this is a crucial point in his career, and it needs to be responsibly managed. It makes sense for me to take the reins while you provide backup, which is, after all, your role. I will be coordinating a PR campaign with long-term reputation management. We can finesse the details, but wanted to loop you into our thinking before you clock up any unnecessary hours and I can start the official handover. Bridget will make her own arrangements with you, at a reduced rate, as the tasks will be low-skilled. I hope that's all clear. I know you are in a rush to get to your 'appointment', so I'll let you get on and Bridget will be in touch directly.' She pats her immaculate up-do and closes her Smythson notebook.

'No.' *Did I say that out loud?*

'Excuse me?' Caroline's expression is priceless. Steve rapidly looks at me, then her, then back at me. 'Don't be hasty, you might want to consider your future,' she snaps.

'Your suggestion is not acceptable. I'm sorry if Steve isn't happy with the way things have been.' Steve opens his mouth to speak, but one look from Caroline and he shuts it, so I continue, boldly, 'I am not offering general household support. If you want to take over, that's fine, but I'm not sticking around to be bossed around by you, Bridget nor anyone else. And thank you for the suggestion; I am thinking about my future, and it involves a much better and bigger job, which is where I am off to right now. Goodbye.' And with that, I slam my laptop shut, punch the air shouting, 'Yes!' then panic I didn't end the call, so open the laptop, get a glimpse of Steve's shocked expression and Caroline's face looking like a slapped arse. I end the call properly and leave the house, ready to start my new career.

Chapter 26

I'm buzzing on the way to Casper's and rather enjoy explaining what just happened to Davina, having made it absolutely clear this was off the record. I did an uptight purse-lipped voice for Caroline and compared Steve's expression to a hostage sitting next to their captor, mouthing 'Send help' when her back was turned. It's strange; despite compromising my integrity and putting myself potentially on the wrong side of the law, I feel empowered and ready to stop being taken advantage of. Before going in, I take a moment to compose myself and get past my nerves. I resolve to 'fake it 'til I make it', which was the subject of a CHAMPS seminar a while back. I am now a TV comedy writing assistant.

Casper doesn't seem to notice the massive shift in me and launches straight in, 'Good, you're here. Correct decision. Next time, bring me a chai latte so we don't waste any time. They're breathing down my fucking neck. I need you to get started on reading in for the episode I want to cover today, particularly dialogue. I want it pacy, but a different pace. Plus, we need laughs. Lots of laughs.' His back is receding, voice fading as he heads down to the kitchen.

No pressure then. But this is it; I'm official and I am not going to muck it up. My phone has been vibrating in my pocket and I steal a quick look. Steve. Well, he can go whistle. Turning it silent, I settle down with the minty fresh pages he has left me and dip my head ready to dive into the scene.

Casper leaves me to it, typing something at his screen, keeping absolutely shtum while I make notes in the margins and highlight phrases as I go. The second I get to the end of the last page and look up, his eyes are on me, expectant. This is the new me, no treading on eggshells, so I launch straight in and he listens, looking pensive while I read out phrases that sound clunky. He interrupts when I criticise Edie's comeback and explains his reasoning. I can see his point, but think we could sharpen it, and so we throw suggestions back and forth across the desk at each other until he says, 'Is that the best you've got?' I flush, lose my nerve and start to stammer something, but he laughs and says, 'Not you, Maddy, Edie!' and, with relief, I laugh and agree. 'Yes. That's it, totally works.' We sit back in our seats and enjoy the moment. A brief moment, because the next thing he says is, 'You might as well sort out the car paperwork. Thanks to your stubbornness, it's taken a week to get sorted. It's signed, so you can post it today. But let's read this through one more time out loud for a laugh count.'

The car comment brings me back down to earth with a smack. After a pretty flat read-through, I head downstairs to find the dreaded penalty notice. It's there, glaring at me from the middle of the worktable, and while Casper has signed the bottom of it, it is left to me to select the 'somebody else was driving' option and fill out my own details. I can taste a bit of sick at the back of my throat, but I've burnt my bridges with Steve on the strength of this and, more to the point, I have loved the last couple of hours working with Casper. I really want this, so no more wavering. I've made my choice. Let's do this. I fill in my name and address and wonder if I am making my bad situation worse with additional crimes, but I can't check it with Ella. I can't even think about Ella without a wave of anxiety. I take a final pause before putting the form into an envelope, delaying the deed.

From Steve, 1.20pm:
She's gone. Please call me.

I almost feel pity. Caroline will have taken advantage and walked all over him, but that is not my problem and, although I am fond of him, I won't miss Bridget's annoying requests. He chose Caroline, blinded by her flattery and grooming. It could have been very different if things had worked out with Jess. We'd have been a great team.

258

I'll really miss Coco. If it all goes tits up, I could offer to be their dog walker...

I know I'll have to respond to him at some stage, so, not procrastinating over the penalty notice *at all*, I reply.

**Hi Steve. It's a shame
but I can't see your new
arrangement working for me.
I'll call later. M**

I have a policy of not speaking to another client while at a different client's house. It seems a bit disrespectful, like being unfaithful. However, I must also let each client think they are the most important. I should explain this etiquette to Davina – that's just the kind of insight she'd be after – rather than commenting on my private life. Which reminds me of the ski trip, which is probably just getting going as I sit here. I've stayed off social media, but apart from Mimi wrapped round someone other than Ed or, better still, on crutches, what do I hope to see? I'm best off out of it. I'm starting on my new career. I've got weekend plans. I will post this bloody form, call Steve from the car and move on, just like Ella said.

The call went as expected. He said he was confident of Caroline's abilities – she's obviously done a top PR job on him – but that as a family, they appreciated my support keeping things running smoothly and that he didn't see Caroline fully inhabiting that part of the role. Roughly translated, he meant Caroline wouldn't walk Coco or mind Sigmund for an hour while Bridget did something terribly important like a laser hair removal appointment. I nearly crashed the car when he offered to keep paying me the same rates, but much as I enjoy the odd skirmish with Caroline, I wasn't up for a long-term engagement. Apart from admiring Steve as a writer, there was really no incentive for me at all. Well, there was a tiny one, to see Caroline fail at getting him his precious *GQ* cover, but I suspect Caroline is the type who takes all the credit for success, but manages to shift the blame if things don't go well. Having always thought hard work would reap rewards, Caroline is the perfect example of just how wrong I was. Another reason to remove myself from the equation all together.

Of course, this isn't how I put it to Steve; I have a few PR skills of my own. I tell him I've taken on a new role but don't get specific – writing is his domain, after all – and mention something vague about having very different working methods to Caroline and not being sure that they would be complementary (i.e. she is a bitch on wheels and I'm not). I wish the family well and say Caroline can contact me if she has any queries. This is when the tone changes.

'The thing is, Maddy, you were flexible about what you would take on and Caroline is absolutely inflexible. She was quite brusque with Bridget this morning.' He sounds like man who has been roundly reprimanded by everyone, me included. He goes on, 'To be frank, Bridget and I have realised just how much you did for us and Sigmund will miss you, too...' This is emotional blackmail and, even if I was feeling a smidge of pity for him, he just blew it. However, a plan B starts to formulate.

'Steve, I appreciate what you're saying.' Too little, too late springs to mind. 'But I meant it when I told you I'm moving in a new direction work-wise. However, if you recall, I was very keen for you to meet another candidate at interview, Jessica. She was unavoidably detained on the day, but her working methods are similar to mine.' I let this sink in for second. 'I'm not sure if she's still available, but I could check if you like.' Two birds – one stone. I hold my breath while he considers my suggestion, then Bridget screeches something in the background that clinches it.

'Yes – do. Please. I'm wondering if I haven't been a little hasty—'

That's enough of that. Mission accomplished, so I cut him off. 'Sorry, Steve, I'm at my next meeting. I'll let you know if Jessica is available and interested.'

Result! I'd much rather hand over to Jess and she'll handle Caroline better than I ever could. I can give her tips on managing the family dynamic. Caroline can sit on her high horse and 'run his PR campaign', which I predict will last about five minutes until he realises that the publishers were doing just as well. I leave Jess an excited voicenote, but tell her to take her time and think it through before deciding. And now, I am pretty much ready for a weekend.

When I get home, there's an email from the BBC about scheduling a chat with a researcher for the dame's programme. Happy to oblige. This is the part of the job I like best; being behind the scenes but involved. I'm looking forward to working with the team on this and watching the creative process.

✦

From Lauren, 3.15pm:
All good for tomorrow? It's
full, so whoever gets there
first, bag a spot. Lx

I've got slightly cold feet about the yoga workshop, not least after my episode with Raj. Would Lauren be pissed off at me if I bailed? And can I cope with that many hours of yoga? I'm paralysed with indecision when my phone goes.

Jess launches straight in, 'You are my guardian angel! I promise I won't let you down.'

'You got my message then?' I hope she's thought this through. I don't want her rushing back to work before she's ready.

'Honestly, Maddy, it's just what I need – no diva demands, no international time-zone fuck-ups. A nice gentleman author.' She's toned it down and sounds serious.

'You realise it's a domestic set-up – his wife likes to go a bit Lady of the Manor.' I don't want any misunderstandings about what she is letting herself in for. 'And then, of course, there's Caroline on the scene. Are you up to the challenge?'

'The wife I'm not bothered about and I genuinely like

262

little kids. As for Caroline – wait, which Caroline is it? I swear there are dozens of them knocking around.'

I give a snort of laughter. 'You know perfectly well – Catty Caroline, the one who puts us down whenever possible.'

'Oh – you mean, mouth-like-a-cat's-arse Caroline? Bring it on. I might have been walked all over by an international supermodel, but a jumped-up wannabe publicist? I could eat her for breakfast and still have room for a croissant.'

'And she's back! I'll put you in touch and give you the full low-down.' I bloody love it when things come together. I'm about to suggest tomorrow as an excuse to skip the yoga workshop, when Jess goes on.

'And it's great you're cool with all the skiing stuff.'

My warm glow is replaced by an instant chill. 'What skiing stuff?' My voice is tight.

Jess pauses while she decides how to proceed, knowing she has put her foot in it. 'Just Instagram.' I wait. She goes on, 'That Ed posted, or was tagged in, you know...' She stutters to a standstill. It's not her fault, I guess.

'I decided to give social media a rest, Jess. Break it to me gently.' Trying to keep my voice steady.

'Oh, OK, just group shots messing around in the snow, clinking glasses, bog-standard *Isn't-my-life-amazing* kind of thing.' I know she's holding back; I can practically hear the gears crunching into reverse.

'And what about Ed and a particular woman – dark hair, short?' Short sounds less glamorous than petite.

Jess goes vague. 'Hard to tell in all the gear.'

'Jess, you are a master at this. She's @MeMeMe. Don't bullshit. Tell me straight or I'll go looking myself. You owe me.' A low blow, but I'd rather know.

She takes a breath. 'OK, this Mimi chick is super keen – that's totally obvious. She's doing most of the posting and, yes, Ed is by her side a lot of the time. It looks very fun, mostly big groups. Doesn't look super coupley, but it's only day one.' Her tone becomes serious. 'I do owe you. I'm going to monitor this situation all weekend, so you don't have to. I'll check in if there's anything concrete to report. I promise. Now, have a glass of wine and start your weekend. I've got your back.'

Chapter 27

From Dani, 8.25am:
Hey Babe any progress with
Casper? Don't wanna jinx it but...

Had pretty much forgotten about Dani's speech request, but as it is Saturday decide to keep her in a holding pattern.

Hey! Hope all is well in NYC.
He's super busy – will try and
find right moment Mx

I hope she can read between the lines, but I seriously doubt it. I am done with work for today. It's all about the yoga, keeping busy, keeping my mind off Ed and Mimi. I got a sweet email from Lauren last night with some handy hints: don't eat beforehand and have plenty to drink, but not so much I need to pee. I decide a banana can't hurt anyone and eat it while contemplating my whatever-the-opposite-of-extensive options are for what to wear. I don't want to look too try hard, but I'm acutely aware that sexy Raj will be there and a girl has a certain amount of pride. Much as I love clothes, sportswear has never been a priority. Rifling through my collection of slightly baggy leggings and washed-out gap vests, there is very little difference between my active wear and my pyjama collection. Lauren wears cool kit. I don't want to show up looking like I just rolled out of bed and once I've had that thought, I'm off to the Sweaty Betty in Muswell Hill. If I get a wiggle on and am there when the doors open, I can still make it to the workshop in time.

Nothing wrong with a bit of displacement activity.

An hour later, I am pulling up at the gym, not only wearing understated but stylish leggings and top with a decent amount of strappiness (not too much), but carrying my own personal yoga mat, cleverly rolled up and tied with what will be my own personal yoga belt. The assistant in Sweaty Betty was impressed by my decisiveness. Fortunately, she was looking at her screen when the total pinged up and my knees buckled. I was so busy being decisive (i.e. in a massive hurry), I never checked the price tags. I had no idea that a sports kit could cost that much, but at that price, it must be good. Presenting my credit card, I asked for a receipt. Maybe I can claim this as a business expense?

Spotting Lauren heading up the stairs, I call out, 'Lauren! Wait!' and run up to meet her. I'd much rather arrive with her than on my own. The others all look like they a) know what they are doing and b) know each other.

'Nice outfit,' she greets me with.

'Thanks – its new.'

'I can tell,' she replies and plucks a price tag off the back of my top, laughing. 'Hope you weren't planning to return it after.'

'As if! I've decided to show my commitment to yoga by investing in the right equipment.' And look OK in front of Raj.

'Well, I'm delighted to hear it, as long as you don't fall into the all-the-gear-and-no-idea category!' she adds and I punch her arm as we go through the swing doors. 'But I was wondering how to break it to you that your leggings went see-through over your bum when you bent over.'

I look at her with genuine horror. 'Oh my god! Seriously?' Which means I'm all flustered as we arrive at the studio, where Raj is hovering at the door.

'At last!' he greets us 'I thought it was just going to be me and the yummy mummies. There's some space up front.'

The studio was as packed as health and safety would allow; everyone faffing around with bits of kit or downward dogging as if their lives depended on it. I had a strong suspicion I was out of my depth and would have made a dash for the door if I wasn't sandwiched between two bendy Wendies and stuck in the front row.

Lauren caught my panicked look and leant over. 'This teacher is great, just do what you can. It's not a competition.'

'Tell that to Raj,' I hissed back. He seemed to have folded himself in half.

The teacher walked in bang on time and a reverential hush fell. She walked to the front of the class and settled herself serenely on the mat laid out for her, cross-legged and not six feet away from me.

Here we go. Hope the kit is worth it.

For the next three hours, all I thought about were my muscles and joints and breathing. The teacher gave a continuous stream of instructions and if I didn't understand what she was getting at, I had a great example on either side of me to look at. Lauren was totally in the zone, but Raj and I caught each other's eye from time to time, and each time I felt a little flutter in my belly that, at first, I was worried was wind – damn that banana – but then recognised as lust. I didn't think about Dani's speech, or Ed and Mimi, or even Casper's points. Shit! The envelope was still in my Casper bag. I got sidetracked by Jess's call and forgot to post it. That realisation was a bit of a downer during the relaxation at the end. I couldn't relax at all for thinking about it, then moved on to imagining what Ed was up to and that made me feel sad.

Once we finished and respectfully thanked the teacher, Lauren and Raj were keen to hit the juice bar for lunch and to compare notes about her sequencing or whatever, but my mind was elsewhere. I made my excuses.

'Sorry, sorry – we're yoga bores. We'll change the subject. Don't go.' Raj put a hand on my arm and I froze, acutely aware of the heat of his skin against mine.

'I've got stuff to do – stuff I forgot to do yesterday – so I'd better head out.' Reluctantly, I moved my arm away to dig for my phone in my bag – a reflex action. This time it was Lauren's hand on my arm, but with a restraining grip.

'Oh no you don't. Apart from the fact it is the weekend, you have just done a full-on class. If you did as I told you, you haven't eaten – so, as a responsible friend, I am telling you that whatever is on your phone can wait and we are going to grab some lunch.' She didn't leave much room for argument and Raj nodded his agreement, which made it all the more tempting. I'd missed the post anyway.

'We solemnly swear to stop banging on about yoga,' Raj added, looking deep into my eyes.

Decision made. 'OK, OK, I did like it, honestly, even though I had no idea what she was on about most of the time. And I am actually ravenous – lead me to the salad bar.'

Over a worryingly healthy lunch, we chatted about our weeks. Lauren had a very hot-right-now musician in the studio for a shoot and had us in fits over his demands. He wouldn't take his shades off, would only communicate via one of his three assistants and threw a wobbly when they had the right brand of mineral water but served at the wrong temperature. Rather wonderfully, Django told him to stop being a dick, sent everyone else away and took him into the studio. Lauren says Django shut the door, put some music on and left her to cope with the entourage, who had no idea what to do with themselves without their master. She said it reminded her of babysitting, so she did what she does with her nieces and set up her laptop with continuous episodes of *Friends* and that seemed to do the trick.

As lunch got more relaxed, she told us she had a hot date lined up for that evening. Someone from the musician's record label she'd been in touch with while setting up the shoot. Their emails had got flirtier and flirtier until she decided to seize the day and asked her for a drink.

'I'm jealous,' Raj piped up.

'Me, too,' I said, before engaging my brain.

'Well, my little lovelies, this seems like a problem we can solve right now.' Lauren sat back and crossed her finely toned arms. 'As long as you don't meet up in the same bar I'm going to.'

'God – no – that's not what I meant,' I started babbling. 'Just your date sounded exciting and organic and...' I didn't really know where my point was going and they were both looking at me – Lauren with an amused expression; Raj with a more ambiguous one.

'Sounds pretty organic to me,' he said. 'Why not? We could mix it up and have dinner, if you have any room left after that mountain of salad you just consumed. I've got to go, but I could pick you up at 8?' He's gathering his stuff; it's all happening so fast and I'm not sure quite what is happening, but manage a feeble nod. As I watch him push through the swing doors, I'm aware several other women are also watching him and I permit myself a smug little smile.

Lauren nudges me and I wipe the smile off my face. 'You can pay for my lunch as a thank you!'

'Cheeky cow! Did you plan that? I don't even know if I want a date,' I protest.

'Yeah, right, you two have been gawping at each other all day. Don't overthink it. Raj isn't marriage material and you look like you could do with a bit of fun.'

'Lauren, it's complicated. I sort of have a boyfriend.' *Why did I say that?*

'OK, what's he doing tonight then?' She is brutally direct.

'He's away. Skiing.' I leave it at that, but she's not done.

'With the lads?' She is raising a cynical eyebrow.

'Worse than that,' I admit and decide to match her directness. 'With my rival. Not just her, a group, but...'

'Say no more, Maddy. You don't have to do anything, but have some fun, for Christ's sake.' And that's the end of the conversation.

From Dani, 2.15pm:
Any progress? Word is I'm the
favourite!

God, she's persistent.

Hey! Course you are. I'll get
something sorted. Mx

Missed call from Jess. Must be bad news or she would have just left a message. Feeling pretty upbeat about dinner with Raj, I decide I can take whatever it is she has to tell me.

'Hey, Jess, you called?' I keep my tone bright and breezy.

'Yeah, I just spoke to Steve. It was good! I'm going to meet him and Bridget on Monday with a view to starting asap. I've got a friend's sofa to stay on for a couple of weeks, so it's all cool. I wanted to thank you.' I know there's more. She could have said that in a message. She needs a prompt.

'Great! You'll be fine; Bridget will love you instantly if you say something nice about Sigmund. But Jess, I've kept my part of the deal – have I missed anything?'

There's an awkward pause.

'Maddy, I don't want to jump to conclusions, but there was a bit of soppy stuff last night. Doesn't mean anything happened—'

I interrupt her. 'Just tell me, I can overanalyse for myself.'

'OK, so Mimi posted a photo of a table with two wine glasses in front of an open fire. The caption said: 'alone at last' and two hearty-eye emojis.'

'Massively cheesy, but she could mean any number of blokes.' My heart is racing, but I don't want to let on.

'She tagged Ed in it. And he liked it. He's a creep, Maddy.'

Ouch – that hurts, but not as much as I thought it would.

'Yep, a creep. And also a cliché.' I want to front this out. 'Jess, you've done me a favour. I've got a date tonight and I felt guilty about it, but not anymore.' There is some truth in this.

Jess's screech fills the car. 'You're a dark horse – how did that happen? I'm so jealous. My only prospect of a date is with Netflix.'

'It gets better, Jess. He's a super-fit yoga teacher. Lauren knows him. She set us up.' Telling Jess makes it real – and why not?

'Lauren? Who is this matchmaker, Lauren, and why don't I know her?'

'You do know her – Lauren from CHAMPS, Django's assistant?'

'Shit, Maddy, you take networking to a whole other level. Well, go for it – I expect a full report tomorrow. Am I still on Ed-watch?' Even though I felt something shift at news of the stupid post, I can't quite let it go, but it's my pride that's hurting more than my heart now.

'If you don't mind, but don't tell me until I ask. I'm going to have a fun night and park all the bad stuff. It's the weekend and I am officially letting myself off the hook, following all the current advice and living in the moment.' I've not had these butterflies of excitement in my belly for a very long time. I am going to enjoy an afternoon of getting ready and just go with the flow tonight.

Even a call from the dame, who had managed to lock herself out while deadheading the roses, couldn't dampen my mood. Buzzing round with spare keys meant a quick whizz round the fancy shops in Hampstead and resulted in a swishy blow dry that made me feel like swinging my head round more than any normal person would ever need to.

It was all worth it for the look of appreciation on Raj's face when he buzzed for me. I put my arm through his, noting the firmness of his bicep and how different it felt to Ed's rather skinny arms. It felt strange as Ed towers over me and – stop. In that second, I resolve to stop making comparisons with Ed and we head up the Broadway, arm in arm, to grab a cocktail.

Chapter 28

The less said about last night, the better.

I felt good in my jumpsuit and wedges – casual with a glamorous twist. The hair was the right amount of curly and I'd kept my make-up minimal, as I didn't want to look like I was trying too hard. The cocktails were fine. Raj was very attentive.

I'd put a lot of effort into not thinking about what Ed might be up to – and it paid off until we left the cocktail bar and headed to a local tapas place where Ed and I had eaten many times. Like an idiot, I started to tell Raj about the hilarious time Ed had tried to order in Spanish, assuming the waiter was Spanish, only he was Polish and had no idea what Ed was on about.

Yep. That's about as funny as Raj found it. He changed the subject to work and asked me a bit about my clients, but that sent me into an anxiety spiral. I had to come up with a plan for Dani's speech; Casper wasn't having anything to do with it and time was pressing. The dame was starting to kick up a stink about the documentary people approaching directors she had worked with who may not be entirely complimentary about her, and when I tried to be positive about my new writing gig, I got palpitations about the driving points. The poor bloke started to look a bit uncomfortable. I was losing him and so went on a slightly drunken charm offensive.

My flirting was on the rusty side and I ended up just inviting him back to mine, where it all got even more awkward. I don't think he knew how to read my signals, which wasn't surprising as I didn't really know what signals I wanted to give. To avoid any more uncomfortable conversations, I led him to my bedroom and wound my arms round his neck for a kiss. He obliged and, although it was a perfectly executed kiss, it just didn't feel right. He was shorter than Ed and broader across the shoulders. While I was making these comparisons, he was stroking my back in a slightly tickly way and I had to stop myself from slapping his hand. Instead, I grabbed it and led him to my bed and started unbuttoning my jumpsuit in a rather business-like manner. He was kissing my neck and murmured, 'Hey, no rush, baby,' and I cringed because I hate being called baby. To be fair, I only realised at that precise second that I hated being called 'baby', but I was also thinking how dumb it was to have worn a jumpsuit on a date that I had gone on with intent.

I think he took my cringe as a shudder of delight because next thing his tongue was in my ear and I yelped.

Not a sexy yelp – a Jack Russell terrier kind of yelp. He leapt back, holding the side of his head, because the yelp had been surprisingly loud and right in his ear. I said sorry, that I had just got a fright. He looked at me, shook his head (still holding his ear) and said, 'Baby, is this what you want?' which was nice of him. I said it probably wasn't, though I appreciated the offer, and suggested a cup of tea. He was halfway down the stairs before I finished the sentence. I went back to my room, sat on my bed and cried. Salty snotty crying. Then I got my phone out and went straight on Instagram and made myself sick with putting two and two together and coming up with Ed and Mimi having an impossibly romantic time in full view of anyone who cared to look. She was clinging to his arm or sitting on his lap in every photo, and don't even start me on the hashtags.

He has most definitely moved on with (I think) obscene haste. I gave it my best shot and just made a fool of myself with a perfectly nice and very handsome guy. I climbed under the duvet, still wearing my best matching bra and knickers and what was left of my make-up, and drifted off into an unsettled sleep.

※

From Ella, 9.42am:
Prep running behind. Pls pls
pls can you pick up sourdough
from Gails??? Come ASAP Ex

Brunch. On a scale of one to ten, my desire to go is below zero. I could pretend the date went really well and that I'm luxuriating in the afterglow, but Ella didn't even know it was happening. I'd rather not have to go there with her, which may be for the best all things considered. Even if I come up with an excuse, three pleases means it's serious and it would be more hassle to let her down than to just buy the bread and show my face. Having made a plan propels me to the shower; I then dress in the abandoned jumpsuit because I can't be bothered to think about what to wear and swap the wedges for trainers. Today, the make-up really is minimal as opposed to a big load of effort to make it look minimal, but who cares? Not me.

From Lauren, 10.30am:
Well…?

No urgency on replying, but I do want to get my version of events in before Raj, but all that matters right now is getting to the bakery before they sell out. I grab some cava from the fridge and find Betty.

I am warmly greeted by Ella at the door of Drippy Tom's incredibly sterile modern box of a flat. For fear of letting her down, I bought four loaves of sourdough and some baguettes for good measure. She is suitably grateful and too frazzled to ask after me. Grabbing the bags of baked goods, she heads down the corridor to the kitchenette, which is cleverly disguised as a cupboard and sadly has no room for two.

'Where's Tom?' I wonder, conversationally.

'Obsessing over the playlist. No use on the food front. Can you start unwrapping the cheeses and arrange them on the board?' She doesn't look up from scooping out an avocado.

'Sure. How many are you expecting?'

'Well, it was ten, but we've had cancellations: Stella and Maya – terrible hangovers, apparently. I hate it when people cancel on the day – rude. I mean, your host will be stressed enough, right? Just don't show up and then create an elaborate excuse...' and so she chunters on. It's ideal because I don't really want to engage and concentrate on a Tetris-style cheese layout in keeping with the hipster cheeseboard, aka a slab of plywood. I'm also pondering how many people there would have to be to make me slipping away less noticeable.

'... Am I right or am I right? Maddy? Maddy!'

Shit. Got no idea what she's been on about, but seems that saying she is right will be the correct response, so I slap on a big smile and say, 'So right, Els, 100 per cent.' This does the trick and she carries on. And on.

'Where shall I put this?' I interrupt and proffer the cheese platter.

'Garnish, Maddy; garnish, for god's sake! Look in the fridge. Baby plum tomatoes on the vine and a dish of Nocellara olives.'

'Christ, Els, what happened to a bag of Doritos and

a jar of salsa as perfect snack food? When did you get so fancy?'

I was trying to lighten the mood, but she whips round and snaps, 'Don't take the piss, Maddy. I just want it to be nice. People from work are coming, Tom's boss and his wife, so stop being snarky and start slicing lemons.'

'Sir, yes sir!' I salute her, which raises a smile and I fall into line.

By the time the first guest arrives, the table looks lovely – a few creative touches added by my good self make all the difference. I picked some grasses from the neighbour's garden and stuck them in a jug and did something sculptural yet tasteful with the napkins. I made freshly squeezed orange juice and poured Ella a glass topped up with Prosecco, so we were all good and ready to receive. I hung back and watched her as she transformed into a suave, sophisticated hostess. Drippy Tom stopped peering at his phone screen and put his arm round me awkwardly and said, 'Cheers, Maddy. You're a mate. She was really stressed out before you arrived. I had to take cover in the bedroom,' and this made me feel good.

Suddenly ravenous, I `m the first to destroy my geo-metric cheese design and smear some avocado on my lightly toasted sourdough, then I withdraw to a corner to eat in peace. I nab one of the few chairs, slightly concerned that the spindly hairpin legs might buckle under me, spread a napkin on my lap and make ready to tuck in. No casual standing around picking at a morsel or two for me. I am here to eat, help Ella a bit and then split.

The other guests look like proper grown-ups. The women are wearing a lot of ARKET, all very monochrome, with the odd pop of colour from a cross-body bag or jazzy trainer. The guys are mainly going for a utility workwear look – navy canvas shackets or Breton T-shirts and more-than-your-average amount of directional spectacles to be seen. There is a genteel muddle of voices, not much laughing. I am chewing on a particularly tough bite of sourdough crust and wondering if I should get some heavy black glasses frames to look like a serious writer, when a voice from above says, 'Hello. I was hoping you'd be here.'

Disturbed from my contemplation, I am eye level with the crotch of some very tatty jeans. Looking up, it's that guy from the picnic. 'Dominic?' I hadn't meant to say that in such a questioning way.

'At your service.' He gives a happy smile. 'Can I get you a top up?'

'That's usually my job,' I reply. 'I was just getting fuelled up,' indicating my now empty but crumby lap. I decide to stand as I feel weird talking to his pelvis. He is a good deal scruffier than anyone else here, much more in line with my idea of how one should look on a Sunday morning. Before I can answer, he grabs the bottle of cava off the sideboard and is pouring me a glass. *Well, why not?* It is clear I am going to have to stick around. Ella would certainly notice if I left.

'Cheers,' I clinked his glass. 'How have you been?'

We end up having quite a giggle. I even tell him about my disastrous date. He goes a bit quiet, polishes his not at all trendy, metal-framed academic specs and clears his throat. 'So, it's all over with that other guy then?'

'We'll see – he'll come to his senses, I reckon. Just thought I'd flex the old dating muscle in the meantime,' I reply breezily, trying to protect my pride as much as anything.

It seems to convince Dom, though. He mumbles something about the loo and leaves me. Not wanting to look like a saddo, I grab the cava and start a circuit of the room, offering refills. Practically no one accepts. My seat is still empty, but going back to it without the excuse of eating would look a bit pathetic. Ella is deep in conversation with a serious-looking, slightly older woman – fifty maybe? I am fascinated by her hair; she isn't exactly grey, but not any other particular colour I can put my finger on. Edging closer, I can see it is a combination of streaks of lots of different shades. Ella has clocked me and kindly makes an introduction.

'Liza, this is my good friend, Madeleine. Madeleine, Liza does some training for us.' I winced slightly at Madeleine – she never calls me that – but, determined to make an effort, I weighed in.

'You never said you got workouts at the office – perk of the job?' They both laughed. At me.

'Not that kind of training, Maddy, management training.' Ella looks a bit embarrassed on my behalf, but how was I to know?

Anyway, Liza thinks it is hilarious and says, 'If only – my gym days are over. Bit of Pilates at the weekend, if I'm lucky.'

Seeing as the ice is broken, I go on, 'I was admiring your hair, Joanna. What colour would you call it?'

Ella is shooting me looks, but, patting her loose bun, Liza smiles as she leans towards my ear and says, 'Expensive.'

'Well, I think it's fabulous. I want to have hair like yours when I grow up.' We both laugh and Ella has to join in. This is a bit more fun, but then Ella asks if I'd help her with the coffee and breaks it up. She follows me to the kitchen.

'Shit, Maddy, I nearly died when you asked Liza what colour her hair was. We're all terrified of her.'

'Why did you invite her then?' I'm genuinely confused.

'She's a good person to have on side. Influential.' Ella looks anxious, eyes darting around the guests, making sure it's all running smoothly.

'It's weird you're doing this on a Sunday morning, Els. Are you getting your work-life balance out of whack?' This is what she usually accuses me of and she smiles at the irony.

'Feels like work is my life these days, Maddy. I envy your freedom to switch things around.' We have a bit of a moment; I always assume she has it all figured out and I'm the mess.

'But *Madeleine* – seriously?' I give her a gentle shove.

'Shut up – I'm being an adult. Don't put me off.'

At that moment, Tom catches her eye and beckons her over. It looks like I'm on coffee duty by myself then. Heading to the kitchenette, I recognise Dom's back hunched over the sink. Tapping his shoulder, he starts. His face goes a bit pink when he sees it's me.

'Room for a little one? I'm coffee monitor.'

'Um, sure, let me dry my hands and I'll get out your way.' He grabs a linen tea towel from the side.

'Or you could give me a hand? You seem like the helpful type.' I indicate the washing-up draining on the side.

'Not really. I just didn't know what to do with myself. I was surprised Tom invited me. I figured there must be a good reason.' He's looking at me. Straight at me.

'Oh, I know full well why I'm here,' I say, as I fill the tank of the coffee pot at the sink. 'Cheap labour.'

I stayed until everyone had left, which was almost exactly an hour and a half after they had arrived. Dom stayed too and we did a good job of clearing up while Ella and Drippy Tom debriefed. The chat flowed easily and I told him I'd signed up for a writing course. I said he'd sown the seeds at the picnic and he seemed chuffed. It wasn't until I went to take the recycling out that I checked my phone.

From Ed, 1.45pm:
Hey x

Chapter 29

I left Drippy Tom's place pretty damn quick. Heading home, I work through all the different things that 'Hey' could mean. Ella shouted after me that she was coming back tonight, so there's the possibility of going over it with her, but if I wait that long, my brain will have gone round in so many circles I'll be dizzy. Could this be the moment I've been waiting for? Has he come to his senses? I'm not going to make it easy for him, that's for absolute sure.

My phone rings and startles me. Is Ed so keen to get hold of me? Nope, Dame Annette. It's Sunday. I'm not going to answer.

It's a client, I have to answer.

'Madeleine, is that you or an answering machine?' Her plummy tones fill the car.

'I'm here, Dame Annette. Is everything alright?' I wouldn't mind a drama to take my mind off things.

'The filming tomorrow, can you come early and make

sure they behave?' She must be feeling anxious.

'Sure, but won't Charles be there?' Her agent, Charles, is a real luvvie lover, oozes schmooze, but I like him.

'Well, yes, but I want you keeping an eye on things backstage, as it were...' She means hang around with the crew and try and get some intel, while the bigwigs blow smoke up each other's arses.

'Of course, I'll get there first thing and keep my ear to the ground.' I'm quite happy around a crew – throwback to my movie days – and this should be more fun because back then the crew didn't want me there.

'Thank you, dear. See you tomorrow.'

Wow, she's softening in her old age. 'Dear' is definitely an upgrade. I ease Betty into an almost-space, slightly hanging over next door's driveway – living dangerously. Bursting through the door, dumping bags as I go, I fling myself down on my bed. This is where I do some of my best thinking and this not wholly unexpected turn of events with Ed needs some close analysis. I was hurt by his decision to go ahead without me and then angry about the obvious hook-up with Mimi. But there was still a tiny bit of me that thought we had so much potential and that one day he would wake up and smell the coffee. The fact that he is contacting me the minute he's got home seems to bear this out – but what does he expect? Is it even meant for me?

Aha! That will be how I reply without giving anything away.

To Ed, 2.35pm:

Meant for me…??

That'll show him I'm no pushover. Might scare him off – but this is Ed we're talking about. He's not easily frightened, at least not by a slightly passive-aggressive text. And I'm fascinated to know what he has to say, because even though I recognise that he has behaved really badly, there is a distinct whiff of unfinished business about this and loose ends are something I cannot abide.

Tomorrow will be a long day – filming always takes ages, plus the dame will be fussing around telling them what they can't do and where they can't go. The sensible move is to make sure my bag is packed and ready, and there are important things to take into consideration like whether the BBC will run to a catering station or if I should take my own snacks, and tuck in a spare charger just in case. Despite all this practical prep, when I hear my phone ping, I can't pretend to be playing it very cool as I don't recall my feet touching the ground. I fly up the stairs so fast. Let's see what he has to say.

From Ed, 2.45pm:
Ha ha! Missed your GSOH Ex

I knew it! He's having regrets and there is no mistaking his tone now. This is flirty, the cheeky sod. My hears races, but I think it's a reflex action with a little 'Told you so' on the side. The temptation to fire something sassy back is strong, but in the midst of all this excitement, let's not forget he is fresh off the slopes with Mimi the Moo-Cow. Seriously, he probably still has snow in his hair, and fascinated as I am to hear his version of events, I will keep my cool – at least until Ella gets home. A considered run-through of my options with her is just what I need and keeping him waiting is the very least I can do.

In the spirit of diversionary tactics, I decide to make something nice for supper. A quick assessment reveals the contents of the fridge will not permit this, so I grab a bag for life and head to Sainsbury's. In an unusual move, I leave my phone at home. It's Sunday afternoon, so work-wise I reckon I am within my rights, and I can't quite trust myself to resist the temptation to text Ed back.

Striding up to the Broadway, I ponder what to make and settle on a Greek salad. We had all that bread at brunch so a salad is just the thing – and if I make loads, there could be leftovers to take for lunch tomorrow in case the BBC don't do catering. Practicalities sorted, my thoughts return to Ed. Didn't I always say we were good together? And that, at some point, he would realise it himself. There is, of course, the matter of what exactly went on with Mimi, but I will keep an open mind and hear his side of the story, for no other reason than my personal satisfaction. My guess is that he doesn't know that I know what he's been getting up to.

The aisles of Sainsbury's only get half my attention as I think about how much things have changed for me recently. I'm positively looking forward to this week, which has not been my Sunday vibe for a long time. I'm feeling so damn positive, I decide I will have a crack at writing Dani an acceptance speech. Why not? I'm officially a writing assistant. Casper has made it clear he's not doing it and how hard can it be? I'll do some research (watch tonnes of them on YouTube) and put something short and smart together. Actually, that's not a bad line given Dani is just over five foot – see? I've got this.

Bouncing home down the hill, swinging a bag of feta, olives and cucumbers, humming a cheery tune, I let myself in. I'm not the tidiest, but the contents of my Casper bag are scattered across the bottom few stairs. The bag itself on its side, flopped over the edge of my teeny desk. Bending down to start scooping up the keys, notebooks and highlighters, I hear a sharp voice bark my name.

Looking up, there is Ella, the light behind her so I can't see her face, but before I can say anything, she snaps, 'Never mind that, Maddy, what the hell do you call this?'

'Greek salad?' I venture, not understanding what the fuss is about. 'Hang on, must have knocked my bag on my way out.'

'No!' she shouts – most unlike Ella. Maybe she's got a day hangover from the boring brunch. 'This letter from the Metropolitan Police, neatly filled out in your handwriting and signed by Casper.'

Oh.

There's no way to joke my way out of this. I start up the stairs with a childish urge to just grab it off her. It's none of her business; she wasn't ever meant to know. But before I can reach her, she marches into the kitchen, turning to glare at me as I follow shamefully behind. We stare at each other, my heart racing, until she breaks the silence.

'Well?' Her cheeks are pink, her jaw clenched tight.

'Why were you going through my stuff?' My guilt has made me defiant.

'I *wasn't*, you idiot. My elbow caught the strap of your stupid bag and it fell over. I was picking your stuff up and this was right there on the top. And actually, I don't need to make excuses – *you're* the one with explaining to do.' She crosses her arms and fixes me with an icy glare.

It's scary seeing her like this. We've had plenty of arguments, but this feels different. This is a matter of morals and while I know I haven't got a leg to stand on, I must make a case for myself because I made my decision and I can't see a way back. I need to play for time because I'm finding it extremely hard to marshal any coherent form of argument.

'Why don't I make us tea and I'll explain? Honestly, it's fine.' *Who am I kidding?*

Not Ella. '*No, it isn't fucking fine!*' I haven't heard her shout or swear like that in years. It's shocking. 'This is what you called me about, isn't it? You and I both know you weren't driving that car. What the *hell* do you think you are playing at?' I'm busted. I need to explain it like Jess did to me.

'Listen, Casper and I made a deal. It's not unusual, apparently. I did refuse, loads of times, honestly I did.' My tone is pleading. I have to make her understand how hard he was pushing me. 'He kept going on and on, offered me money, all sorts, and I kept saying no—' Maybe she'll get it if I can just get to the bit about the nanny.

'But then you didn't,' she interrupts, her arms tightly folded, standing stiffly by the fridge.

I desperately try to make things normal. 'Ella, please, I've got a nice healthy supper for us. Let's talk it through. Jess knows this nanny...' She's not having any of it.

'There is nothing to talk through, Maddy, apart from the possible repercussions – I don't think you realise how serious this is. You could face prison!' She is furious and I'm pretty sure she's not just trying to frighten me. I'm scared enough anyway and not sure how to respond.

The time for fudging things has passed. Honesty is the best policy.

'He said I could name my price. I asked to be named as his writing assistant, I *demanded* it.' Is there a tiny possibility she'll respect my chutzpah?

'Not good enough. You *are* his writing assistant, whether he calls you that or not. Now, how about I show you the verdicts where people have been convicted of perjury for doing exactly this? Or the newspaper head-lines – remember that MP's wife? They both went to jail. *Jail*, Maddy.'

Shit. That does ring a bell. I'd found a way to make it feel OK in my head, focusing on my future and not what I'd had to do to get there. Hearing what Ella's saying cracks the whole thing wide open and sends me into panic.

'But, Ella, how would anyone find out? No one would ever know. Hang on, you wouldn't – would you?' Fear

291

prickles my neck. It would be a great tabloid story and the end of any kind of career I might have. Writer or PA. My bravado is long gone. I feel nothing but the grip of anxiety.

'I'm sorry. I didn't mean to be a bad person. Casper wouldn't take no for an answer. I was scared I'd lose my job; he was so angry, pressurising me. Jess said taking points is a thing and I just wanted to do something creative. This seemed like my chance.' My voice is shaking with panic, but I have to make her understand. 'I had a taste of something better and it was being taken away.' My voice catches and I try my best to stay strong and hold back the tears. 'I was trying to get something good out of a bad situation.'

Letting out a sigh, Ella slumps into a chair at the table. I immediately sit opposite, leaning across to plead with her. This is how we have solved so many problems over the years, at this table and many others, but there's such a look of disdain on her face that I feel just awful.

'Ella, I'm scared. Apart from the fact that I can't afford to lose this job, I really love the writing. It's like I've finally found my thing and I'll never get another chance like this – Casper will make sure of that. He was calling and texting me day and night. I gave in. Please say you won't tell.' I'm genuinely terrified. 'I don't know what I'm more afraid of, Ella, going ahead with the chance of being found out, or backing out and facing Casper.' Dropping my face into my hands, try as I might to hold it together, I can't stop crying. 'I'm sorry. It's a mess. I'm a mess. Don't hate me.'

Her expression has softened a bit. She's chewing her lip.

Seeing myself through her eyes, I'm ashamed. I knew what I was doing was wrong and I've known it all along. The end does not justify the means. Time to brace up.

'You're right, Ella. I know you are and I didn't talk to you about it because I knew the answer without asking the question. I won't send the form back. I'll tell Casper I'm not doing it.' Fresh tears form as the reality of all this hits and I keep thinking of more repercussions as I lay my head down on my arms, giving in to the sobs. I'll lose everything.

'Maddy, come on, you're doing the right thing! We'll figure something out; it can't be that bad.' Ella's being kind, but she doesn't understand what Casper could do in terms of my reputation. It's a small showbusiness world out there and he is not famed for his discretion.

For her sake, I wipe at my face and try to pull myself together. Though a watery smile, I manage, 'You know what, Els; it probably is that bad,' and I can't help a weak laugh.

'Let me help you. I hate seeing you like this, because, honestly, you don't deserve it. Your clients wouldn't last five minutes in the real world, plus you've shown a talent for writing. Let's put a case together for you to present to Casper. If you're calm and reasonable, he'll see sense. For a start, if it did get out – not through me; I'd never do that to you, you idiot – but if it did get out, it'd look far worse on him than it would on you. He's the name the papers would be plastered with, you'd just be a side product.' She's got a point. 'Let's Legally Blonde the shit out of this, Maddy.'

That film was the reason Ella became a lawyer, so I

know she means business. Greek salad forgotten, I put the kettle on at last while she gets one of those big blue legal pads and a pen and we meet back at the table with our laptops to brainstorm some ideas and facts. Me downloading news stories about high-profile perjury cases while she sends links to court reports of driving offences. I revisit the suggestions I made to Casper earlier but flesh them out. Actual candidates and costings for hiring a driver, setting up an executive cab account and details of a fancy motorbike limo service. I reckon Casper might just go for that – I'll get him some designer leathers and a Louis Vuitton helmet. I keep looking over at Ella and feeling a wash of relief; being in full-on work mode, she is oblivious to my grateful gaze. She's always believed in me; it's time to believe in myself. Her conviction is rubbing off on me and I almost start to believe it might be OK after all.

A couple of hours and an oil tanker's worth of tea later, we have an expertly prepared document for me to present to Casper. I suggest emailing it over to him and then running for cover, but, in my heart, I know I have to face him. The timing isn't brilliant, but I'll go first thing, before I go to the dame's. Stretching out my crumpled shoulders, I reach over to give Ella a big hug.

'You're the best,' I mutter into the side of her ponytail.

She pulls back with a serious expression.

'What? I'll do it, Ella, I promise. No going back.' I know that look and she's got me worried.

'I believe you, hon, but there's something I wanted to talk to you about before all this kicked off. It's the reason I came back here tonight and, despite all this…' she gestures to the table strewn with notes and dirty mugs, 'I can't put it off any longer.' I wonder what she's about to say; it certainly doesn't feel like good news. She rushes on, 'Remember I mentioned Tom and I were talking about moving in together? Well, now he's pushing for it, wants to do it as soon as possible.' Poor Ella looks so worried when she should be happy.

'Oh.' I sit upright, feels like I've been kicked, bizarrely, in the back, where I was least expecting it. I rally. 'Of course he does. You're the best. Will you move into his? Should I find a new flatmate? Jess needs—' She interrupts me in full babble.

'Thing is, we want to live here. His place is more suitable for renting out, plus I have the second bedroom.' She's speaking softly, reasonably, trying to soften the blow.

'*My* bedroom?'

'I wasn't in a rush, but Tom's really keen. I wanted to give you as much warning as I could to think about what you want to do.' I can see she's torn, but I know exactly what I want to do. I want to stay here with my supportive, clever best friend. Even if it means living with Drippy Tom. 'I won't get in your way. I could cook for us all and stay in my room a lot. I don't need the bijou office; you can have it back…' I tail off as her face crumples. This is very un-Ella.

'Maddy, this is hard enough,' she says with a wobble. 'I'm sorry, but things move on. You need to move on.'

Chapter 30

How things can change in just a few hours. Sashaying up to Sainsbury's considering quippy responses to Ed seems like another lifetime. He's been forgotten in all this. Absence really does seem to have done its thing because there is another message and even a missed call from him. If only I'd known during those weeks of chasing and plotting that all I needed to do was ignore him. I should reply, but I just can't be arsed. Honestly? I have more important things to worry about right now.

Big day tomorrow. I try some yoga breathing while also contingency planning. Even when my world is falling apart, I need to have a plan. Perhaps when I am mostly unemployed, I will do more yoga. I'll ask Lauren to recommend some local classes. Although I'm pretty sure tomorrow morning will be a shit show, I have let Ella give me a shard of hope. I will give it my best shot and do everything I can to make Casper understand.

It's ridiculously early, but rather than lie in bed worrying, I get up and shower. I'm going to dress like someone who knows what's what, someone not to be messed with. Someone like Ella, in fact. We're about the same size and she is still in her room, so I tap on the door wrapped in my towel.

Flinging the door open, she says, 'You're not bottling it, are you? Don't make me have to get angry.' The look on her face gives me no option of backing out.

'Of course not! I was wondering if I could borrow something to wear. I'm trying to look the part.'

'Like a suit of armour?' Not bad for this early on a Monday morning.

'Ha ha. Just a suit would do. Basically, I want to channel you on your way to kick ass, in a professional way.'

'Help yourself,' she gestures to her wardrobe. 'I need to get on, but you've got this, Maddy. He'll see sense – he's not a monster.'

Turns out that is exactly what he is. Right from the get-go, things did not go well. He was surprised to see me, which I thought could work to my advantage, but it just meant he was on the back foot. I hadn't even got to the end of my pitch before he started shouting expletives. Determined to keep my head, I let him go on until he ran out of steam, which was way longer than I could ever have anticipated. Turns out he knows an awful lot of ways of saying, 'You are a duplicitous young woman' – none of which are polite.

Once he had sputtered to a halt, so red-faced even his scalp was glowing, I went in for round two and tried the 'It would be your name in the papers' route, which led to accusations of blackmail, even though I reminded him I'd get in just as much trouble as him if I spilled the beans. He'd run out of swear words by now, so was just going for volume and I had to stand there taking the full force. I couldn't think of a way to bring the situation back to any kind of sensible discussion, plus I needed to get to the dame's. Thinking I'd weathered the worst, I took advantage of his next pause for breath and leant over to put the proposal on his desk. I was about to suggest he gave it some thought when he grabbed my wrist, tightly.

'You have made a big fucking mistake, missy, and you *will* live to regret it.' Still squeezing my wrist, he leant over and growled in a low voice, 'I never want to see your face again – not here, not anywhere. Understood?' Unable to speak – he's not letting go of my wrist – I manage a nod. He releases his grip. I step back, rubbing the spot he's been holding. Seeing my whole future falling away, in a fit of desperation I manage to say, 'Um, about Top Notch—'

'Fuck off and leave my keys!'

I fumble in my Casper bag and gingerly place them on his desk. The adrenalin has worn off and my hands are trembling. I flinch as he stands to make his final point, aware of the burning sensation on my wrist.

'You were a good assistant until you started to get ideas

above your station. I did you a favour and this is how you repay me.' Dropping his voice to a nasty hiss, he finishes with a flourish, 'Get. Out. Of. My. Sight.'

Without waiting to see if that really is it, I leave on unsteady legs, grabbing the back of the sofa to steady myself, but not wanting to break pace – just to get out as quickly as possible.

My hands are shaking so much by the time I reach Betty, I can barely open the door, but once in I slam it shut and hit lock. The fear has kicked in and I half expect Casper to come launching out of the front door with another barrage of fury. I've weathered many a tantrum, but nothing like this. For the first time in my career, I felt physically unsafe. Clenching the steering wheel, I curse my naivety. I let Ella convince me he would see sense because I wanted to believe it, but I should have known better. As my heart rate settles, I try to console myself by knowing that I have done the right thing, but what a mess I've made. As soon as I feel safe to drive, I head off. I wish I could just go home, which won't be home for much longer, and hide under my duvet, but instead I have to get my head in gear for a day of wrangling the crew at the dame's.

Time to employ the PA's superpower – the ability to compartmentalise. That's one for my how-to guide.

Squeezing my way up the narrow lane, trucks and vans blocking the road indicate that the crew have already arrived and, despite everything, I feel a twitch of excitement. There's a gaggle of folk huddled round the catering truck holding polystyrene cups and bacon butties, while grips and sparks unload endless reels of cable, metal poles and tripods. It still amazes me how much equipment filming entails. Stepping carefully over the coils of wires up the garden path, I call out as I lean in through the door, which is standing ajar.

'Hello? Dame Annette? It's Maddy – shall I come in?' I'm impressed at how well I've managed to pull myself together, trying to ignore the burning skin on my wrist.

'Morning room,' she calls back. *Is that the same as the drawing room?*

I can hear Charles' voice, so in I go. Putting on a very peppy face and smiling broadly, I say, 'I see the crew are getting set up. Do they know where they can and can't go? Can they use your loo?' I'm covering up my wobbliness with forced efficiency.

'It's all in the contract, Maddy, don't you worry. Nice to see you again. Remind me who else you look after these days?' Charles stands up give me a double kiss. I see the dame's face sour over his shoulder. You'd think he'd know better than to mention other clients in front of her, but he goes on: 'I hear Dani is doing a good job on Broadway. There are rumours of a Tony nomination.' Aha. He's got his eye on Dani now she's a proper actress.

With impeccable timing, the Dame cuts in, 'Maddy, tell them to mind out for my borders. If I see them trampling the flower beds, I will have something to say.'

'Of course, I'll go and make myself known to the director. Give me a shout if you need anything.' I flash a tight smile at Charles, who gives me a wink. The old bugger knows exactly what he is doing.

Once I've said hello to the director and producer, there's not really much for me to do. So, taking a cup of super strong tea from the urn, and chucking in a load of sugar, I go and perch on the dame's garden seat and take a moment to process this morning. Rubbing my wrist, the skin is still red. Tugging my sleeve down to cover it, I wonder if this counts as assault. Whichever way you cut it, things are pretty much as bad as they could be.

I don't want to let him frighten me off; dare I contact Top Notch directly about the writing work? Maybe they can go over his head. Who am I trying to kid? Casper's a lead writer on a hit show with a third series in the pipeline. There is no way he will have me working anywhere near him and if they ask him for a reference, well – let's not go there. Sitting there with my spirits falling ever lower, I feel the comforting vibrate of my phone in my – well, technically Ella's – pocket.

'Jess, hi.' I try and sound normal, despite my world crumbling around me.

'Hey, Maddy, just a quickie, I'm at Steve's and Bridget can't remember how to get visitor parking permits. Also, how far did you get with Mindfulness Minis?'

I can picture Bridget lurking in the background, so keep it professional, 'Sure, no worries. I can email you the link and the nursery said they would put him as high as they could on the waiting list, but not above siblings. I did explain. She's probably just wants you to give it another go.' I can't help myself. There's a bit of scuffling at the other end. Sounds like Jess is on the move.

'Are you OK, Maddy? You sound odd.'

'Yeah. Bad day. Casper. I really don't want to go into it.' I'm just about managing to hold it together and there are people everywhere.

'Is it about the car thing? Or Top Notch?' She sounds genuinely concerned.

'I really can't talk now, but let's just say it will be me on the lookout for a new client and my writing career is over before it started.' If I say more, I'll get upset, so I pretend the dame is calling me. 'I'm coming! Got to go, Jess.' And I ring off.

Looking over at the crew, I see they're laying tracks up the garden path and, as I head back, a grip steps a giant boot into the geraniums. 'Hey! Careful!' I shout as I speed-walk over. 'Please mind out!' He takes not a bit of notice, the other boot joining the first as he does something fiddly with a spanner while planted firmly in the middle of the border. 'Hi, listen, can you be careful of the flowers please?'

Looking up, he smiles, cheekily, 'Course, darling.' But makes no move as he carries on doing whatever it is.

Exasperated, I head off to find an AD. Maybe they can speak a language I can't and I stop a frazzled-looking woman with a headset. 'Hi, I'm Maddy, the dame's assistant. Can you remind the crew to be careful in the garden, please?' I say as I gesture towards the grip. 'Sure, yes,' she replies, though I'm not sure she's really listening. 'Yep – she's right here,' she says into the microphone, while fixing me with a look. 'Maddy, right? They want to do a piece with you. Is it OK if we mic you up now before we get started? We'll do your bit in a break once we are running.'

'My piece? What are you talking about? I'm just here to support Dame Annette.' This is the last thing I need.

'Exactly! Perfect for providing some context, you know, for the 'real' Dame Annette.' She's looking expectant.

'I don't think that's a good idea. I'm a behind-the-scenes sort of person and I wouldn't have anything interesting to say.' I know exactly what they are hoping for – me saying something controversial by accident. No way am I agreeing to this.

She's listening to her headset intently, then turns to me with a shrug. 'Dame gave us full access, so you're on. The sound guys are over there; the gaffer's expecting you.'

Gesturing towards a large truck parked outside the gate, she bustles off before I can come up with any more objections. The grip winks at me as I stomp past him, resolving to be as boring as I possibly can so they regret wasting their time on me. I'm a strictly behind-camera person.

There's some apologetic fiddling around while I thread a wire up through my blouse and attach a pack to the back of my trousers. Then some 'What did you have for breakfast?' type questions to test my levels and I'm released.

I pop back inside to make sure the dame is happy. She's in her element being fussed over. I see her swell up with pleasure as the make-up girl tells her what great skin she has, then deflate slightly as she adds, 'for your age.' Spotting me, she twists in her seat to say, 'I can hear footsteps upstairs; they do not have access to upstairs. *You* are meant to be keeping an eye on things.'

I turn back huffily before I can respond. Once upstairs, it's clear they have taken absolutely no notice of the rules – there are kit boxes everywhere and the worst kind of evidence that someone (probably more than one) has been using the en-suite. On a mission, I stomp off to find that AD and tell her in no uncertain terms to get things sorted. She eyes me warily. I'm guessing to see how seriously to take me, so I threaten to have filming pulled completely. I don't think I can actually do this, but she's not to know.

Just then, the very well-known and very pompous presenter arrives to do his bit, and several members of the crew flutter around him. The dame greets him graciously and they settle down in the morning drawing room while the lighting is adjusted. The dame spots me in the shadows and hisses, 'There's a large man trampling the roses, for goodness' sake. *Do* something.'

A young spark is unwinding a fat rope of cable, heedless of the plants he is squashing under its weight. In very firm terms, I suggest he might want to be a bit more careful, and before I can be sent to reprimand anyone else, I take myself off to the flower bower at the very bottom of the garden. I feel very on edge and decide to ask Lauren for an emergency relaxation class recommendation.

From Jess:
'Call me. ASAP.'

Being on a call will make me look busy, so I do.

'Talk to me, Jess. This crew are driving me insane.

They're a bunch of complete idiots; I'm having to herd them like a bunch of naughty toddlers. What is it with TV people? They think they're so bloody special – it's not exactly saving lives, is it?' I feel much better for a bit of venting. 'What's up? Bridget driving you nuts?' So relieved it's not me anymore.

'Nothing like that. But I spoke to Olive, my pal, and no one at Top Notch knows anything about you. Casper definitely hasn't told them.' She's whispering and muffled. 'I can't talk now but thought you should know. Speak later.' I wander slowly back towards the house, trying to ignore the various misdemeanours I see the crew committing. I'm just here as glorified law enforcement. Struggling to digest what Jess has told me, I consider the options.

Had Casper not had a chance to tell them yet? I'm sure he said it was all agreed and he's in daily contact with them. Could he have forgotten? Highly unlikely. A horrible realisation dawns on me. Could it be that he was never planning to? He was so reluctant to acknowledge me and terribly vague about when I could go to a production meeting. Was he was just fobbing me off, telling me what I wanted to hear? Is he that much of a bastard?

Deep in concentration, it goes noticeably quiet as I stop by the improvised production office they've set up in the kitchen. Everyone is looking at me.

'What? Has something happened?' Concerned for the dame, I look from face to unfriendly face.

'Your mic was open,' the producer says, curtly. Slamming her laptop down, she leaves the room.

Chapter 31

The atmosphere for the rest of the day is distinctly frosty. I am swiftly relieved of my mic and pretty much ignored by the entire production team. Charles makes his excuses and leaves after his moment with the presenter, so I stick close by the dame. The day drags as the crew bustle around, ignoring me, intent on whatever task is in hand. And to think that this was a day I'd really looked forward to being part of the team.

At last they are done and start packing up. There is a stand-off over who is responsible for the disposing of rubbish sacks, but I am taking no prisoners, so the AD chucks them in the back of her car and slams the door, leaving without saying goodbye.

Stressed, anxious and confused, I havn't been able to string a coherent thought together with all the commotion and the dame's demands. In the quiet of Betty, I have a chance to think. But none of it makes sense. Casper definitely told me I was official with Top Notch. I guess he could argue that I said I'd take the points and now I'd backed out, but there is no way I would be having that, or any conversation with him. Casper is done with me, that was clear, but Top Notch? it just doesn't seem fair. My head is going round in circles.

From Lauren, 6.20pm:
Yo! There's a Pranayama class
at the Quaker meeting hall
7.30pm. I'll go if you will?? Lx

I'd forgotten about my SOS to Lauren, what kind of torture was Pranayama? I got Siri to send back a question mark. With a kiss. Immediate reply.

Breathing!!!

Well, breathing sounds like a very good idea. I don't want to be home when, or if, Ella gets in. I'd have to relive the scene with Casper this morning, as well as admit he's been stringing me along and I've been taken for a mug. If I tell her he hurt me, she'll pressure me to report him. I don't have my head around the whole moving out thing just yet. Any delaying tactic sounds good to me right now.

To Lauren, 6.29pm (via Siri):
Breathing sounds good. See
you there. Mx

Briefly stopping home to change, dropping Ella's suit at the cleaners, and even walking as slowly as I can, I'm still there early, so am delighted to see Lauren's tall, rangy figure heading towards me from the tube station. I think efficient PAs are incapable of being late.

'I came straight from work; I just need a minute to change. You OK?' She always seems so chilled.

'Um, yeah. Actually, no. Helluva day.' I manage a weak smile.

'I hope that numpty Raj isn't the cause? He's a sweetie, really – just a bit of kid in the candy store.'

'God, no – nothing like that. I'm talking the big stuff. Client sacking me, flatmate kicking me out, dissing a TV crew over a live mic and, on top of all that, I think I've been lied to about my dream career progression. That kind of day.' I attempt a carefree shrug.

'Whoa – sounds heavy. Shall we skip this and just go for a drink?' She puts a kindly hand on my arm, concern on her face.

'I dunno, Lauren, my head is so messed up. I don't even know what I want.' I concentrate on my feet, coming over a bit wobbly.

'Right. I'm taking charge. This is only an hour. We do it, you get to lower your stress levels and then, after class, if you want to grab a bite or a drink, I'm all yours.' She slings an arm over my shoulder in a brief hug and it registers that this is just the way I would react with Jess.

'Cheers, Lauren. You're a pal.' And I mean it.

The class is super relaxing and the teacher has a lovely

hypnotic voice. He talked us through breathing patterns and, although I don't get a lot of the talk about side ribs and back chest, it is very soothing. The last part is spent flat on our backs and I drift in a lovely state of semi-consciousness. As we slowly rouse ourselves, I mutter to Lauren, 'Breathing is great. I should do it more often.'

'I know, right? You're a natural.'

She looked so serene and together, I wasn't sure if I wanted to spill my messy life. I'm supposed to be the organised one. We sat in our coats at the juice bar at Planet Organic and I started to explain about Casper, keeping it as unemotional as I can. I even told her about the driving points. It felt good to offload. I trusted her and, when I slowed to a halt, she put both hands on the table, leant in and said, 'Maddy, this guy is a bully. A plain, old-fashioned bully. You shouldn't be scared of him; you've done nothing wrong.' Sounds so simple.

'That may be true, but he has all the cards, Lauren. He's the name; I'm nothing. You don't know what he's like.'

She banged the table and I jumped. Her expression was fierce. 'I know *exactly* what he's like. I had a boss like that. She was a bitch and made me feel useless – questioning everything I did, loading more and more on me so it became impossible to do in the time I had, and then making me feel shit for not being on top of things. They do it because they can, because we let them. They're just people. They fart and snore like everyone else, but I was a mess. Couldn't sleep, worked late into the night and then, one day, something snapped. I walked away and promised myself never again.' She paused, smiled, sat back and continued, 'I started working with Django, got serious about yoga and meditation, and look at me now.' She picked up her juice and slurped the last mouthful.

'Living the dream?' I ventured.

'Life is good,' she shrugged. 'Work-life balance, interesting job, sleeping well. No complaints.'

Put like that it didn't sound unreasonable. Time to stop facilitating everyone else. Right on cue, my phone pinged.

From Dani, 9.26pm:
Babe, I need a speech. Has
Casper agreed??

I hesitate for a second, then reply.

I'm on it. Speak tomorrow.

Raising my juice cup in a toast, I say, 'I hear you. Thanks, Lauren, now I have work to do.' Knocking back the last of my carrot and ginger zinger, I gather my stuff and give her a quick squeeze as I set off home down the hill with a plan – a plan that is giving me a thrill of excitement.

Approaching the house, there's a tall figure leaning against the big gnarly oak tree opposite our door. This is a pretty safe part of town, but I'm a bit shaken from today, so I cross over and loop around from the other side where there is a streetlight. Hold on, I recognise those enormous CDG Play Converse.

'Ed?' I venture as I approach from out of the shadows.

'Maddy. At last. I've been waiting. Guess one of your clients had an emergency?' He's doing jovial familiarity, but it's not working.

'No. I've been at a class. Actually, it's none of your business where I've been. Why are you here?' Having once been desperate to see him, today has just been endless. I haven't got the emotional capacity for anymore and I have an idea to put into action.

'I've been trying to talk to you, but you didn't call me back. Can I come in?'

He starts towards the door and, just like Lauren said, something snaps.

'Ed, I'm shattered and I have stuff to do. Can you just tell me what is so urgent?' I'm desperate to get started on my plan and then have a nice soak in the bath.

He's taken aback. 'Oh. OK, well, it's not the sort of conversation I'd want to have in the street, but the bottom line is: I miss you. I'm an idiot and I'm ready to try again.' He opens his arms for a hug. I admit a hug is tempting, but the way I feel right now, a hug from almost anyone would be tempting.

'What about Mimi? Your romantic getaway? I'm on Instagram, Ed, I saw it all.' No mincing my words.

'Yeah, well, Mimi is all about the Instagram, Mads. Nothing happened. Well, not much, and then she turned psycho, really clingy and needy and, well – not you.'

x

He does his boyish smile and looks out from under his eyelashes. 'You were right, Maddy, it *is* you. I miss you.'

Wow. The words I'd dreamt of hearing, but strangely they aren't doing it for me. I give it a moment to sink in.

Nope. Still nothing. Ed is looking at me expectantly. I have to say something.

'Thing is, Ed, I've got an awful lot to think about. Important stuff and I can't be dealing with this right now.' And that's the truth. Without waiting for a response, I put my key in the door and head in – no looking back.

Funny how things turn out, I muse, as I run a bath. That is pretty much the scenario I had dreamed about, probably without the not-much-with-Mimi bit, but, emotionally, I'm just not feeling it. I chuck in an old goody bag gift of fancy bath oil that claims to be 'invigorating and uplifting' and thank CHAMPS. I decide to use all of it as I am in need of a large dose of both of those qualities, park the whole Ed situation and focus on Dani, because I am going to write her a goddamn cracker of a speech.

Lying in the bath, I let my mind wander and practise a few lines out loud, drying a soapy hand to record voicenotes, but it's not working for me, so reluctantly I leave the heavenly fug, dry myself off and settle down on my bed with my laptop on my knees. This suits me better and I bang out a whole load of witty quippy phrases. Once that's done, I go back over them, striking any that sound similar, or jar in tone, and start to uncover a thread that sounds modest, but with a dry undercut of humour. Play up the Brit angle, allude to her old reputation. Strike that, not the American way, go with fresh start, thank the American theatre world for the opportunity. It's way too long, but I'm on a roll and easier to go back and cut. I was sure of my opening:

'The producers said to keep it short and smart – well, I'm just over five foot, so here we go!'

I'll call L-a in the morning and see if there's a desk at Workspace for me to finesse and then send it off. Glad to have a plan of action, I turn all my devices off, get under the covers and recall the melodious voice of the teacher earlier, counting beats to my inhalations. Almost at once, I drift off.

I feel so refreshed when I wake up a solid eight hours later, I have to remind myself of the horror show of a day I had – but something has shifted. I reckon I was feeling guiltier about the driving points than I was admitting to myself and I think I had some kind of closure with Ed.

From Jess, 9.03am:
Walking Coco first thing. You
around? Jx

That works; it's a nice morning and I'll take my stuff so I can head straight to Workspace if L-a comes through for me. I've got a draft of a speech and I think letting it breath for a bit is just the thing. I dress in an American Vintage clingy, long-sleeved T-shirt with some wide-leg canvas trousers, topped off with massive hoop earrings, and reckon I can fit in wherever the day takes me.

To Jess:
Meet you by the café 9.30 Mx

It's a fresh morning and, marching through Highgate Woods, I notice the bird song. I leave the path to cut through the woods in a direct line to the café and am delighted to be love-bombed by a fluffy toffee-coloured ball, 'Coco, baby!' Bending down to receive a flurry of kisses, Jess is not far behind, hair now bubblegum pink, out of puff but relieved.

'Christ – she just took off. I thought she was doing a runner.'

Once our greetings are done and Coco is diverted by a squirrel, we head to the coffee counter, pick up a couple of flat whites and settle on a bench by the field where we can see Coco dashing around with her regular playmates.

I quickly bring her up to speed with what went on with Casper. She didn't even know I had changed my mind about the points. I'm not sure why, but I leave out the wrist grab.

'I still reckon you'd have gotten away with it, but I get it. Now – listen to this; I checked in with Olive at Top Notch and she said Casper's wired so tight he's going off at everyone. The goodwill has pretty much run out. They keep asking him who he's working with, because there is some improvement, but he still won't tell them. I 'may' have said I knew who it was, but I didn't give her your name. I wanted to check in with you first. Let me hook you up with Olive. She's cool; she knows everyone there. You should talk to her – just give me the go ahead.' Jess makes it sound easy, but even in a dip, Casper is one of their big-name writers. I'm a nobody, who Casper hates.

'He could just deny it all and he certainly won't want me to be involved. What's the point?' I'm voicing my fears.

'The point is you've been doing the bloody work!' She's right. And at this stage, what have I got to lose? I'm not going to overthink this. Any ray of hope is better than none at all.

'OK, Jess, do it. Tell her. And thanks for having my back. I have to get something over to Dani, so I am going to love you...' I lean over to give her a peck on the cheek, 'and leave you. But keep me posted. And by the way, Coco needs a groom. Don't let Bridget book her into Pets at Home. She came back looking like a cockapoo convict.' I can't help myself. I rush off, equal measure excited and anxious, but I've already had Casper's worst once this week and I'm still standing. Time to stop running scared.

L-a offered me a spot that works out exactly right for New York, timings-wise. The girl on reception is expecting me and I get straight down to it. The change of scenery and hit of adrenalin has done me good. I get a few strange looks as I whisper my speech out loud while timing it, pausing for laughter (please god) and making changes on the screen as I go. It was only allowed to be ninety seconds and I was determined to make every second count.

At 12.53pm, I composed an email to Dani. I hinted that Casper had been involved, then thought why the hell should I? I deleted that bit and wrote the truth: Casper wouldn't do it, but I'd been working with him as a writing assistant (which is true) and put something together for her, which I hoped she liked but she was free to reject. Nerves were about to set in as I re-read it for the fifth time, when L-a came in – looking for me, I guess – so, without further ado, I hit send. Scream!

Chapter 32

L-a invited me to join her for a bite and, frankly, it would have been rude not to. I keep wondering if Jess has made the call to Olive and what that might set in motion, so lunch was an excellent diversion and we had a good chat over delicious eggs benedict. She said the CHAMPS do had given them some leads, but also been a lot of hassle. What did I think about doing something in the next couple of weeks on a smaller, more targeted scale?

'Sounds like a good idea, but it would be hard for CHAMPS to arrange something like that. There are members who just turn up for free drinks and a goody bag.' I'm thinking of Caroline and her cronies, the all-talk-and-no-action brigade.

'Well, that's why I was keen to catch up with you, Maddy. You seem to know the assistants to the more creative types, and that's who we want to be associated with. How about you pull together a small group, I lay on a sit-down lunch rather than just drinks, and invite some of our marketing people? No hard sell, I promise; just like minds seeing if they can help each other out.' L-a looks at me expectantly. It's an interesting proposition and nice to be asked.

'Well, I'm real friends with Steve's new assistant, Jess, and there's Lauren – who looks after Django, the photographer.' She's nodding thoughtfully. 'Sounds cool. If you each brought one or two more suitable sorts, we'd have half a dozen, which sounds like a good number to me.'

I'm starting to see her vision. 'Jess knows an assistant at Top Notch Productions – she's not in CHAMPS—'

'Perfect,' L-a interrupts. 'I'd love an intro to someone over there. Let's do diaries and make this happen.' This could be a fun thing to do and, more importantly, gives me a good excuse to get in touch with Olive directly, just in case she doesn't get the full story from Jess, who does tend to go for drama over substance.

We put in a couple of potential dates and she swishes off in a rustle of Miyake style pleats, leaving me with a delicious fresh mint tea. Nice as all this is, my real problems haven't gone away. I need to plan my next moves. I should check the CHAMPS message board for jobs to replace my Steve and Casper hours in the short term.

Email from Dani – that was worryingly quick. Deep breath, then open.

'Babe!! I LOVE it!!!! It sounds just like me – but a cleverer funnier

me. Who needs Casper? Fingers
crossed for the win! I *really* want
to give this speech. You've got it
babe xxxxxx'
P.S. Can you get my Cartier watch
fixed. It's in my bedside drawer.

My mouth does something it hasn't done for a while. A
big, genuine smile. What a relief. I'd been so anxious about
her reaction. I quickly type my reply:

EVERYTHING crossed. I'll
be watching. You deserve this.
Mx

We both do, I reckon. Win or not, I did this all by myself.
Casper was nowhere near it and full credit to Dani, who
was prepared to take a risk and run with it, even though it
could backfire. She's happy to give my speech in front of
all those VIPs, as well as the press. Even if nothing more
comes of it, this has done wonders for my confidence.

P.S. I'll sort the watch

Keeping my feet firmly on the ground. I send emails to
Lauren and Jess explaining L-a's idea, adding it would be a
good excuse for us to have a fun get-together, and suggest
inviting Olive. Feeling quite productive, I pack up my stuff
and head off.

My route takes me past Ed's office and that's the direct route, not me making a detour. I cringe when I remember lurking outside trying to accidentally-on-purpose bump into him. Looking back, I can see that I was possibly a bit intense, trying to pretend everything was cool by overlooking the signs that it wasn't. I just wanted it to work out so badly. I decide to take the long way round, because the last thing I want right now is to bump into him.

Last night was a weird one. I got no satisfaction being proved right about him missing me once I was gone, and there's no coming back from the fact that he had to go off with someone else to realise what a good thing we had. But it's given me space to really think about things and about my priorities. Being around Ella and Drippy Tom has been quite instructive. No game playing, mutual support, total honesty but also respectful of each other's work. I think I must be maturing because, in the cold light of day, these traits seem more attractive than boyish good looks and a killer leather jacket. I was putting up and shutting up with a lot where he was concerned: trying to second-guess what he was thinking and making excuses for his laid-back approach to communicating. I'm pretty damn sure he wasn't spending ages composing light-hearted texts to hide the yearning for attention and loitering near my office in the hope of an 'accidental' meeting. He says he wants to give things another go, but what's changed? Me.

Even though things are pretty shit overall, having taken some ownership of my life over the last twenty-four hours has felt really bloody good. And not just Ed, it's my work, too. I've been drifting, for longer than I care to work out. I do get a buzz from achieving what my clients ask of me, but when did I give up on following my dream? Writing a speech for Dani is certainly more rewarding than getting her watch fixed and even working with the TV crew basically boiled down to shooing people out of the flower beds.

My life may be a mess right now, but I can't rely on anyone else to sort things out for me. Isn't sorting lives out what I'm supposed to be good at?

At Dani's, I head to her bedroom to rescue her watch. The contents of her bedside drawer make me blush; let's just say Casper's comedy gift won't have been her first encounter with a vibrator. Using a tissue to have a rummage around, I locate her Cartier Tank. She bought it for herself when she signed a deal with Channel 4 years ago. Honestly, if I'd paid that much for a watch, it wouldn't be squashed in among sex toys, but whatever. Gingerly removing it, I drop it in a little suede pouch on her dressing table and stash it in the inside pocket of my bag. Going on the tube approaching rush hour, I'm not taking any chances.

Cartier is quiet and, after a quick check, they said all it needed was a new battery and a clean (too right) and I could wait. I settled in to one of the comfy padded velvet bucket seats, took a photo of a beautiful display of diamond rings and Instagrammed it. Upping my social media game wouldn't do me any harm. I scan the US entertainment pages to see what they are saying about the awards; it seems Dani is favourite to win and there is much speculation about who will be wearing what. I reply to some queries from Jess about stuff Steve (Bridget, really) is wanting and I can't help but ask how Caroline is getting on. Apparently, she had gone very quiet since her grand entrance and Steve is starting to have his doubts.

The very smart young woman at the counter gestures for me to come over; the watch is all sorted and ready to go. I zip it back in my bag and set off to brave the crowds. Feeling pretty knackered, I head home.

Letting myself in and shedding my jacket, I go straight for the kettle and it isn't until I have a brew in hand that I sit down at the kitchen table and look at my phone. *What the hell?* Why is a photo of a shop display case proving so damn popular? Reading the comments makes no sense.

'Amazing news!'

'Congrats to my favourite presenter!'

'Who's the lucky guy????'

'Jealous!'

'How did I miss this? Love you!'

Brow furrowed, I keep scrolling back – I don't even have that many followers, but my post is being tagged and reposted with added comments. It is something to do with Dani.

'Shall I buy a hat?'

'Please get hitched in the UK, Dani!'

Dani is getting *married*? This is crazy; there's no way I wouldn't know if she was serious about someone. Had

I missed clues over the weeks she'd been away? Been too wrapped up in my own emotional turmoil? She'd have said something when she was here, wouldn't she? Unless she was being sensitive about my break-up. Unlikely.

I check her account, the private one, but all it shows are pictures of her posing by posters of the show, and nothing new on her public one either, though that was run professionally.

And then I twig. Some of Dani's superfans follow me. Sometimes I get tagged in her posts and people will chase any connection with their idol. My innocent photo from Cartier had led one of them to deduce I was in there collecting an engagement ring. It had all blown up in the space of less than an hour, but it wasn't showing any signs of stopping. The likes and comments are rolling in faster and faster. *Shit*. What to do? Delete? Post a denial? Ignore? While my mind and belly flip-flop, my phone rings. It is Stephanie, Dani's scary agent.

I answer with a strangulated sound.

'I've had the tabloids on about a surprise engagement. Surprised me alright. What the fuck is going on, Maddy?'

Chapter 33

After a rather tetchy call, Stephanie said to leave it with her – a reputation management lawyer owed her a favour. We agreed I should give Dani a head's up in case the press hassled her. I felt the need to grovel, although I'm not sure I did anything wrong. I seem to spend a lot of time feeling guilty for things that are in no way my fault.

I decide direct is the best approach, so I phone Dani and catch her at lunch. Fortunately, she finds it hilarious and says she wishes someone *was* buying her a Cartier engagement ring. All she wants to talk about are the awards; there are only a few days to go and given the amount of good luck muffin baskets she is receiving, she is quietly confident. She asks if she can change a line in the speech. We run through it and she is right, it sounds more like her.

'You're so cool about this. Casper wouldn't let me change a single precious syllable. He helped me for the

National Television Awards and had a total meltdown when I added three words. That's why I was nervous to ask him again, but win or not, Maddy, I won't be asking him in the future. Now, who do you think I should wear?'

She tells me her mum and sister are coming over, which reminds me to alert my mum. She'll love all the inside info. Maybe it would be nice to go and watch round there. Imagine hearing Dani saying my lines. Mum would bust a gut.

It is impossible not to get swept up in Dani's bubbly enthusiasm. I miss having her around. There is never a dull moment and, although there is a lot of drudgery, she sometimes takes me to openings and awards ceremonies as her plus one. Another client like her would be ideal, because with my housing situation being so precarious, I need to be able to make rent.

Changing out of my work clothes and into my leopard print onesie, I allow myself a little reverie about not needing to find a new client because Top Notch called and said Casper had had a nervous breakdown and I was the only one who could help him recover. I picture Casper lying in his super-king deluxe bed under his 500-thread count sheets, looking wan and saying, 'Maddy, please forgive me...' Catching sight of myself in the mirror in my onesie, with my fluffy paw slippers and my hair sticking out all over the place, brings home how unlikely this is, but optimism is all I have right now.

Hearing Ella's key in the door, I stay in my room in case Drippy Tom is with her. I don't think he's ready for my current look. Jess sent Olive's details, so I compose an email introducing myself, mentioning Casper as if Jess hasn't been updating me regularly on their conversations, and explain about Workspace and L-a's idea. On the verge of getting rambly, I include my phone number, the proposed dates and hope she can make it. Job done. I send it off and wander into the kitchen to touch base with Ella.

She's horrified when I tell her how it went down with Casper and offers to look into unfair dismissal, but with the points thing it's too complicated and – honestly? – I just want to move on. She acknowledges that I've lost two clients and says not to worry about rent, which leads me to ask about Drippy Tom moving in. She says they are prioritising their partnership applications for now and realise it will take some time and effort to get his place ready to rent out, so that takes the pressure off for a bit. She looks knackered, so I make us some beans on toast with Marmite and cheese – just how we like it. She's got work to do and I head back to my room, planning to watch some serious catch-up telly. There's a missed call from a number I don't know. And a voicemail.

'Hi, Maddy, this is Olive. It's not exactly about the lunch, which sounds great, but please give me a call as soon as you get this. Whenever.' She sounds eager.

I could sit and puzzle what this is about or I could just call.

'Olive, hello. This is Maddy Sparks.'

'Maddy the mysterious – at last. We need to talk,' and with that, she launches straight in. Seems my daydream about Casper wasn't a million miles from the truth. He is completely losing the plot and throwing tantrums at anyone and everyone. There has been a crisis meeting and the executive producers have decided to put a writers' room together. There is serious time pressure and Olive told them she had a pretty good idea of who had been working with Casper. They are interested in talking to me. She thinks there might even be a possibility of coming on board, but no promises.

I can hardly make sense of what I am hearing. My heart is galloping – then reality bites me on the bum.

'Olive, I would *love* to be involved, of course I would, but without going into too many details, Casper and I had a massive falling out. Not only do I no longer work for him, but I can't imagine him letting me anywhere near this.' And that is an understatement. I remember the look on his face as he gripped my wris. At that moment, I hated Casper with every fibre in my body.

Fortunately, Olive is undeterred. 'Maddy, it's out of his hands, but if you want it, it's up to us to make it happen. Can you give me something to take to the bosses? We don't have much time.' She is loving being in the thick of it all and sounds almost as excited as I feel.

'I've got the scripts we worked on together, with my mark-ups. Some were just verbal, but I remember the conversations. I could talk them through?' *Sod Casper.* I was already sacked; what more could he do? And I clearly recollect all the suggestions I've made.

'Perfect! I'm going to try and get you in front of the

exec or the script editor. Think about your pitch and stop worrying about Casper.' She sounds pretty confident.

'Thanks, Olive, I really appreciate this.' She is throwing me a potential lifeline.

'Jess says you helped her out massively, that you're one of the good guys. I'll be in touch tomorrow.'

I need a moment to process what has just happened, then hug myself and let out a squeal. In the moment, I love Olive – and God bless Jess for gossiping!

'Maddy...?' Ella was tapping on my door. 'You OK in there?' She pokes her head round, looking anxious. Poor girl has had to put up with so much drama because of me recently.

'I'm fine – better than fine, I'm great!' She looks a bit confused, but I don't want to jinx it. 'Just a bit of interesting work news.' Satisfied with that, she is gone.

Instead of working myself up into a frenzy of nerves, I go and get my Casper bag – untouched since that awful morning – and sure enough, there are the scripts with my notes on. I write a list of page references and attach one to each cover. I watch back episodes we had talked through and make a document detailing my input. I'm sure what Olive meant by a pitch, so I make notes along the lines of the conversations I'd had with Casper; how he hadn't developed some of the characters – especially the women – and how the comedy set-ups had become formulaic. Finally, I make a couple of quite radical suggestions for future developments. Casper would hate them. Good.

Now, final decision before getting a good night's sleep.

What to wear? Not formal, but not too casual. Serious but also creative. My fashion rule when I'm not sure what to wear but want to make an impression is to go vintage. And I know just the outfit – a Jaeger suit rescued from Mum's wardrobe. She hates when I call it vintage, but it had been lurking in there for decades. I'll wear it with a boat neck T-shirt and boots. Sorted. I'll be ready for whenever Olive gives me the call.

She is true to her word and by the time she phones, I am showered, dressed, packed and ready to go. They can't see me until the afternoon, but Olive suggests meeting for lunch to give me the low-down. We agree on a café near Long Acre that will offer some privacy but will also be near her office.

I need to keep busy so set about firming up the details for the networking lunch. Lauren is going to bring a stylist she worked with and Jess wants to use the invite to get closer to a model booker she has crossed paths with. L-a seems happy with the cast of characters and we set the date. I got the pick-ups organised for the dame's documentary crew. She doesn't seem fussed if I am there or not, so that is a relief. I check in with Lauren about setting up a shoot with Dani; the award rumours had made Django even keener. I have a feeling that if she won, her schedule will go crazy, so I make sure to loop Stephanie in.

Finally, I suggest to Mum that I come round to watch the awards with her if she's prepared to stay up late enough.

A whirlwind of efficiency and it is still only eleven. I have ants in my pants so decide to set off and walk the last few stops. A final check of the contents of my bag – *not* my Casper bag, but a serious-looking leather messenger bag I'd borrowed from Ella. I check my face, hair and the back of my trousers for toilet paper (a recurring nightmare), then pocket my lipstick and, feeling good, set off.

Striding through Bloomsbury, I try not to be over-whelmed by the enormity of what might be about to happen. What did my Granny Heather used to say? Expect the worst but hope for the best. Maybe Olive is all talk and no action; maybe Casper can veto any involvement from me; maybe the producers just want to pump me for info and then move on. I'm so lost in these thoughts it takes a moment to register someone shouting my name. Breaking my stride, I look around, confused, and spot a man lolloping across the very busy road. As he approaches, I recognise Drippy Tom's pal, Dominic. He's fast approaching.

'Hey, Maddy, you're a very brisk walker.' He's a bit flushed and out of puff.

'I'm on my way to a meeting. This is a weird coincidence.' He looks quite smart, in a cool English teacher kind of way.

'Not really, I teach at Kings,' he gestures to a building a block or so up. We stand a bit awkwardly for a minute.

'I'm seeing someone about a writing job,' I offer 'At least I hope that's what I'm doing.' I remember how engaged he was when we chatted at the picnic.

'That's fantastic news!' He looks really chuffed. 'At least I hope it is,' he teases.

'It's a bit complicated to explain, but cross your fingers for me.' It's nice to share my excitement with someone. He holds up both hands, fingers crossed. 'If I'm investing this much, you have to let me know how it goes. I'm guessing you're seeing them somewhere round here?'

'Wow – you really *are* clever!' It's possible he's blushing or he might still be pink from the lolloping, but then he looks at me seriously and says, 'Let me know how it goes. We could celebrate or commiserate. I'd better get on, the undergraduates will be getting restless.' He sets off back across the road.

'I don't have your number...' I call after him.

'I've got yours,' he shouts back over his shoulder. 'I'll drop call.'

He waves as he heads off and I see his fingers are still crossed. Cute. I didn't remember him as cute. Maybe he has new glasses.How come he has my number? Never mind that now, Olive awaits.

Chapter 34

I knew who Olive was the second I walked in. Her jet-black hair was in a messy pile on top of her head with a heavy fringe almost obscuring dark, lively eyes. Wearing a baggy, washed-out band T-shirt tucked into a dark denim skirt, there was a large canvas promotional bag full of stuff threatening to spill by her feet. One phone face down on the table, she was two thumbing at the speed of light on another. I took a moment to gather my guts, keen to make a good impression, before heading to her table with a broad smile.

'Hi, Olive...?' I offered tentatively, in case I had it wrong, but, before I knew it, she had grabbed me for a double kiss.

'Maddy, hey! I feel like I know you already. Jess talks about you all the time. Wow – your upper arms are so buff. Want a coffee? Or straight onto food?' She was going a mile a minute and I felt completely at ease with her, but – note to self – treat this as a pre-interview.

I slid into the other chair and looked at the menu, but without further ado Olive leant over the table and, in a conspiratorial voice, said, 'Casper! What the fuck? He's gone batshit crazy these last few days.'

I had a flashback to our last conversation, but was not about to share that with someone Jess said could take gossiping to Olympic level.

'We haven't spoken in the last couple of days.' I'll leave it at that, but Olive isn't having it. 'Why aren't you working for him anymore? Did you quit 'cos he's such an arsehole?'

I'd prepared an answer for this as I knew it would come up. 'We had a difference of opinion and I decided to stand my ground.' Again, keep it simple and keep it classy.

'Come on, Maddy. You were his PA for ages, then Jess told me you started helping with his writing, then – kaboom!' She smacks both hands together, causing the people at the next table to stop and stare. 'World War Three.' She's fixed me in her sights and isn't giving up easily.

'The writing started by accident, but I loved it and it seemed to be working out. He offered to pay me for extra time, but I wanted to be acknowledged and he wouldn't do it.' It sounded convincing when I planned it and, despite everything, I didn't want to badmouth him to Olive. People can be in and out of favour very quickly in TV land.

'For that he fired you outright? There's more to this, Maddy. I know there is, go on. You can tell me – I'm the soul of discretion.' Hmm. I do want her on side; it's clear I have to offer something more, so I tread very carefully.

'OK, but this is just between us.' No pun intended.

She leans in with a satisfied expression and makes a zipping-her-lips motion, so I go on. 'Casper asked me to do something else for him, as his PA, and it was something I wasn't comfortable with. I did my best to reason with him, but he wouldn't let it go. He was under pressure, as you know, and he lashed out. That's it.' She's looking thoughtful and not fully convinced, so before she comes back with round two, I deflect her, 'Who am I meeting at Top Notch? How can I impress them? Olive – I can't tell you how much I want this, no – *need* this.'

That does the trick and she attempts a potted explanation of the hierarchy at Top Notch and runs through the main players, telling me indiscreet stories about who was seen coming out of who's hotel room at MIPTV Festival and who fiddles their expenses. I try to keep track and get her to tell me more about who I'll be meeting. She says it will be Sophie, the executive producer – super smart, doesn't suffer fools gladly, but tells it like it is – and Jo, the lead writer, who is quiet, but doesn't miss a trick. She explains they are under a tonne of pressure to improve ratings, but also resisting attempts by the American parent company to send over some of their writers. The show has such a British sensibility and that's a big part of its appeal, even in the US, plus they don't want to be seen as failing to turn it around. Things had started to improve, but ideally they want Casper out of the way as he's being so obstructive. All eyes are on them and you're only as good as your last hit.

The reality of my situation sinks in, from a fantasy to the chance to make my dreams reality. I'll never get an opportunity like this again and, as my lunch is placed before me, a wave of nerves hits. I can't eat the mushroom risotto that sounded so delicious. Trying a forkful, the texture of the porcini on my tongue turns my stomach. Olive is chattering away about looking forward to meeting Lauren and the others at the Workspace lunch, but I'm spinning out. Leaning back in my chair, as far away from the glutinous risotto as I can, I take sips of my water and concentrate on what Olive is saying, about wishing she could be in CHAMPS, how awful the Carolines sound, but she slows to a halt when she realises I haven't touched my food or said a word.

She leans over the table and takes both my hands.

'Maddy, you've got this. You're holding all the cards – insight and a track record. They were super interested when I told them you were bringing in marked-up scripts.'

I stare back at her; the closer we get to my appointment, the less confident I feel. Olive can tell I'm still panicked.

'Come with me.' She tugs my sleeve and we head to the ladies. 'OK, I'm going to show you something and you have to do it with me, and then do it just before you go in. Right?'

I'm worried she's going to offer me an illegal pick-me-up – I know all about these TV industry types – but instead she puts her hands on her hips, feet apart and thrusts her chin up. 'Copy me. It's called Wonder Woman pose.'

At a loss for a good reason not to, I do as she says and she babbles on, 'It's a proven science thing. I watched a TED talk. It does something to your cortisone. Or testosterone, or both! Come on, we hold it for two minutes.' She's relentless and so we stand there in the loo until I get the giggles and then she does.

'Thanks, Olive, I do feel better, but I need a minute to clear my head and go over my points. I'll see you in there.' She high-fives me and heads out to ask the waiter to bag up my risotto. 'Waste not, want not,' she says as we head out in opposite directions.

✳

From Mum:
Sounds super! I'll have a nap
and then make dinner. Love
Mum xxx

If she only knew what was going on. Maybe I'll tell her, depending on how this meeting goes. Perhaps she'll be genuinely proud of my achievements rather than just blinded by stardust. Looking back, it would be fair to say Mum always supported me in my creative endeavours. It was me who was prepared to walk away at the first whiff of failure. Well, not anymore.

I present myself at reception as ready as I'll ever be. As I'm led through the open-plan offices, I catch sight of Olive giving me a double thumbs up and smile gratefully back. Thanks to her, I've got some idea of what to expect.

Both women rise to greet me and it's immediately obvious who is who. I make self-assured eye contact with them both and, pleasantries over, we sit.

Sophie, dressed in a sharp navy jacket and incredibly well-cut trousers, opens, 'Maddy, this is a little awkward as we've been informed you were assisting Casper. I'll be frank; he denies it completely, but we're having some trust issues with him right now, so thought it best to hear it straight from the horse's mouth, as it were.' She looks at me very directly and I decide – on the spot – no bullshit, no waffle. I briefly explain how it unfolded, leaving out the driving points and present the marked-up scripts. They each take one and I sit quietly as they go through them. They swap, then there's the third and, although the silence is disconcerting, I bite my tongue.

While Jo is looking at the third script, I suggest talking through the other points with Sophie.

'We get the picture. I think we're good for now.' Her tone isn't giving anything away.

Feeling it slipping away from me, I blurt out, 'He said he'd told you. He promised,' hating the note of desperation in my voice.

They share a look. Again, I have no idea what message is passing between them.

'I have a question for you, Maddy,' Jo says. She's softly spoken and has auburn curls framing her face. 'Have you any thoughts for moving *Just Between Us* forward?'

I weigh this up – she may mean little tweaks or maybe this is the moment to be bold.

'I've got a couple of ideas that may seem pretty out there...' I pause for a reaction, but she just looks at me impassively. I outline one of the points in my pitch, which they haven't read yet, about disrupting the dynamic and trusting the fans to come along – maybe attracting new ones with some controversy. 'I think we need to lose at least one, maybe two, of the key characters. This could open up so many new possibilities.'

Liza is nodding thoughtfully. 'And any ideas of how you would go about that?'

I reckon this is make or break and offer up my big idea, how Grace – one of the senior designers at the agency – offers to mentor Edie, taking more and more interest in her career. As they become closer, Edie's feelings deepen and confuse her. She tries to talk to Jake about it, but he feels threatened and angry, and demands she finds a different mentor. I suggest it would take a while to develop, but, ultimately, they start a relationship and Jake, feeling humiliated, leaves the agency altogether.

As I wind up, I present them with a hard copy of my pitch. There's an uncomfortable silence, which I'm screaming inside to fill with pleas and promises, but manage to hold my nerve. Sophie stands up and reaches out to shake my hand. I start to gather my papers up.

'Could you leave those with us, Maddy.' It's not a question. I get a bad feeling; are they going to use these against me somehow, or Casper? Were we breaching some contractual agreement? I look up at them, both standing now, but their faces are giving nothing away.

'So, um, if there's anything else you need from me...' I trail off into the silence. Nothing for it, but to take Sophie's outstretched hand. I can't resist a final attempt. 'Can I just say that my experience with Casper has made me realise that writing is what I want to be doing. I know I've got a tonne to learn, but I'll work so hard, put in all the hours, because, honestly, this is it for me. It's taken me a while, but now I know what I want to be when I grow up.' I smile and shrug. That wasn't part of my plan, but I have to make them understand, because in these last few weeks I've discovered my passion and I may never get a chance like this again.

Sophie raises her eyebrows. 'Right. Well, if that's it, we were due on a conference call two minutes ago. Thank you, Maddy, and good to meet you. You've certainly given us food for thought.'

Chapter 35

Glancing around the busy office, no one is interested in me. I'd hoped to spot Olive, a friendly face, but there's no sign of her. With an overwhelming sense of anti-climax, I wait for the lift, lost in thought. Looking up as the doors open, I'm face to face with Casper. I gasp, but quickly recover. Even though I have every right to be here, it doesn't stop my heart pounding.

He looks furious. I can't be sure if he already looked like that or if it was a result of seeing me. I flinch as he steps out of the lift and manage to dive in. He turns and opens his mouth to say something, but with perfect timing the lift doors close. I lean against the mirrored back wall, rubbing my wrist where he grabbed me, adrenaline pumping. Thank God I didn't see him on my way in, because even actual Wonder Woman wouldn't have given me the nerve to make any sense after that encounter.

My thoughts were racing between what Casper thought

I was doing there, reliving the fear I had felt the last time I saw him, going over what happened with Sophie and Jo, and I just couldn't settle on any decisive interpretations. I came to the philosophical conclusion that it was now out of my hands. Casper can say what he likes, but at least I've had a chance to give my side. As for a result, I'm not sure what I expected, but I know what I'd hoped. An on-the-spot offer of a job. A girl can dream.

Leaving the building, the fresh air is cleansing. I'm away from that toxic man and resolve to stop worrying about what Casper thinks or does. According to him, Top Notch knew all about me anyway. He never admitted that he was lying to me. Me and my network of lowly assistants worked it out between us and even managed to get me in front of the top execs. Casper underestimated me. Never underestimate the power of an assistant.

True to his word, Dominic has texted. He's finishing up at work and I'm too buzzy to want to go home, so we arrange to meet nearby.

The steamed-up café is full of what I assume to be students. Feeling ancient, I navigate my way round the book bags on the floor and make for the only empty table. A small group next to me are, heads together, in serious discussion and I overhear the word 'existentialism', so decide not to interrupt to ask if they'd watch my stuff. I make the bold decision to order two large lattes, which the very young guy on the counter says he will bring them over. Seeing such fresh young faces makes me realise how far I have come.

As I sit and wait for the coffee and Dominic, I keep going over what just happened and checking my phone for a heads up from Olive, but nothing. My gut feeling is that it didn't go badly, unless they thought my ideas were ridiculous, but they didn't show any signs that I could read. They hadn't even said when or how I might hear from them, and, of course, there is still the large Casper-shaped obstacle to factor in. Unable to resist any longer:

To Olive, 3.55pm:
Let me know if you hear
ANYTHING. Maddy x

I see Dominic arrive, stopping just inside the door to wipe the steam off his specs. My pulse speeds up a little, which catches me by surprise, which makes me blush, so by the time he spots me I'm a bit flustered and do a weird half standing-up thing while waving. Not cool. He gives a wave back and points to the counter. I shake my head and point at the other chair. He smiles and heads over, not noticing the students noticing him. He leans down to kiss my cheek hello, which I wasn't expecting, I was turning to say hi, so he catches a spot at the very edge of my lips. We laugh awkwardly and he eases into the chair.

'Well?' he says, holding up a hand with fingers still crossed. 'It was bloody difficult operating my clicker like this. How'd it go?'

I pull a grimace face, then realise it's not a good look, so stop and shrug. 'I really don't know; it wasn't bad exactly, but they didn't give me any feedback and then I bumped into my old boss, who fired me and hates me, and I couldn't find the friend of a friend who knows what's going on—'

He interrupts, holding both hands up: 'This is way more complicated than I was expecting. You're going to have to give me some context.'

The coffees arrive and I end up telling him everything. He nods and listens and asks the occasional question – or 'point of clarification' as he calls it. When I get to the driving points, I feel ashamed I was going to go through with it, but relieved I made the right decision. Scrutinising his face, it doesn't look like he's judging me. At last, I get to the present moment, notice he's finished his coffee, realise mine is cold, and then just as he leans forward to give his opinion, my phone, which is on the table next to me, starts to vibrate. 'It's Olive.' I hold it up to show him and we both pull the same cartoon panic face.

'Answer it,' he says. I nod, compose myself, and do.

I've barely managed 'Hello' and Olive is off, in a stage whisper, 'Oh my God, Maddy. It's all kicking off! I'm calling from the loos. Everyone has been in and out of hush-hush meetings all day. I wanted to see you after, but I got called away. Casper came in for a US conference call, but Sophie took him in to her office and I couldn't hear, but I could see her showing him some papers – I think the ones you brought in. I was trying to lip-read, but he came bursting out, slammed her door and left the building without taking the call. Then, all the execs went upstairs and none of us knew what was going on, but you could cut the atmosphere with a knife.' She finally takes a breath.

'That sounds intense, but do you have any idea about *my* meeting, Olive?' Dominic is watching me intently, which helps me stay calm. 'Did you get any feedback from Sophie or Jo?'

'Shit – I've got to go. Someone's come in,' and she's gone.

'I'm none the wiser,' I tell Dom, 'but it does all sound extremely dramatic. Slamming doors, whispering in toilet cubicles – you know the kind of thing.'

'I so don't,' he replies. 'It doesn't really go down like that in academia, but, I tell you what, I am fully invested in this, Maddy. I won't be able to sleep until I know the outcome.' He's smiling.

We chat about this and that and I find myself telling him about Dani and the speech. He's the first person I've told and he thinks it's brave and brilliant. That's not something anyone has said about me in a very long time and it feels fantastic. I'd much rather be perceived as brave and brilliant than steady and reliable. That's not to say there isn't a place for steady and reliable, but it's not exciting or challenging.

'Well, I'd best be heading home to mark essays. I wish I could make that sound more glamorous, but that's the way it is.' He pats the laptop bag he's just pulled onto his lap. 'If I get them all done without pulling my hair out, there may be a takeaway involved.'

'Well, I'd swap the word glamorous for stressful if you're

making comparisons with my life. Thank you for listening – next time, I promise to ask all about you.' Chatting with him comes so naturally, I hadn't noticed how time has passed and fully taken my mind off my troubles.

'Next time sounds promising. In the meantime, I'll keep these crossed for Dani and that's not a sentence I ever thought I'd hear myself say.'

We gather up our belongings and head for the door. Once outside, we stand facing each other, a bit self-consciously.

'I really hope it all works out well for you,' he says. This time when he leans in to kiss my cheek goodbye, it lands perfectly.

I catch a whiff of Jo Malone's Lime, Basil and Mandarin, one of my favourites, which sends me off to the tube with a spring in my step.

Chapter 36

I swear every minute of the next day feels like an hour. I do my best to keep busy, but the longer I don't hear anything, the less confident I feel. I have to come to terms with the fact that if things don't work out with Top Notch, I will have to have a major life rethink.

I've decided to stop looking for more clients. It's been a mostly fun ride and I've certainly learnt a lot, but now I am going to follow my dream. I will find a way to make it work. I can live off baked beans and eke out the money from Casper. Even if I have to swallow my pride and ask Mum and Dad if I can move home, I'll do it and I won't care what they, or my sister or anyone else thinks. My course at the City Lit starts soon and I will work my butt off to be top of the class.

A call just after lunch shakes things up. Casper. I don't answer. Just seeing his name on the screen makes me anxious. He leaves a message and I anticipate a blast of vitriol. This will be good practice for my new tough persona. Not wanting the sanctuary of my bedroom tainted by him, I pop my headphones in and take a walk.

'Well, it seems I've lost my instant access to you.' He sounds different. 'Seeing you at the office made me think. It's a shame we aren't working together anymore.' That's a polite way of referring to him telling me to fuck right off. 'You were a good assistant, kept me in check and, unlike most of your generation, had a sense of humour.' To be fair, we did used to have a laugh and I quite enjoyed his acid tongue.

'Fact is, things here are starting to slide. I could do with a safe pair of hands. I know you're ambitious, I get it, and I could help you. I *will* help you, but I was under a shitload of pressure, and you just kept pushing and pushing.' There's a pause and I wonder where this is going, because that's not how I remember it going down. My pace quickens as my hackles rise. I'm practically power walking though the Broadway.

'I fucking hate leaving messages,' he goes on. 'Forget about the car stuff. Come back. We can discuss terms. I'm sure we can work something out, but I need an answer. Today. There's shit going down and I want you on my side.'

Well. Exhaling the breath I didn't realise I was holding, this was most unexpected. Funny how things go – first Steve and now Casper realising they were onto a good thing once they'd blown it. And while I'm at it, add Ed to that list. I'm on a 'Go Sister' roll, because, if nothing else, these last few weeks have shown me that sitting around feeling taken advantage of doesn't get you anywhere. I mistakenly believed that keeping my head down and working hard would lead to success, when in reality I was just helping everyone around me achieve their aims. When did I decide to use 'Put up and shut up' as my mantra? Well, not anymore, this sister is going to start doing it for herself.

✦

Mum opens the front door as I am raising my hand to do my signature knock.

'I was looking out for you – it's so exciting. There's nothing on the telly yet, so let's have supper and then we can settle ourselves in in good time. I don't want to miss the red-carpet interviews.'

I don't have to say a thing – she's chattering on and I'm happy to let her. It's rather sweet. I always wondered who watched those inane interviews on the way into ceremonies – turns out it's my mum. I half listen as she's telling a long story about Elijah being top of his class. He's only in kindergarten for heaven's sake. I surreptitiously text Dani:

**Everything crossed – watching
on telly x**

I don't expect a reply; she'll be being primped and preened and squeezed into something fabulous, but she'll see her phone at some point and know that I'm thinking of her.

Mum's filled the kitchen with steam as she frantically shakes her wok around.

'Is Dad eating with us?' I wonder aloud as I open the window to avoid the smoke alarm going off.

'Oh no – girls' night tonight. He's off at Tai Chi and then having a drink with Simon.' She's getting chopsticks out of the drawer, the free wooden ones that come with takeaways. 'I'm glad I saved these – your father never uses them.'

We settle ourselves at the table and douse the plates with soy sauce. Mum hops up again, 'I'm going to open the cava now, with dinner, and then, if Dani wins, we can have another glass to toast.' She's thought it all through and we happily clink glasses.

'Since when has Dad started going for a drink of an evening?' It's hard to picture.

'Since I told him not to interrupt us watching our programme. He'd only spoil it by talking and he doesn't care a bit about the frocks.' If I ever wonder where I get my love of clothes...

Half an hour later, we are tucked up on the sofa with huge bowls of ice cream and popcorn. Mum won't buy 'fancy' ice cream like Häagen-Dazs, but she's pushed the boat out with a Mint Viennetta. I can revert to childhood and forget all my worries.

The coverage is starting, so we settle in to praise and criticise and we grab each other's hands when Dani arrives. She looks spectacular, glamorous and, I have to say, really classy. She's wearing Stella McCartney, flying the British flag, and some fabulous Tiffany diamonds. Her hair is a much softer blond, lots of honey tones, and her make-up is subtle – she's ditched the signature red lips for a more sophisticated look. She is grinning from ear to ear and making the most of her entrance, waving, posing for selfies and being charming and polite.

'She looks gorgeous,' Mum coos.

'Doesn't she?' I reply with a pang. 'And so happy. I miss her.' It's different with Dani; we're not exactly friends, but definitely friendly.

'Do you wish you were there?' Mum asks, sympathetically.

'Are you joking? I'd be having a nightmare worrying about cars and schedules and those bloody diamonds, carrying everything from phone chargers to safety pins, but not having the one emergency item she'll need, plus I probably wouldn't have slept for days. I'm much happier here with you and my Viennetta.' And I mean it. Mum squeezes my hand and I nearly tell her about the maybe job interview, but then Meryl Streep arrives and we are hooked.

Awards shows go on and on, but we get to see tasters of a few Broadway numbers and, just when it was starting to drag, they announce the nominations for Best Featured Actress in a Play. The camera swoops over the nominees sitting in the audience and I can see Dani gripping her American agent's hand tightly, seated at the end of a row – which is promising. She is smiling, but I can detect the tension in her jaw.

'Come on, come on,' I mutter through clenched teeth as we sit through snippets of each one performing. None of it sinks in, except seeing Dani, even briefly, in her stage costume – a complete transformation.

'And the winner is...' I stop breathing while the host makes a show of fiddling with the envelope, reading it first and then smiling, pausing, before loudly proclaiming, 'Daniella Nichols!' in a fake English accent.

Mum and I scream and grab each other, bouncing on the sofa so the popcorn spills, just as Dad comes in the front door, shouting, 'Hello – what the bloody hell's going on here?'

'Shh!' we hiss simultaneously as the audience applauds and the camera cuts back to show Dani kissing her agent on both cheeks, being hugged by her mum and then smoothing her dress down, ready to make the journey to the stage.

I hadn't told mum about writing the speech in case it didn't happen and now there isn't time. Dad leans on the back of sofa behind us as Dani launches in. I can't help mouthing every word along with her, delighted at the laughs from the audience, which she pauses to acknowledge, while worrying she'll go over time and get cut off. Then, just as she is wrapping up, making her thank yous, she looks directly into the camera and finishes with, 'A special thank you to Madeleine Sparks back in the UK, who helps me in so many ways.'

I sit staring, eyes fixed on the screen, mouth open.

'Did I just hear right?' Dad says as he ruffles my hair. 'Did she just thank *you*?' He sounds proud.

'Oh, darling!' Mum's got tears in her eyes. 'I never realised you were so important. How wonderful. Can we record it? Wait until I show my book club.'

I admit feeling tearful myself – I never knew she cared so much either. I'm sure it was the speech that swung it. Mum was spot on; we assistants rarely get any recognition, but we're always first in line when things go wrong. Wow.

Before this momentous event sinks in, my phone, which I had tucked down the side of the sofa for surreptitious check-ins with Twitter etc., is bouncing around like Elijah after eating Haribo. Seems everyone was watching – Jess sent about twenty emojis in a row, a text from Lauren says: 'Nice one!' and even Ella: 'SO, SO proud!!' My Twitter alert is pinging away merrily. Mum is juggling remotes, trying to see if she can rewind and record the show, shouting at dad to call and tell my sister, but Dad is off to the kitchen to get a glass to join us with our cava.

Next, there's a message from Ed: 'Let's celebrate!' *Twat. Now* he wants to know me. And then Dominic: 'Glad to see my finger crossing is working. Next up – new job.'

I reply with a fingers crossed emoji, surprised and touched by the fact he was watching.

Chapter 37

It got so late I decided to stay over in what used to be my bedroom. It took me ages to fall asleep. Eventually, Mum wrestled my phone off me as I couldn't stop checking what people were saying, watching my followers go up and scrolling through the press coverage.

I just about made it to Dame Annette on time next morning, feeling a little blurry, and gave my customary ring on the bell.

'Morning – it's Maddy.' I try to sound perky through the intercom.

'Madeleine – I wasn't sure you'd come...' She buzzes me in. 'Parlour' she calls imperiously as I shut the front door behind me.

'Hello. Weren't you expecting me? It's Thursday.' I'm not sure what she means.

'I know perfectly well what day it is, but now you are

a star in your own right, I thought my little jobs may be beneath you.'

Now would be the perfect moment to tell her I'm putting my rates up. Is she being nice? It's hard to tell. 'You watched the awards? I'm so pleased for Dani; it was such a brave move going over there.'

'Never mind that.' Gracious as ever. 'A little bird tells me you wrote her speech.' It takes me a minute to work this out – Charles! I'm amazed at the speed of the theatre grapevine. 'It wasn't at all bad, perhaps I'll get you to write one for me when the time comes.' She inclines her head, modestly.

'Of course, I'd be happy to,' seems the right answer. We can cross that bridge when (if) we come to it. Meanwhile, real life goes on and there are lots of the usual to get through, which takes my mind off other things. Once we've gone through everything, she offers me a cup of tea, which I gratefully accept. As soon as she leaves the room, I check my phone.

A sweet text from my sister, an even sweeter one from Needy Steve saying congratulations and that he missed me, and the one I'd been waiting for:

From Olive, 10.55am:
Casually told EVERYONE at
work that you wrote Dani's
speech!!

Olive may be a drama queen, but God love her for banging my drum. If it gets back to Sophie or Jo, it can't do my case any harm, can it? Still no actual progress, but no news is blah blah. I'm sitting gazing at my phone, lost in thought, when it rings. Casper. Again.

All my good vibes instantly disappear and I feel panicky and scared. The dame will be back any minute. My assistant's instinct is to answer. My back is sweaty and hands a bit shaky when it dawns on me: he's not my client anymore and I don't owe him anything. I hit decline just as the dame returns with a tray. I will talk to him – when I'm ready.

'I thought we'd have a biscuit,' she says, putting the tray with china cups and saucers down. Seems I am in the good books. In a chatty mood, she is soon telling me to be wary of Charles, 'That man promises the earth and rarely delivers.' It's as if she knows he's been sniffing around.

I drink tea and eat shortbread to avoid answering and she rattles on to more familiar territory, the last award she won. Not for a support role, of course, for the lead – and so it goes on.

✦

Back at home, still debating what to say to Casper, I'm delighted to receive a call from Dani.

'Hello – is that the Leading Actress in a Featured Role?' I greet her.

She laughs happily, 'It's the leading actress with a stonking hangover. Fancy bringing me round a Maccy D's?'

I fling myself onto my bed for a good catch-up and

she regales me with hair-raising tales of what went on at the after party. 'Now don't you be posting any of this on Twitter!' she warns. I thank her for the namecheck and she tells me Casper is about the only person she hasn't had a message from.

'I'm not sure what's going on with him. He sacked me a while ago and now he wants me back,' I admit in a rare breach of confidentiality.

'Course he does, you're a super assistant. Which reminds me, what do you think about coming out here for a bit? I could with the support and I've taken an apartment with a spare room. It's yours if you want it and you could help me out as much as you did in London. I'm sure I could hook you up with other people here. We could have such a laugh, Maddy – New York, baby!'

'That sounds amazing, but – it's a lot to think about. Can I get back to you?' My hope, of course, is that I will not carry on being a freelance, part-time assistant, but I daren't burn all my bridges.

'Don't take too long – when word gets out about my spare room, there'll be a cat fight. Laters, babe – got a sold-out play to perform tonight!' and she's gone.

I lie back on my bed for a minute to think about this latest offer. It's a very tempting alternative. Suddenly I'm in demand, but still no word from the one job I desperately want. I've got to slow my spinning thoughts down. A swim! That's what I need.

✦

My first few lengths are splashy – I can't find my rhythm. I picture myself in New York with Dani. Hanging out in her dressing room, heading out after the show, on every guest list in New York, then falling into a yellow cab at the end of the night and heading back to her apartment. Then, a vision of working with Casper pushes in, where I've negotiated a decent gig that includes working on *Just Between Us*. Top Notch know the full story now; I don't have to trust him to tell them. Then, as my strokes become more regular, a different picture comes into my head. I'm sitting in a room, round a big table with other people, a huge whiteboard covered with ideas and a production assistant bringing in a cardboard tray of coffees, just like in the movies. This is the scene I decide to build on as I ease into a good pace. I think it's called manifesting – I read about it. I embellish my vision. I'm wearing an L F Markey jumpsuit and surprisingly have a pair of glasses on my head – surprising as I don't wear glasses. I can't exactly picture the other people, but they are all very cool in a slightly nerdy way, and we're laughing and calling stuff out and someone is sticking Post-it notes up, and then the door flies open and Casper bursts in and shouts, 'Stop!'

I gasp and swallow water. Spluttering, I stop, much to the annoyance of the person tailing me. I get out the way by ducking under the lane dividers and, still coughing, grab my towel and head to the changing room. Feeling the chill, I head straight for a hot shower. My breath settles and my muscles feel nicely tired. Standing under the steamy showerhead, I try and get back to my lovely daydream, but I can't get Casper out of my head. Going back to work for him would not be a good idea, whatever promises he is making. He's lied to me, bullied me and hurt me. I'm not prepared to ride on his coat tails anymore. He's shown his true colours and there's no coming back from that. I just need to tell him.

Chapter 38

Well, my drawers are as tidy as they have ever been and the spice rack is alphabetised. I'm doing my best to keep busy and productive, but also finding it impossible to focus on anything. In the spirit of compromise, I half-heartedly consider some assistant positions on the CHAMPS job board – maternity cover for a terribly young actor, who sounds like he needs a nanny more than a PA. The job description includes choosing his clothes, which could be fun, and planning his meals, not so much. There's also a very part-time role for a camp comedian in Camden, so I could still do my course, but my heart is not in it.

The days since I met with Sophie and Jo have dragged – all that excitement seems like an age ago and even Olive has gone quiet. Last I heard was when she accepted the lunch invite and said things were changing hour by hour – nothing concrete to report.

I'm trying to concentrate, reading one of the books on

the reading list for the course I signed up to, when my phone rings.

'Hello, is this Madeleine? It's Gerry from Sophie Swayne's office.'

OK. This is happening. Not sure exactly what is happening, but I'm excited and terrified.

A brief conversation later and I have exactly twenty-five minutes to transform myself from scruffy mess to smart professional. Too churned up to plan an outfit, I stand in front of my wardrobe devouring a peanut butter sandwich. I settle on a second-hand Margaret Howell suit, a little frayed round the edges but still classy. My hair is doing its own thing, so I pin it up as best I can, and throw on some make-up. A bold lip, for sure. Lipstick is like armour. There isn't time to overthink anything as I slip on my lucky silver bangle and a squirt of Chanel No. 5. Still hungry and anxious about bad breath, I pop some gum and power walk to the tube.

Bang on time and only slightly out of breath, I'm about to announce myself to the receptionist when Olive appears and steers me away. 'I'll walk you round,' she says, brightly, gripping my upper arm. As soon as we are out of sight, she hisses in my ear, 'I may have mentioned about the drugs.'

I stop dead and face her. 'What? What drugs?' At that moment, I hear my name being called. It's Sophie, standing at the door of a different office. With a last bewildered look at Olive, I head over.

'Madeleine, thanks for coming in at such short notice.

As you may know, we are working in a rapidly evolving situation. Please – take a seat.'

Olive's bombshell has shaken all the composure I'd worked so hard to cultivate and I just look at Sophie like a dope. 'Um, sure.'

'I'll cut straight to the chase. As you are only too aware, there have been problems with *Just Between Us*, as well as Casper's attitude. He is, for the moment, out of the picture. We've been looking at various options to turn the situation around and trying to do so without interrupting the process. I have recently been led to understand that, as well as the input you shared with us, he also placed you in a most unfortunate and, let's say, delicate situation. We value loyalty, we value it highly, and we thank you for your discretion.'

'Right.' I have no idea where this is going, but need to seem like I do. 'Discretion is key in my job.'

'Absolutely, but for obvious reasons we can't see a way to build you in to the *Just Between Us* writing team. It's a shame, but there it is,' she says with finality.

'I'm really sorry, Sophie, but I'm confused. I thought I'd proved my value to the show and if Casper isn't involved anymore, what's the problem? Please, give me a chance.' My dream scenario is disintegrating rapidly.

'I don't deny that, but the latest revelations mean things are now out of our hands. The US are taking over and giving it to someone tried and tested. They've been looking for a reason to cut him and now they have it. A drug scandal on top of everything is the last thing we need.'

I don't want to seem stupid, but she's not making sense. 'Again, I'm sorry, but I don't know what you are talking about. Casper isn't into drugs, not that I'm aware of.' Is this what Olive was talking about? Maybe he has totally lost it.

'Madeleine, your loyalty is commendable, and that is part of the reason, coupled with signs of raw talent, that we want to offer you a role as an assistant script editor, under Jo, on a brand-new show we are putting together. We need to stay relevant to a changing audience and some fresh blood is just what we need. What are your thoughts?' She folds her hands and looks expectant.

'Fantastic, that sounds fantastic. Of course, I'd love to be involved.' It's hard to keep up, but I really need to know what she means about Casper. 'It's a dream come true, but—'

Sophie cuts in. 'Great. Things you need to know – you'll be part of a team, a mixture of experienced and new faces. We think being in right from the start will suit you, as you'll be part of the whole process. There is one thing to flag up; the job doesn't start for three months, so that gives you time to sort out your current job situation and I suggest you take a holiday, because once you start, it will be twenty-four seven, seven days a week. You will think about this show every waking moment.'

There's so much to take in, but before I can say anything, she is ushering me out of the door and beckoning Jo over, who says, 'Welcome aboard,' and ushers me into a different office. Gesturing me to sit, she offers tea, but I'm really preoccupied with what Sophie said about Casper.

Jo asks me about what programmes I am into, what my most recent binge had been and what I loved watching growing up. Well, this is one of my areas of expertise and I forget my concerns and chatter away. She nods, made a few notes and then gives me a copy of the book the show is loosely based on. She says I should read it before we next meet and get a feel for the characters, but ignore the dated language and societal assumptions. She also asks if I knew what I was letting myself in for, reiterating what Sophie said about crazy hours, but adding deadlines and demanding directors into the mix, and despite having previously thought I would hate to be tied to a desk, I hear myself telling her wholeheartedly that I can't think of anything I would like more. Maybe I'll achieve my long-held dream to be one of the crew and not an outsider getting in the way and annoying people.

I walk back to reception in a daze. Olive is waiting to see me out.

'Olive, I honestly don't know what half of that was about – Casper, drugs?'

'I hinted he'd been pressuring you to score for him. Wasn't that what your falling out was about?' she says, matter-of-factly.

'Christ – no – it wasn't that at all.' I'm engulfed by a horrible realisation. 'Olive, I can't let this happen.'

'Oh, Maddy, don't overthink it, I only implied it. Everyone's been desperate for a reason to get him off this series, right from episode one. He's only been told to take a break and sort himself out. Never mind him – what about you?'

'They offered me a job,' but I'm distracted. If Casper has been taken off his own series because of what I said to Olive, that's not right. I've had it with bending the truth and dodgy morals. Leaving Olive looking bemused, I dash past reception back to the room I left just minutes before.

I can't let myself think about the possible outcome of what I'm about to do, but I absolutely know I can't live with myself unless I do.

Bursting back into the room, a man I have never seen before is on the phone and looks up in surprise. 'Can I help you?'

'Sophie Swayne,' I blurt out, 'I need to see Sophie Swayne – now!'

Bemused, he points across the passage at a closed door. Before nerves kick in, I knock and enter. Sophie is there with half a dozen other people, seated round a table. Every face is turned to me. I falter. 'Sophie, I need to talk to you, urgently.'

She is not at all happy, but comes to the door, half closing it behind her, and looks at me quizzically. 'It's not true, what Olive told you about me and Casper,' I blurt out, trying not to think about the consequences of what I'm about to tell her.

She looks stricken. 'That you didn't work on the scripts? Jesus Christ—'

I quickly interrupt, 'No, that *is* true, absolutely, but

he didn't ask me to buy drugs. It was something else. Illegal, but not drugs.' I need to shut up before I make this any worse. 'He shouldn't lose his job because of a misunderstanding.'

She crosses her arms and narrows her eyes. 'I think it's best we don't go into what he did ask you to do, I'd rather not know, but please don't think it was because of Olive's tittle-tattle that he's taking this break. We're hoping it won't come out publicly, but there have been allegations made by a crew member about inappropriate behaviour and that is what we are investigating while Casper takes some time off. Now, I appreciate your ethics, Madeleine, but I know you are friendly with Olive, so listen to me: Do *not* share this information with her or it'll be all over Popbitch. Now, if you'll excuse me, I am in the middle of some particularly delicate negotiations.' And she goes back in, closing the door firmly behind her.

OK, phew. I've made an idiot of myself in front of one of the most important women in TV production, but I can live with that. Far more than I could live with myself if I'd got the job based on a lie.

And then it sinks in – I got the job!

Afterword

The networking lunch turned into quite the celebration. L-a had arranged it beautifully, in a space furnished like a super-cool loft apartment, with bare brick walls and exposed metal piping. A chef cooked up delicious sharing plates behind an open-plan steel counter. After some friendly introductions, we took our seats around a large Ercol table with a huge glass jug of wildflowers in the centre.

The assistants had all made an effort and dressed up, and L-a gave a little speech welcoming us, introducing her team and then popping a bottle of champagne. 'I am delighted to welcome you all here to Workspace, with special thanks to Maddy for pulling you behind-the-scenes heroes together.'

As she raised a glass, Olive chipped in and raised her own glass, 'To Maddy – the soon to be Script Editor.'

Everyone turned to me. '*Assistant* Script Editor,' I corrected her. I'd been hugging this excitement to myself, luxuriating in letting it sink in, but Lauren clapped, Jess whooped, and L-a and her team were congratulating me. Clinking glasses all round, I realised my exact title didn't matter, and how lovely to be sitting and celebrating with some of the people who had played key roles in the craziness of the last few weeks that had all led up to this point.

Lauren and I had booked Dani in for a shoot with Django on her next trip home. Dani was delighted and I had earned back my credibility with Scary Stephanie. Jess was looking forward to be taking over looking after the dame, and although her heart would always be in fashion, she was still rebuilding her confidence and happy to wait for the right role to come along. Dom and I had kept up a jokey chat via text, but yesterday I'd taken the step of suggesting a quick drink, which was happening later. And just before leaving home this morning, I used that extra Casper money, which had been burning an uncomfortable hole in my pocket, to book a flight. Dani's spare room was waiting. As was the whole of New York.

The Start.

Acknowledgements

Writing a novel was a long-held dream of mine, but the years slipped by and I left it rather late to start, so I am particularly grateful to those who encouraged me along the way.

First and foremost, to the memory of my mother who always believed I would write a book. Next to Jo Lal, whose disbelief spurred me on. When I finally did get stuck in and then stuck, Thalia Suzuma from The Literary Consultancy helped me over the hump and showed me how to shape it into something resembling a novel.

Heartfelt thanks to Martha and Josephine: my first readers, who took the time to give me honest and constructive feedback; and the next round: Hilary, Tiphaine, Geraldine, Emily and Mary, who helped me stay positive with their kind words and advice.

Adam, Martha and Phoebe for having confidence in me, listening to me and being part of my process, never wavering in their positivity and encouragement.

And finally, Jo, again, who has pulled out all the stops to help me get this over the line.

Printed in Great Britain
by Amazon

32365493R00205